Shadow Bender

Fay E. Simon

Published by
Rogue Phoenix Press
Copyright © 2015

ISBN: 978-1-62420-191-2

Credits
Cover Artist: Greg Palko
Editor: Christine Young

Dedication

I dedicate this book to my Heavenly Father, my mother, Georgia M. Simon, rest her soul, and to Mari Asim, Sandra Katis, Wendy Loizos-Schnell, Brandon Wyse and Greg Palko who have given me moral support.

Prologue

Sudicorp Research Center, Los Angeles, CA

Sudicorp Research Center, known for its long-standing reputation as a place for scientific research for the betterment of humankind, was nestled in the heart of East Los Angeles where a bunch of grungy warehouses rested. The Sudicorp building looked deserted and quiet, except for the dim light in a window on the tenth floor.

Dr. Thomas Franklin, dressed in a white lab coat, stood in a large room within the building.

A ruggedly handsome fellow in his late forties, he wrestled with a machine oddly similar to a futuristic rifle with the look and feel of metal. The lens, which sat at the end of the metallic barrel, held a dark blue crystal, the size of a golf ball. The lights in the room gave off enough radiance to cast shadows.

"Haven't you got that crystal situated yet?" came the angry words of Drake Carver, CEO of the Research Center. Carver squinted behind his horn-rimmed glasses. They had been working on this experiment since five in the morning. The clock on the wall now said two minutes to midnight.

After readjusting the crystal, Franklin looked up. "It did work. Three times in a row, but the crystal has to be aligned just right," he said in a British accent. "Now that I've programmed the prototype to my brain waves, this thing will tear away any shadow from its origin."

"Why? So you can tear shadows apart?" Carver paced around Franklin and the gun bearing the crystal.

"You don't understand. I'm not tearing the shadows apart; I am separating them from the object of origin. For example, I will separate that chair from its shadow. From there, I will be able to command it. The theory is to remove the shadows away from what makes them. These lone shadows become a living entity. They can be controlled and given orders," Franklin looked to Carver.

"So this is what you dragged me in here for? You're trying to make shadow people?"

"No. A new kind of army; shadow soldiers at my command," explained Franklin, pushing back a few strands of light brown hair from his eyes. "It's all in bending the photons or using negatively charged photons. That's where the crystal comes in. We've discussed this before."

Carver looked around the lab, there were a number of tables with bits and pieces of metal parts and clear lenses scattered over them. On a table nearest Franklin was set a framed photo of a pretty, young woman with shoulder length dark hair and dark eyes. The smell of burning wires drifted about in the stale air. Drake Carver wrinkled up his nose then looked back at Franklin and the metallic gun holding the dark crystal.

"The cute girl in the photo, your girlfriend?" asked Carver, as Franklin adjusted the crystal for the umpteenth time.

"That's Francie, my future wife."

Carver lifted an eyebrow and smiled at the photo. "Frances DeWitt?"

Franklin stopped what he was doing and stared at his boss in disbelief. "You know her?"

"In another lifetime, my friend. Don't let me distract you."

Franklin went back to adjusting the crystal and said, "There. That should do it. Now watch!" Franklin lifted the gun and pointed it at a nearby office chair. When he pulled the trigger, a loud whirring noise exploded the silence and something began to happen. Its projected shadow on the floor began to stir without any movement from the chair. Had this been a cartoon, it would have been amusing, but to witness the shadow peeling itself up from the floor and pull away from the chair made Carver gasp and shudder. A creepy tearing sound, like the ripping of fabric, echoed throughout the room.

"What the crap was that?" Carver took a step back and looked around.

"That was the sound of the shadow tearing itself from the chair," replied Franklin with a grin. "Fantastic, isn't it?"

Slowly, the chair's shadow crept toward them. "The shadow is moving. Stop it! Stop it now!" Carver demanded as he took several more steps back.

The shadow grew taller and moved across the tiled floor menacingly.

"No worries. Watch this," Franklin turned to the shadow and with great authority said, "Desine movment. Sustine me mandato. 'Cease movement. Wait for my command'." Instantly, the shadow stopped advancing.

"What the crap was that?" Carver's eyebrows knitted together.

"Latin. The commands work best in Latin." Franklin grinned at Carver.

"Why?"

"Ancient language, I suppose. Greek works sometimes. Watch!" Again, Franklin looked to the shadow and said, "Μετακίνηση προς τα εμπρός δύο βήματα και στη συνέχεια να σταματήσουν, 'Move forward two steps and then stop'." As before, the shadow obeyed, taking two steps forward before stopping.

"That's incredible!" This time Carver moved to the stationary shadow. It looked as if he stood next to a black mass from a haunted house or some CGI from a horror movie. "Can I touch it?"

Franklin shrugged. "Go ahead. Try it."

Gingerly, Carver reached out to the shadow. As he did, his hand went right through it as if it were a spirit. Yet, he flinched.

"I feel something, but nothing solid. Like a spider's web, thin and fragile. That's creepy." Carver moved away from the thing and sat on a chair that *had* a shadow.

"Latin seems to work the best. There're a number of times that Greek commands are not understood. Can you imagine what we can do with the power to control shadows? No terrorist or any foreign power would ever know what hit them if they tried to invade the US."

"So, this is what you've been looking to do all these years, create a weapon?"

"No, not just a weapon, acquire more power. Wait until you see what I can do with the darkness..." but Franklin's voice trailed as the chair's shadow attacked him. Viciously, the thing lashed out, ripping the sleeves of his lab coat.

Quickly he gave the command in Latin, "Desine movment. Sustine me mandato." The shadow froze.

Carver stood up and stumbled back. "Wh...What happened?"

"That's what I was saying. Latin commands are better."

"This thing nearly killed you. It's too dangerous," Carver straightened his self. His hands shook and he desperately gasped to catch his breath.

Then, without warning, the chair's shadow lunged at Franklin again. Instinctively, he threw up his forearm to protect his face. The shadow raked sharp, unseen claws over his arm, once again ripping the sleeves of the lab coat. Red body fluid squirted out over the linoleum and the white lab coat. Franklin shrieked in pain as he held his bleeding arm. The shadow hunched over and prepared to launch itself again.

Chapter One
Francie's Bakery—Los Angeles, California

Twenty-eight year old Frances DeWitt stood behind the large display case of pastries and muffins. Behind her sat rows and rows of various types of fresh bread, from rye to nine-grain whole wheat. Every morning at this time, a crowd of people pushed into the tiny bakery for hot drinks and tasty sweets.

For the last hour and a half, Frances, or Francie as her friends called her, had been bagging the sweet of choice for dozens of customers, along with their drinks. Miguel and Pedro worked in the back doing all the baking that had begun at four am, so that all the goodies would be ready for the morning rush at seven o'clock. Annalisa, a dark haired woman who had arrived from Texas a few years ago, was dressed in a pink uniform with a white apron like Francie and worked behind the display case of pastries, serving customers and ringing up orders at the register.

Five years had passed since Francie started her bakery. Her life's dream had come true. The sweet savor of fresh bread and bakery goods permeated the small unit, but this was the sweet smell of success for Francie DeWitt. Not many women her age could truthfully say they owned their own business. If she hadn't inherited money from her Aunt Paula when the dear woman died, she would never have been able to be her own boss.

The tinkle of a bell sounded when the door opened. There before her stood Thomas Franklin and his lab assistant, Lon Jamison, a young man of thirty-something. Franklin smiled cheerfully and eyed Francie lovingly.

"Good morning, sunshine!" He greeted her. The door closed behind him and the bell tinkled again.

Subtly, the smile faded from Francie's face. "Lloyd, you're here again. Good morning," she tried to sound professional behind her annoyance. "Do you want the usual?"

"Yes, please, a blueberry muffin and coffee," he kept smiling as Francie filled his order.

When she placed the bag containing the muffin on the counter top next to the register, Annalisa set a disposable cup filled with coffee next to it. Francie placed the lid on the cup and said, "That's okay, Lloyd. We've known each other for a while. It's on the house."

"That's so kind of you, Francie. Thank you," his British accent flowed through. "Have you considered my invitation to dinner this evening?" Suddenly, he caught her hand with both of his and brought it to his lips. Francie flinched as the world around her vanished.

Her mind seemed to pierce Franklin's very soul and a roiling mass of blackness engulfed the scene. Dark shadows danced in the eerie dimness, crawling about the growing black mass. Immense fear clutched her heart, and she began to gasp and choke.

"Are you all right, my dear?" Franklin's voice brought her back to reality. Quickly, she claimed her hand.

"Not tonight. We've talked about this remember? I don't want to be rude, but I'm just not interested." Francie shook her head to rid her mind of the visions of darkness, as she wrinkled up her nose and narrowed her eyes at Franklin. He only smiled and nodded. Picking up the bag and coffee, he turned to leave. Lon Jamison caught his arm and asked in a whisper, "Why does she call you Lloyd? Your name is Thomas."

Franklin didn't look at his sandy-haired lab assistant, but replied, "That was another lifetime," and with that, he opened the door and left. Jamison shook his head and followed.

Annalisa adjusted her dark hair as she leaned in to whisper to her boss. "He's cute. Why don't you give him a chance?"

"I did once, but it just didn't work out. No fireworks," replied Francie, as her thoughts wandered back to the vision of darkness and the shadow that had revealed itself when Franklin had taken her hand in his.

"No fireworks? So, now we have to have fireworks? Well, he's pretty hot to me," Annalisa smiled. "Hah, hah, hah!" she stuck out her tongue in mocked panting.

"Be my guest. He's all yours," Francie started to turn away, but Annalisa pulled her back.

"Come on, Francie! I've been working for you for the past four years, and we've been friends longer. What do you want in a man? Lloyd comes in here every day. He keeps asking you to go out with him and I have it from good authority he has a terrific job at that research center near Spring and Flower."

"I don't know what I want. There's a darkness about him. For some reason, I don't feel Lloyd is for me. Let's drop the subject. I don't want to think about him." Francie abruptly pushed passed her friend and employee and began helping other people.

Annalisa frowned and mumbled to herself. *Darkness? What the heck does that mean?*

Chapter Two
Sudicorp—Same Day

In a sterile looking office filled with windows and a few pieces of scattered stiff-looking furniture sat Lewis Avery - Chief of Safety and Security. He adjusted his chair behind the clear, Plexiglas table as he read over several of the papers scattered across it. Running his fingers through his short, ash blond hair, he sipped his coffee as he studied the documents in hand.

Now and again, he'd glance out of the window and mouth the words; "Hades experiment" and "umbrakenesis."

The paper in hand read:

The Hades Experiment has been approved by the Office of the President of the United States for the study of umbrakenesis; the control of darkness and shadows for the purpose of discovering a new defense for humankind.

Due to controversy, this experiment will determine whether umbrakenesis is a science or of the occult 'magic', and if possible, capapble of enabling the absolute control of darkness and shadows.

No animals will be harmed or killed in any experiment. No risks are to be taken with the lives of any living creature.

The project will be funded by a little known department out of Homeland Security.

If at any time Drake Carver, CEO of Sudicorp Research deems it necessary to abort this project, he has the authority to make that decision.

The person in charge of the experiment will be Dr. Thomas Franklin, PhD in Physics and Masters in Paranormal Psychology. Dr. Franklin will have complete use of all facilities, equipment, and staff of Sudicorp for the completion of said experiment. Next to Drake Carver, Dr. Franklin is in complete control of the Hades Experiment.

This approval from the Office of the President will expire three years from the date of this letter.

As Lewis looked up from the papers, Drake Carver burst through the door.

"I know you're the boss, Carver, but out of courtesy, could you please knock before flinging the door open." Lewis barked.

"Lewis, have you signed the approval for the Hades Experiment? I need it now," Carver sounded cold and demanding.

"No time to greet a long time employee? Not even a smile?" asked Lewis.

Carver said nothing.

"Looks like you needed it nine months ago, from the date. You've already started the experiment, haven't you?" Lewis gave his boss a cold stare.

"Up until now we were receiving the funds. Since we didn't forward the approvals, the funding may stop and we can't have that. Please sign the papers," Carver stated, his hands shook, even the bandaged one.

Lewis noticed the tremble and the injury. "What happened to your hand?"

"Nothing serious. I'll live."

After a long sigh, Lewis narrowed his eyes at his boss. He never liked when Carver avoided answering a direct question. Lewis bit his lip then tossed the papers on the desk. "Another need to know situation, huh, Drake? He nodded to the damaged hand.

"You know these docs read like a comic book. Secondly, the proposed procedures are extremely risky and dangerous. If they don't kill the people conducting the experiment, the entire building and its environs could be destroyed. There are twenty pages of pros and cons, which includes a list of risks. As head of Safety and Security I cannot, in good conscience, approve this project." Lewis leaned back in the chair and stared Drake Carver in the eye.

Carver sat down quietly and said, "I know I should have told you about this experiment before, but there wasn't time. Come to the lab with me, and Franklin will show you what he's accomplished so far."

"What has he accomplished? From what I've read, he's trying to control darkness and shadows. With the amount of electricity he needs, the entire place could blow up or he might create an electrically charged grid and kill everyone that comes near it."

Drake Carver adjusted his glasses and arose from the chair. "Come on. Let me show you why you need to approve the project. After seeing what Franklin has done, I don't think you will continue to refuse."

Lewis got up and followed Carver.

They had to walk past a series of closed doors and several observation windows where a few tables filled with test tubes, microscopes and Bunsen burners sat.

Finally, they came to a door labeled Room 606. Carver slid a card key through the slot on the door just above the doorknob. A soft "click" sounded. Carver twisted the knob and opened the door, but something pushed it closed.

"Do not disturb?" Lewis said with an ounce of sarcasm.

"That's never happened before. I'll try again," Carver said, as he slid the card key through the slot and turned the doorknob again. This time, the door jerked forward and pulled Carver with it.

Inside, the lab looked like it had earlier with the stilted tables and office chairs scattered about. Franklin was nowhere in sight. Lon Jamison, his lab assistant, stood wide-eyed and pale as a sheet.

"What's going on? Why did you slam the door in my face?" Carver waltzed in with Lewis in tow.

"I didn't," replied Lon, shifting his eyes from side to side. With shaky fingers, he ran them through his sandy colored hair.

"There's no need to lie," Carver reprimanded.

"I'm not. I didn't shut the door. It did," he nodded to the shadow on the wall.

"Huh?" Lewis looked around. "What?"

"The shadow; it shut the door on you," Lon Jamison moved away quickly, flew past them, and left the room.

"What's he talking about?" Lewis stepped into the room and the door closed automatically. Carver reached out to the shadow on the wall, but it dwindled in size and skittered away like an insect.

The two men exchanged looks. Carver motioned for Lewis to follow him deeper into the lab. "Franklin! Franklin! I've brought a visitor. He's anxious to see your achievements," Carver called out. As they moved closer to Franklin's workbench, the framed photo of Francie DeWitt, the pretty brunette wearing a pastel print dress, came into view. Once again, Carver hesitated, and this time picked up the photo. His features softened and a smile crept across his lips.

"Pretty woman," remarked Lewis with a grin. "Franklin's wife?"

"No. He says 'future' wife," replied Carver, setting the photo back in place on the workbench.

"Seriously? What does she see in him?" Lewis examined the photo then set it down.

Without a sound, a black mass formed near the entrance. It stretched as tall as a man would and moved quietly toward the two. No longer did the shadow slither across the wall. It came toward them upright along the floor, as a three-dimensional being. Lewis turned and jumped back at the sight of the dark creature headed toward him. Carver flinched at Lewis' reaction then let out a gasp when the shadow was almost upon him.

All at once, Franklin appeared as if out of thin air and commanded in a loud voice, "Et parce mihi exspectare iubet." Instantly, the shadow stopped short and waited for further instructions.

"My apologies, gentlemen. I didn't expect company so soon. We didn't mean to startle you." Franklin extended his hand. "Lewis Avery, good to see you again."

The two men shook hands. "Nice job. You nearly scared the life out of me. What is this thing?"

"The shadow of my lab assistant, Lon Jamison. Lon was the young man that spoke to you briefly before running out of here," Franklin gave a lopsided smile.

"I take it he wasn't prepared for the results?" Lewis also gave a lopsided smile.

"Precisely! You haven't been in the lab lately. You need to visit more often," Franklin smiled. Lewis said nothing. Tension grew between the men and Franklin changed the subject.

"I believe Drake brought you here to see the progress of my work," Franklin continued as he picked up the metallic gun from the workbench. The dark crystal gave off an eerie radiance as the florescent light struck it at an angle.

"He did. What is this crystal? I assume you analyzed it." Lewis stared at the strange gem. Franklin didn't reply.

"By the way, where did you come from? There is nowhere you could have been in here that we wouldn't have seen you." Lewis looked around.

"I was here. Your attention was on the shadow," Franklin lied. "Well, what do you think?"

"So far, I'm impressed but bristling with questions," Lewis remarked as he looked about the lab.

"Allow me to show you what I've accomplished so far," Dr. Thomas Franklin picked up the metallic prototype. "This contraption looks much like a conventional gun, albeit the metal and copper wiring. I've programed the small computer chip inside to my brain waves. The dark crystal I found in Greece some years back. It contains some properties unlike anything I've ever seen. Therefore, I thought to test the power of the laser through the crystal."

Franklin handed him the gun. "Lasers don't use copper wiring." Lewis turned the gun over and over in his examination.

"Correct. However, electricity does. May I?" Franklin reached for the prototype.

Lewis handed it to him. "Drake, please hand me the dust broom at the workbench over there," Franklin motioned to the work area not far away. Carver walked to the broom, picked it up, and brought it to him. The good doctor leaned it against his workbench and motioned for the others to move back.

"Please note the shadow it casts on the floor."

Then he raised the gun and aimed. When he pulled the trigger, a weird dim light shot out from the barrel, went through the crystal and struck the broom.

The broom quivered and a loud ripping noise sounded, like fabric being torn. In a moment, the shadow pulled away from the broom and stood up right from the floor, now a three-dimensional entity.

"Good heavens! I've never seen anything like that. May I touch it?" Wild-eyed, Lewis looked to Franklin, who nodded his approval. Gingerly, Lewis moved to the broom's shadow and reached out. His hand went through it with ease. He flinched and moved back to Franklin.

"Feels like fine cobwebs or spider webs," Lewis remarked. "Amazing! So, you're tearing shadows apart to control them?"

"No, I'm not tearing them apart. I've only separated them from their object. When independent, they are no longer two-dimensional. They become three-dimensional, with a mass that is like thin webs, but a solid mass, nevertheless," Franklin explained.

"Drake said they responded to Latin commands, why?" Lewis ran his hand through the broom's shadow again.

"After trying different languages, even ancient Egyptian, Latin seems to be the one they will obey most of the time without dissention."

"Dissention? You talk as if they were alive."

"In a sense, they are. When no longer attached to an object or person, they have no direction. Without it, the consequence would be disastrous." Franklin looked from Lewis to Carver.

"Disastrous, huh? Drake, is that what happened to your hand?" asked Lewis.

Carver moved his bandaged hand behind him. Even Franklin glanced at his own bandaged arm and moved it out of sight. Lewis noticed and grabbed Franklin's arm and pulled back the sleeve of his white lab coat. His limb was bandaged as well, and blood seeped through the pallid gauze.

"And you as well, Franklin?"

"Minor accident. No reason for alarm."

Seriously? So there is no chance these things could run amok? From your wounds I'd say they could."

"As long as I have control, no. They answer to me."

"What if something happens and you can't control them? Say something makes your brainwaves disconnect from these things. Can they be stopped? Don't mean to shatter your theory, but it is my job to ensure safety and security." Lewis questioned.

"Of course, Lewis, I understand. To answer your question, artificial light as we have in this building will do nothing to them," Franklin said, as he pulled a lighter from his pocket. Then he grabbed a piece of scrap paper, flicked the lighter, and lit the paper. As soon as the shadows saw the flame, they retreated across the floor.

Quickly, he shook out the flame and continued, "Fire will keep them at bay, however, sunlight, *true* sunlight will destroy them. I'd show you, but I really would like to link the shadows back to their objects."

"Of course. However, how do you know sunlight will destroy them if you haven't tried it?"

"I have tried it. A red ball around here is without a shadow. Such a sacrifice for science," Franklin said in sarcasm. Lewis nodded.

"Would you care for tea?" Franklin looked to Carver then to Lewis.

Carver nodded to Lewis, "Just say 'yes'."

"Yes. Thanks!"

Franklin looked to the shadow of his lab assistant and said in Latin, "Oremus hospitio aliquid tea. 'Pour some tea'."

Instantly, the human shadow moved to a table next to the wall. After picking up a couple of china cups and a teapot, it moved back to Franklin's workbench. Then it set the cups on the bench, poured the tea, and set down the teapot. It picked up each cup and offered one to Lewis, who accepted it. The shadow offered the other to Carver. He took it.

Franklin turned to the shadow and said, "Quod est in omnibus. Sustine me mandato. 'That is all. Wait for my command'." The shadow moved back in line with the broom shadow and waited for further instructions.

"Since it cannot speak as humans, the shadow cannot ask if you wish for milk or lemon, or even if you want sugar. And I have yet to have it pick up the saucers along with the cups," Franklin beamed with pride of his accomplishments.

Lewis grinned as he shook his head. "Half of me is afraid of this thing and the other part marvels at the achievement. Bravo, Franklin! You've made amazing progress. I'm blown away. Congratulations!"

"Thank you."

"One last question; if you use a laser, why high voltage electricity as well?"

"In order to control shadows and darkness, I must bend light photons, negative energy if you will. Laser uses electromagnetic waves. I cannot use electromagnetic waves to bend photons, as it is both a particle and wave. What went through the crystal looks like laser, but is not. Brainwaves are electrical. They are grounded within the gun by the copper wiring. There is no danger of electrocution, as I have embedded certain precautions. I shall loan you my notes if you wish," Franklin sound very agreeable and willing to answer questions.

Lewis pursed his lips and nodded as he sat down the teacup. In the far corner, he noticed a black mass forming itself.

"What is that in the corner? The black mass over there," Lewis pointed to the void of darkness morphing into a shape. He'd seen many strange things, many ghastly experiments in his years with Sudicorp, but none as disturbing as an independent shadow obeying on command and struggling to act on its own.

Without a word, Franklin turned slowly and deliberately toward the distant shadow and said in a loud voice, "Egredere, et sta meae. 'Come forth and wait for my command'." The mass stopped morphing; however, it refused to obey. It just stood at a distance, quiet and still, as if glaring at its master in defiance.

Drake Carver shuddered and he swallowed hard. Lewis Avery stepped back slowly, his stomach trying hard not to churn. His heart pounded in fear.

Again, Thomas Franklin said in a loud voice, "Egredere, et sta meae."

Still the black mass refused to obey. This time Franklin grabbed up a strange, metallic headband and situated it on his head. Then, he moved toward the misshapen mass with his arms spread out. The others did not see the whites of his eyes disappear and turn solid black, as he said for the third time, even louder than before, "EGREDERE, ET STA MEAE!"

This time, the shadow slowly glided across the tile in direction of its master's voice. When it stood about four feet away from Franklin, it halted abruptly and awaited further instructions.

Carver and Lewis exhaled slowly. "What was that about?" Lewis sucked in a lung full of air.

The whites of Franklin's eyes returned and he staggered back a little, nearly unnoticeable. As he removed the headband, he turned to Lewis. "Sometimes my brain needs a little boost. Therefore, I have to use this headband. As you can see, there are six sensors embedded within. As they lay against my head, the brainwaves increase and intensify the commands."

"Your brainwaves control the shadows?" Lewis' eyebrows knitted together awhile he glared at the shadows standing to attention. Franklin handed him the headband. Accepting the band, he examined it carefully then looked up, still waiting for an answer.

"Yes, my brainwaves, with the commands in Latin, control the shadows. These creatures must have someone or something to keep them in check. When they are attached to an object or person, they are governed by the movement of that object or person. However, without such attachment, they tend to get out of control." Franklin moved to a stool and sat. As he turned away from the men, he closed his eyes a moment and struggled for air.

Franklin was sitting with a hand to his chest. "Are you okay?"

At first, Franklin didn't respond. This time, Lewis saw him gasping.

"Franklin, are you all right?" He moved to the man and placed a hand on his shoulder. Franklin looked to him and nodded.

"I don't think so," Carver said reaching for the telephone, but Franklin grabbed his hand.

"I'm all right. Just need a moment."

"You don't look all right," Carver replaced the telephone receiver. Lewis could see the weakness in the man's blue eyes and his pale, drawn face.

"Really, Carver, I'm fine," he paused a moment, then continued. "It takes a lot out of a person to control these bloody things. The headband just augments the strain. I am fine." Franklin finished speaking and took in a long deep breath.

Lewis set down the headband. "You seem to be in control now. I'll approve the experiment. Take it easy Franklin."

"Thank you Lewis. Will you join us for lunch?" Carver looked to Franklin, who nodded his approval. Lewis shifted his gaze from one man to the other.

"I said I'd approve the experiment. Lunch is not necessary." Lewis sounded abrupt.

"Lewis…"

"The approval will be on your desk within half an hour. Take it easy Franklin. Carver." With that, he sped past the shadows that were still at attention. When he reached the door, he slid his keycard across the slot. The door opened.

As soon as he left the room, Franklin turned to Carver. "He still doesn't like me, does he?"

"You tried to kill the guy, who can blame him?" Carver leaned in to get a better look at Franklin's face. His features looked more relaxed.

"You appear to be better now." Carver started to move away.

"I still need to test the abilities of the project as we've discussed," Franklin arose from the stool and pulled himself up to his full height.

"I know. I hope that doesn't mean you're going to attempt to kill him again."

Franklin shot him a dirty look, but said nothing.

"Meet me in the lobby." With nothing more said, Drake Carver turned and left. Franklin's eyes turned solid black again as he glared at the shadows.

Chapter Three
Karaoke Bar—Evening

The karaoke bar always had a large crowd on the weekends, but on a weeknight like tonight, not so much. The small, round tables scattered about seemed nearly empty except for Francie DeWitt and her cousin Meggie Caulder. Pushing back her chestnut-colored hair, Francie grinned at the list of songs in hand. Meggie laughed and pointed to the song 'Music of the Night', pretending she was the Phantom of the Opera by standing up and acting like she was twirling a cape.

The tiny one-person stage, now empty, seemed to be waiting for the next superstar.

A handsome young man with short curly dark hair served as the DJ for tonight's karaoke as he turned on the machine and set up his display of CD's.

The simple atmosphere displayed no frills, just plain round tables, straight back chairs and a couple of posters advertising American Idol and America's Got Talent decorating the walls.

"So, why don't you do 'Music of the Night'? It'd be cool to hear a woman sing it," remarked Francie as she sipped a glass of water without ice.

"I'm thinking about it but I'd really like to do 'Let it Go'." You know that song from the animation; Frozen," Meggie replied.

"I don't think you know it that well. Do something you really know all the words to."

"Maybe you're right. So, Lloyd brought you to this place. Guess you like it since you wanted to come back." Meggie grinned like a mocking schoolgirl.

"I like it because they have a great song selection."

"Why don't you like Lloyd? He's so adorable!" Meggie looked off into space with that glassy lovesick look in her eyes.

"Puppies are adorable. Kittens are adorable. Babies are adorable, but a grown man is not adorable," corrected Francie playfully. "I don't dislike him. There're no fireworks. You know?"

"You and fireworks! Come on. If only he'd look at me. I'd snap him up in a minute."

"Be my guest. I want true love. I don't want a relationship built on a physical attraction," explained Francie.

Meggie sipped her soda. "What's wrong with physical attraction? It works for me."

"Meggie, you're too easy to please."

"So, you admit you're attracted to him?" Francie's cousin grinned impishly.

"In a distorted way. He's sweet, kind, and thoughtful, but I am not in love with him. He annoys me with the stalking, among other things. Every morning at seven-thirty, he's there for coffee and a blueberry muffin. Every evening, around seven when I'm about to close, he's there for whatever. I've told him so many times why it doesn't work with us and he still says I should give him a chance." Francie half lied. Actually, she had strong feelings for the man, but due to the strange visions received when he touched her, she'd broken off the relationship. The darkness she kept seeing around him terrified her.

"What other things annoy you?"

"Maybe annoy is the wrong word for *the other things.*' Something about him just isn't normal. There's darkness around him," Francie looked away hoping she didn't sound too crazy.

"Darkness? What does that mean?"

"I don't know. Darkness. I…I feel it. Sometimes he creeps me out."

"That doesn't make sense. Darkness? Fireworks? Loosen up, cuz. That is the only thing wrong with you. Wound too tight!"

Meggie looked up from her soda to see Franklin coming through the door. His eyes lit up when he saw Francie DeWitt. No longer in his white lab coat, he wore a pale blue denim shirt and jeans. As he approached the table,

Francie tried not to let him see her roll her eyes. Meggie's face lit up and she grinned like a child meeting Santa Claus.

"It's my good fortune this evening; two of my favorite, beautiful women. Meggie, Francie," like a gentleman Franklin took the hand of each woman and kissed it.

"Hey, Lloyd! Come join us," Meggie motioned for him to sit next to her, but instead he sat by Francie. Meggie's smile faded into a pained look. Nothing hurts more than unrequited love.

Meggie excused herself to prepare for her song. "Looks like you two need alone time. I'll just go tell the DJ what songs I'm going to sing."

Francie reached out to stop her, but Meggie was too quick and she found herself alone at the table with Franklin, the man that annoyed her so.

"I come to the bar every night, hoping you'll be here. I've missed you so much," Franklin looked at her lovingly and tried to take her hand, but she quickly moved it away.

"No offence, but you come to the bakery twice a day. How can you miss me?" Francie held back *some* of her rudeness.

"I miss being with you like this. If only you'd give me another chance…" Francie cut him off.

"Lloyd, I gave you two chances. I just don't feel the same way. Give Meggie a chance. She'd make a wonderful wife." Francie looked into his blue eyes and saw a hopeless case.

Ignoring anything said about Meggie, Franklin replied, "I can make you happy, Francie. I would give you anything you wanted. I have a good job at Sudicorp. You'd have a good home."

"Please quit stalking me. I don't know why, but I can't get a judge to put a restraining order against you."

"Francie, please…"

"No, you listen. Stop following me around."

"Francie, look at me. Look at me," Franklin said gently. Their eyes met.

"I am in love with you. Look into my eyes and tell me you don't care whether I live or die and I will leave straight away, and never bother you again."

This unexpected demand of truth hit her like a ton of rocks. She did care about him, but in love? She wasn't sure. For a moment, she said nothing.

"I am waiting for an answer," Franklin gently demanded.

"I do care whether you live or die. We have a physical attraction. Just understand that I don't want a relationship built on that. I need to be in love with the man. Do you understand?" Exasperation washed over her. Again, this wasn't the entire truth, but she feared any ounce of hope would keep him hanging on. As it was, she'd still given him a wisp of promise.

A faint smile crept across his lips. "A physical attraction? I can work with that."

"Good night! Selective hearing much!" Francie muttered to herself as she scooted away from him. Again, she rolled her eyes. "I don't see fireworks when we kiss and there are other things, things I just can't explain."

"Fireworks? What do you mean fireworks?" His brows knitted together and he narrowed his eyes at her, trying to understand.

"When I kiss you, I don't see fireworks…" her voice trailed.

Meggie came to the microphone as a few people filtered into the room. The hour grew late and the lights dimmed. The spotlight hit her. "Good evening ladies and gentlemen. My name is Meggie and I'm going to sing an old standard: You Made Me Love You. I believe this song became famous when a teenage Judy Garland sang it to the framed photo of Clark Gable."

Meggie turned to the DJ and nodded. He put on the CD and the intro began. As Meggie sang, she looked straight at Franklin. He tried to look away, but there was no mistaking that she meant the song for him. Generally, he kept his composure, but having a woman he had no feelings for sing to him made him squirm with uneasiness.

Meggie truly had a great voice and when she hit that last line, Franklin looked guilty. Francie seemed sad.

The crowd, what little there was, applauded wildly and begged for more. Meggie smiled and took a bow. Franklin didn't react.

Even though her cousin had a great singing voice, nothing attracted the male population more than a song from Francie DeWitt.

Upon stage, the spotlight hit her and Francie began, "My name is Francie. I usually sing duets with my friend Lloyd, but tonight I'm going to sing solo an old country favorite made famous by the late Patsy Cline, I Fall to Pieces."

She nodded to the DJ and he slipped on the CD. In a few moments, she began at the musical cue; "I fall to pieces, each time someone speaks your name. I fall to pieces, how can I be just your friend..."

Something about Francie's voice seemed to stir every man in the room to a heated passion. They tried to hold back, but something made them climb on stage for her.

Franklin looked around the room and said under his breath, "Strong emotions always drew me to her, but the sound of her singing voice makes me quiver with an insatiable craving."

As he glanced about the room, he noticed that the few men there, including the DJ, seemed to be drooling for her as well. Why?

Francie couldn't finish the song when the DJ came toward her with wanton in his green eyes and reached for her. She had to stop singing.

In shock, she stood still as the music played on, and the other men, including Franklin crowded the stage for her, to appease their desire. Men reacting to her song came as no surprise, but for them to climb up on stage after her in the middle of a song was a shock.

Franklin realized Francie had stopped singing. Seeing the flock of men around her, he raced to the rescue, pulling them away and escorting her off stage.

"Thanks Lloyd! I don't know what's wrong with the men in this place. I've never seen them react like that." Francie shuddered from fear. The incident nearly overwhelmed her.

"I'm sorry this happened. We've been here before, but as you've said, never have the men reacted like this. Perhaps it's because we've always sang duets." He pulled the chair out for her. After she sat, he pushed the chair in.

"You aren't hurt, are you?" asked Franklin as he sat next to her.

Meggie hugged her cousin. "You okay, Francie?"

"Yeah, I'm okay. Just a little shook up. What's going on here?"

Francie was puzzled, but Franklin acted like he wasn't too surprised. Some of the heat died down, but his face flushed a little and he mopped his brow with a napkin. Because he had strong feelings for her anyway, whatever stirred the male libido to the max, made him pant for his want of the woman.

Several numbers went on stage after this, until finally, the DJ said, "We'd like to welcome Lloyd Maxwell and Francie DeWitt. They haven't been here in a while. We apologize for the reaction of the males in here this evening when Francie tried to do a solo. Maybe we can get Lloyd to sing with her."

Franklin looked to her and smiled. "Endless Love?" Reluctantly, she half smiled and nodded. They both stood up with a roar of applause and climbed upon the stage as, accepting the mikes from the DJ, they told him their selection.

At the musical cue, Franklin began.

Francie sang the reply.

As they sang, that old warm feeling she once felt for Franklin returned. The glow in her face showed genuine passion for the man with whom she sang.

In turn, he moved closer to her and caught her hand.

When they looked into each other's eyes, Francie looked past the darkness, only to see the man she had fallen in love with, the man who loved her unconditionally.

The song ended.

For a moment they stared into each other's eyes as they held the final note. Then, as in the past, their lips met and they held each other as if they were the only two in the entire world. As the evening wore on, Francie and her cousin thanked Franklin for his company and got up to leave.

Franklin arose from his chair and asked, "Did you ladies walk or drive?"

Meggie replied. "We walked. I live close by. But you know that."

"Please allow me to drive you home. It's not safe for two women alone at this hour, especially after the men's strange behavior this evening." Franklin offered with eyes only for Francie.

Meggie and Francie exchanged looks. Francie agreed and they walked out of the bar with Franklin.

When they reached Meggie's home, Franklin walked the women to the door. In spite of everything she'd said to him, Francie felt obligated to invite him inside. After all, he did rescue her from her adoring male fans and their raging hormones.

With fake cheerfulness, Meggie excused herself. "Thanks for a lovely evening. If you don't mind, I'm headed for bed. Work tomorrow."

"Wait! Meggie..." Francie reached out for her, but Meggie grinned and pulled away.

"I'm sure you two have catching up to do. Night!" And with that, she trotted off to the next room.

"Looks like we're alone," Francie said awkwardly, as she motioned for him to come in then closed the door behind him.

"If I make you uncomfortable, I don't have to come in. I can leave now." Franklin seemed so meek and pitiful.

"No, it's okay. Have a seat," she motioned to the sofa before them. The room seemed a bit cluttered with mismatched furniture and some Native American dream catchers of various colors hanging from the ceiling.

The two sat next to each other on the sofa. The moment felt even more awkward than when Meggie first left the room. For a long, strained moment, no one said a word.

"Tonight was pretty weird, huh?" Francie broke the uncomfortable silence.

"It was. Your singing was magnificent, as always." Oddly enough, Franklin appeared at a loss for words. Gently, he placed an arm around her.

"Thanks! You've always said kind words about my singing. Let's talk about you. What was the name of the company you work for?" She tried to change the subject, afraid of where he might lead the conversation.

"Sudicorp. It's a research company."

"What do you research?"

"Oh...things that would better the world."

"For instance?"

"The cure for selected diseases, testing products for consumer purchase, and..."

"And what?" Francie turned her eyes to his. She felt the warmth of his body. The scent of his Pierre Cardin cologne filled her nostrils and the closeness made her tingle all over.

The floral fragrance enveloping Francie waltzed about her. The man leaned in and crushed his lips to hers. Instinctively, he wrapped his arms around her and she started to melt. Her arms wrapped around his neck. The kiss became more intense, more feverish with the deep heat of passion.

At that instant, a scene flashed in her mind's eye. She flinched, broke the kiss, and laid her head against Franklin's wide, manly chest.

The vision: outdoors and overcast skies, while people milled about wearing medieval clothing. Many of the men dressed in chain mail armor, like knights. The women wore long dresses with various hats and veils. A castle overlooked the village in the background.

A man who looked very much like Franklin, dressed in the same chain mail armor as the other knights, stood with a beautiful woman who had two small children with her.

Some sort of low hanging mist or fog crept along the ground. The knight picked up each child and kissed it. Still holding the female child, the knight leaned over to the woman and kissed her. The name Arianna came to mind. The names of Rowena and Gregory impressed the mind as the name of the children. The boy named after his father.

The next scene revealed the same knight, who looked like Franklin, sitting inside a thatched cottage before a crude table speaking to a veiled woman who sat gazing into a large bowl. They exchanged inaudible words. The knight arose in anger and stormed out of the cottage.

A battle scene flashed at a crude, handmade bridge. The same knight appeared to lead a charge against the opposing army. Blood, body parts and inaudible screams filled the air.

"Francie, what's wrong?" asked Franklin quietly. "Have I offended you?"

For the moment, she said nothing. Yet, she clung to him and, pressing her head against his chest, she allowed the vision to play out.

The vision continued: the knight returned home with his seemingly victorious army, only to find the village destroyed, its inhabitants massacred.

Devastated by the scene, the knight and his army ran in various directions to find their homes and loved ones. The knight found his family slaughtered, their bodies hacked to pieces in a pool of blood. Inaudible cries of anguish arose from the knight as he threw back his head and uttered something toward the heavens. Then he sank to his knees and wept at the bloody remains of his family.

25

The final scene showed the knight ripping through a sea of men, hacking them to pieces, stabbing some, beheading others and running many through with his sword.

The terror and pain stabbed Francie as if she had lived the horror. Tears welled up in her eyes and she shook all over from the massacre she'd just witnessed.

"Francie, what's wrong?" Franklin pushed her back a little. She looked into his face. Without a doubt, he was the knight in her vision. His hair looked longer and shaggier, but there was no mistaking the face or the eyes, especially the sadness in those beautiful blue eyes.

"Francie. Talk to me. What's wrong?" Gently, he shook her. His lower lip quivered a little, fearing the worse for the woman he loved.

"Was it you? The knight? The entire town destroyed. Everyone dead." She stared into his eyes unwavering, tears streamed down her cheeks.

"What? What are you asking?"

"I saw a man who looked like you; dressed as a knight wearing chain mail armor. He had a family. There was a battle at a bridge, but the town was attacked. All dead...."

"Stop! Stop! How do you know this?" Franklin narrowed his eyes. "How do you know this?"

"I saw it when you kissed me. There's a woman, Arianna. A girl child, Rowena. A boy named after his father, Gregory."

"You know all of this from a kiss?"

"Your touch. So much pain. So much, sorrow. I can't bear to see anymore." Pushing him away, Francie tried to get up, but he pulled her back.

The story sounded all too familiar. The nightmare and grief filled his soul again as it did the day his family died. Oh, how he wished for death rather than relive the horror!

"Francie, how did you see this?" His hands shook as he fought to hold back the tears.

"Get away from me!" she pushed him hard and jumped up. Grabbing her purse, she headed for the door.

"No! Wait Francie! Don't leave," Franklin caught her arm.

Her mind reeled from the flood of visions and emotions. For an instant, the room swayed and she thought she might pass out. Franklin's voice filled the back of her mind, but she shut him out. Jerking away, she flung open the door and ran for her car parked in front of the house.

What was he? What did I see? Francie questioned the vision. In the past, she had seen inside the very core of selected people, but never had an ocean of information and grief hit her as it did tonight.

The click of the lock sounded, unlocking Francie's car. She tried to open it, but Franklin grabbed her around the waist and cried, "Stop a minute! Talk to me!" Holding her close to him, he whispered softly in her ear, "Please tell me how you saw this."

The warmth of his breath added to the sensuality of the moments prior to the visions, but the bloody battle and attack of the village loomed up in her mind.

The stench of burning flesh and burning wood filled her nostrils. For an instant, Francie felt as if she'd been physically transported to the village of the dead. Cries of grieving survivors rose up from the returning knights of the bridge.

The ghastly odor of smoke and death made Francie cough and choke.

The vision cleared away and the sound of Franklin's voice brought her back to reality. By now, her breathing had become labored, and the night, her car, Meggie's house all began to swirl around in a murky haze. A great lump of terror lay in her stomach and she fell back against Franklin.

Gently, he caressed her hair and kissed her face and temple. Franklin whispered again, "It's all right. I'm here. I will protect you."

Francie lay back against his broad chest and closed her eyes for a moment. "Take a deep breath, my love."

She obeyed and the oxygen quelled the terror.

Franklin's voice whispered softly, "I'm going to loosen my grip. Don't run from me. I won't hurt you. Just turn slowly and look at me."

Franklin loosened his grip and Francie slowly turned around in his arms and stared into his deep blue eyes. Her breathing slowed to normal.

As if possessed, Francie began speaking in the voice of another woman, one of high breeding with an English accent.

"Release me and the children. Let us go. Release the darkness before it consumes you." The image of the woman called Arianna from the vision overshadowed Francie.

27

Franklin let out a loud gasp, releasing Francie altogether as he stumbled back in shock. "Arianna!" He gasped.

Wild-eyed, he exclaimed, "Are you a dream or a ghost?"

The woman repeated the words. "Release me and the children. Let us go. Release the darkness before it consumes you."

Francie saw her chance to escape and took it. Opening the car door, she slid under the steering wheel, and slammed the door shut. The click of the locks rang out. In an instant, the engine turned over and Francie took off as though the devil himself were chasing her.

The image of Arianna vanished, leaving Franklin reeling in the wake of a specter and the terrified woman he loved. Quickly, he blinked several times then ran for his own car and zoomed off into the night.

Chapter Four
Pursuit by Night

The roar of the engines from Francie's Honda and Franklin's BMW shattered the stillness of the night as they squealed around the little residential area where Meggie lived. Every vision Francie had ever seen she had taken at face value, no symbolism, no riddles. What had she witnessed tonight? Was it possible for a man to be alive in the present if he had lived in the twelfth century? That would be more than seven hundred years ago.

A car coming toward her swerved to keep from collision then did a zigzag from left to right. The BMW tailing her jerked to the right to keep from ramming the oncoming car. As he looked in the rear view mirror, Franklin's eyes flashed solid black. His car picked up speed.

Once more, Francie felt like hyperventilating or maybe throwing up. Gasping for oxygen, she hit the gas and headed into the heart of Los Angeles.

The two cars roared into the city, speeding past closed shops, fast food stands and some high-rise office buildings. Franklin's BMW braked at the intersection where Francie's car had zoomed through.

Francie and her car seemed to have vanished. Looking about him, Franklin searched for any sign of Francie's car.

Not even a police officer to stop reckless drivers. Where'd she go?

Quietly, he proceeded down the street, eyeing every corner for a hint of where Francie might hide.

For the next thirty-five to forty minutes, Franklin drove around in what seemed like circles through the empty streets. Tired of the charade, he pulled under a streetlight and got out of the car. Looking straight ahead, Franklin stretched out both arms and in a loud voice commanded in Latin,

29

"Veni ad me, et tenebrae. Venite ad me tenebrae. Find mulier exspecto. Veni ad me, et tenebrae. Veni ad me, Umbram. 'Come to me darkness. Come to me shadows. Find the woman I look for. Come to me darkness. Come to me shadows'."

In answer to the summons, roiling black clouds moved around Franklin. Shadows great and small danced like dwindling demons to their master's call. Soon, the streetlights winked out one by one, and the darkness created an eerie illumination of the man who summoned them.

In the still of the night, a car rolled farther into the alley adjacent to the roiling darkness and out of sight.

Chapter Five
Franklin's Lab at Sudicorp

Dr. Thomas Franklin jotted down a few notes in his journal on the Hades Experiment as Lon Jamison held a blowtorch in front of a group of human shadows, keeping them at bay. The cellphone before him rang, but Franklin ignored it.

The young man blanched white and his hands shook as if he had the St. Vitus Dance.

The cellphone ceased ringing.

"Dr. Franklin, will you please command these things. I don't...don't think I can keep them back much longer," Lon's forehead beaded with tiny pearls of sweat and some even streamed down his face. A slight quiver in his voice gave away his terror.

At first, Franklin didn't seem to hear him, as he continued writing in his journal. The door slid open and Drake Carver marched in.

"Aren't you answering the dang phone today?" Carver's face was distorted in frustration. Then he noticed Lon with the blowtorch holding the shadows at bay.

"What's with them?"

No answer.

"Franklin, are you listening? Answer the stinking cell and command those dang shadows." Carver's voice rang with agitation.

At last, Franklin looked up and saw the plight of his trembling lab assistant with the blowtorch.

"Sustine me mandato. 'Wait for my command'." Franklin said calmly and the shadows moved back and stood to attention. Without looking at Lon or Carver, he returned to his notes.

31

Lon relaxed and turned off the blowtorch then set it down on the workbench next to Franklin. Pulling a handkerchief from his pocket, Franklin handed it to his lab assistant and retuned to writing.

As Lon mopped his face and forehead with the handkerchief, Carver glowered over the doctor, awaiting acknowledgement.

Finally, Franklin finished writing and looked up. "Good morning Drake. Sounds like you're in a vile mood."

"Don't get smart with me. The only time you don't answer your cell is when you are moody and depressed. Bad night?" Carver glared.

"I should ask you the same, since *you* are the one irritated." Franklin looked first at Carver then at Lon.

"I need to know if you have succeeded in controlling the darkness. The Commander and Chief want to know. If yes, then we need details."

"You shall have the results tomorrow. I have one last test to perform this evening," Franklin replied. Looking to Lon, he asked, "Are you quite all right? You're as white as a sheet."

"Sir...that's...that's technically incorrect as sheets come in various colors and floral patterns," Lon answered, still with a quiver in his voice.

"I'm aware of that, Mr. Jamison. However, there was a time when sheets were completely white, women neither voted nor smoked in public, and children were seen and not heard."

Twenty-six year old Lon Jamison replied, "I've heard of such things, but it's all before my time. Children being seen and not heard I just can't imagine." After giving a blank look and a forced smile, Lon folded the handkerchief and handed it back to Franklin.

Holding up his hand in refusal to reclaim it, Franklin grinned mischievously, "Keep it. You may need it again."

With eyes wide and laced with terror, Lon strained to smile and said, "Thank you, sir." And with that, he nodded to Carver and left the room.

"Poor lad. The shadows scare him half to death. He hasn't actually seen the darkness. That should be a revelation." Looking to a disgruntled Carver, Franklin asked, "What's the matter?"

"There was a story of some streetlight malfunctions and a few injuries that happened early this morning at one am. One eyewitness claimed they saw silhouettes moving about in the darkness, breaking store windows and attacking them. This person said they were clawed." Carver glared at Franklin.

"Your point?"

"This was a result of your experiment, wasn't it?"

"Obviously."

"No one is supposed to get hurt or killed. What in heaven's name are you doing?"

"I'm doing what you gave me permission to do, my job."

"Things didn't go well with Francie, did they?"

Franklin fell silent and closed his journal.

"I hate when you do this. How many years have we known each other and you still clam up?" Carver removed his glasses, pulled out a handkerchief, and started rubbing the lenses vigorously.

"This evening I want full control. No interference from you or anyone from Sudicorp," Franklin looked Carver in the eye.

"Agreed."

Picking up a small device that resembled an old-fashioned transistor radio, Franklin switched it on and said, "This device is an EVP 'electronic voice phenomenon' recorder. This is the same as that used to record voices and sounds of spirits, ghosts, or if you prefer, paranormal sounds. The human ear may not detect the voice or sound, but more than likely, this device will record it." Franklin moved to the three shadows standing at attention, waiting for their master's command. Placing the EVP recorder close to them, he held it there for about a minute then turned back to Carver.

"I'm going to play it back. Listen closely," Franklin rewound the recorder and played it back. Carver swallowed hard.

The voices played back sounded high pitched and eerily haunting:

"He thinks we're stupid. See how he treats us?"

A reply, "They don't know. They think we are controlled by humans."

A caution, "Don't let them know."

A soft 'click' sounded as the recorder switched off. Carver pulled Franklin away from the shadows. "Are these voices of the shadows?"

Franklin glanced back at the three-dimensional silhouettes then looked to Carver and gave an affirmative nod.

"What do they mean? If you aren't controlling them, then who is? This is not good. You need to pull the plug on this now. If you lose control..."

"They talk, we learn, and I will not lose control of anything. I know what I'm doing. This morning, I discovered their ability to communicate with each other. This is a phenomenal break through. That's why I need to record it in my journal.

"As for what you heard on the news, I will keep a record of that as well. Leave it all to me." Franklin removed his white lab coat. Grabbing his sports jacket, he put it on and motioned for Carver to follow him.

"Have you ever met anyone with the Song of the Lorelei? They also bear the gift of a soul reader, knowing the past and future of whoever they read." Franklin kept talking as he and Carver reached the door. Franklin slid his keycard across the slot and the door slid open.

"I've never actually met one, but I have known people who have. Why?" Carver talked as the two walked down the white, sterile looking hallway.

"Francie has the Song of the Lorelei. When she sings, it affects every male in earshot of her. I thought the DJ and the few men in the room were going to stampede the stage to get to her. I have deep affection for Francie as it is, but for me, it was most uncomfortable, maddening. When I heard her sing, I wanted her so much I would risk all, life and limb, to acquire her body and soul. It felt down right painful." Franklin stopped walking and Carver halted as well to look at him.

"Her song is that alluring?"

"It was past alluring. To hear the song of a siren, a man reacts with wild abandon. Completely on impulse with no regard for the consequences. Nothing fills the mind but wanton craving for the creature uttering the song. It was like nothing I'd ever felt ...overwhelming ...dominating...raw lust. Do you have any idea what that was like?"

"No, I don't believe I do. Are you sure she's a siren?"

"Later that evening, she read my soul. I believe she had done so in the past, but never acknowledged it. I am quite sure that was what came between us. I know she loves me. She never says she doesn't love me, but won't tell me why she doesn't want to be with me."

"You keep saying she's going to be your wife. Why?"

"I won't give up on us."

"What did she see?"

"She knows who I am. Apparently, she saw my life prior to our meeting each other."

"That part of you even I don't know. You would never share it. All I recall is you asking me to kill you."

"If you'd been a true friend, you would have honored my request," Franklin replied coldly and began walking as Carver followed.

Chapter Six
Another Sterile Lab inside Sudicorp

Inside this sterile looking, all white lab within the heart of Sudicorp, Lewis Avery watched over a glass chamber containing a roiling black cloud suspended within. It didn't appear particularly threatening, but at times, it discharged invisible bolts of electricity, which crackled and nearly shattered the glass. Lewis made sure another clear chamber encased the original.

From time to time, he checked the readings on the voltmeter setting on a little stand before him. When he heard the "click" of the door, he turned to see Carver and Franklin entering the lab. Lon Jamison stood on the other side of the chamber, monitoring the way the cloud seemed to roil at selected times, then expanding and shrinking. He took notes each time the cloud changed.

"You have quite an experiment here. I've never seen anything like it. Suspended darkness. Looks a lot like a condensed dark cloud," remarked Lewis as the men drew closer.

"I am so pleased you're impressed. I've made some significant progress wouldn't you say?" Franklin gave a wry smile. Lewis nodded.

"However, I am concerned about what I'm hearing on the news. The attack from claw marks…shadows?" Lewis moved away from the voltmeter and stood eye to eye with Franklin.

"What makes you say that? Claw marks don't have to mean shadows," Franklin walked around Lewis, eyeing him like a contagious disease.

"No one reported anything like that until you started this experiment. What about the report of moving silhouettes breaking store windows and streetlights popping out?"

"You can't blame me for burglaries and used up light bulbs." Franklin motioned for Lon to bring him the notes of the darkness monitoring. His lab assistant handed him the clipboard.

"Are you listening to me? The weird stuff started with this experiment. I approved the project with the assurance from you and Drake that no one would be injured or killed. Currently, there have been two injured and damage done to several stores. Sounds like what I witnessed in your lab."

Looking up from the clipboard, Dr. Thomas Franklin narrowed his eyes at Lewis and said, "I resent the fact that you are accusing me of endangering the people of this city and that I've been less than honest with you. Think twice before you choose to stop the experiment. It may not be the wisest decision." Franklin finished speaking and handed the clipboard back to Lon.

"Lewis, don't provoke him. You know accusations without valid proof cannot stand up in Sudicorp, just as it doesn't in the world outside of here. What you have is speculation," Carver reminded.

"I know that and I will get you the valid proof, even if it kills me," stated Lewis with a touch of venom. Without another word, he shot one last look of defiance at Franklin before leaving the lab.

"Remember, the last test is this evening. No matter what happens, you will not interfere, understood?" Franklin said without emotion.

"I know. Just do it. I'll deal with the aftermath." Carver pushed up his glasses and gave a long drawn out sigh.

Chapter Seven
Office of Lewis Avery

The digital clock on the desk of Lewis Avery read seven pm. Lewis tossed the paperwork he'd been reading back on his desk and rubbed his eyes with both hands. He'd had a long day and he thought about going home.

At that moment, his cellphone rang. He picked it up, swiped a finger across the face, and said, "Avery, safety and security."

A garbled voice came on that said, "The three…" There was a crackling sound and then, "have been taken." Another crackling sound and, "Franklin knows…" then the line went dead. The voice sounded a lot like Drake Carver, but he couldn't be sure. If anything went missing involving the research or experiments, Franklin was the go-to man. As much as he hated it, Lewis knew he'd have to talk to him, right now.

After checking his gun in his shoulder holster, Lewis called for two men to meet him in the parking lot. They should be able to catch Franklin before he left for the day.

The parking lot looked deserted. Only a few scattered cars remained. Dr. Thomas Franklin approached his BMW and pressed a button on the remote and the locks clicked open. As he reached for the door handle in the rapidly fading light of day, he jerked around when he heard someone call his name.

"Franklin! Stop a minute. I need to talk to you!" exclaimed Lewis as he slowly walked toward the doctor.

Without a word, Franklin opened the car door, slid in under the steering wheel and slammed the door shut. The engine turned over and the BMW backed out so quickly, Lewis and his men had to run to get out of its way.

"STOP FRANKLIN! I JUST WANT TO TALK!" Lewis shouted, waving his hands in the air. As the car moved forward, it picked up speed and deliberately tried to run him down. Lewis drew his gun, but had to hop on to a nearby car to avoid injury.

Franklin's eyes became solid black. "I will kill you Lewis Avery!" He growled in a distorted voice.

The BMW screeched out of the Sudicorp parking lot with a black Toyota Camry close behind. Twists and turns with increasing speed led the two cars barreling into the streets of Los Angeles, very close to where Franklin had chased Francie the night before.

Streetlights popped on as daylight faded rapidly. In the Toyota, Lewis squinted to ensure the accuracy of where they headed. Ty Barnett, dark haired security specialist and direct report to Lewis, sat in the passenger seat with his gun drawn. "I thought Dr. Franklin was alone. Maybe I was wrong, but it looks like someone is in the car with him."

"I agree. I thought he was alone, too. Can any of you see who's with him?" Lewis asked. He never acted on impulse, but tonight seemed different. Even though he felt like a lamb to the slaughter, he couldn't back down and he had no time for another plan of action. Biting his lip, Lewis quivered a little. Fear? Not him. After all, he was head of Safety and Security.

Mac Waller, another security specialist, sat in the back seat, also with gun drawn. "I thought I saw something or someone slip into the car before he got in. I can't make out any features. Too dark."

Suddenly, the BMW began to weave in and out of the cars it approached. A number of horns honked in an effort to let the speeding cars know they were there, braking in shock as the two cars ignored them.

Drawing a gun from his belt, Franklin rolled down the window, poked the barrel out, and began firing.

Cursing under his breath, Lewis swerved and exclaimed in anger, "The son of a bitch doesn't care who he kills! Innocent people are out here."

"Should I shoot?" asked Ty, waving his gun.

"Wait! Don't want to shoot civilians. I'm going to try to force him over to the side."

Lewis hit the accelerator, shot out into the left lane and tried to force the BMW to the side of the road. Again, Franklin stuck the gun out of the window and fired several times. The Toyota dropped back and moved into the lane behind the BMW. Then it moved into the lane at the right and picked up speed. This time, Lewis pulled the Toyota over, bumping the BMW to move to the far left.

An overpass loomed up ahead as the Toyota pushed the BMW into the guardrail, forcing it to a dead stop. Lewis and his men jumped from the car. The dimly lit overpass displayed growing shadows dancing about like fireflies before a light. Franklin emerged from his car, crouching as he fired several shots in Lewis' direction. This time, Lewis fired back.

After a moment, the sound of flesh and cloth ripping and tearing rang out, and the screams of Ty and Mac stabbed Lewis in the heart. Something or someone had attacked his men. Ducking between the cars, Lewis peered around the front of the Toyota. In the dim, orange streetlight, he saw the lifeless, bloody hand of one of his men. Another moment passed, before the thud of dead weight hit the ground next to him. Mac lay in shreds, covered in blood.

The door of the BMW slammed, and took off down the busy street.

Glancing at the bodies of his men, Lewis drew a deep breath, got back into the Toyota and started after Franklin.

He knew very well that he should call in the death of his men and ask for back up. Even though he wasn't an official peace officer, he still had to abide a code similar to one. However, he didn't. What he wanted to do to Franklin shouldn't have any witnesses. A few years ago, another incident involving Franklin occurred that had ended in death. Both of Lewis' men had died this night. He had to prevent any more deaths.

Something didn't add up. He only wanted to talk to Franklin, so why did he run? Why did Franklin shoot at him? For a while, the two cars sped up and down streets, side swiping a parked car every now and again.

By now, the sunset heralded the night as the BMW led the Toyota down an alley and came to a screeching halt. Lewis couldn't stop fast enough, and plowed into the rear of the Beemer. Both men leapt from their cars firing at each other. A thick darkness formed around the men. Only the headlights from each car pricked the darkness.

A sharp, searing pain stabbed the left side of Lewis. He kept firing until the gun clicked empty. Franklin caught his jaw with a right jab. Lewis threw a left jab then a right hook. The rustle of shuffling feet sounded all around them. Amid the punches, Lewis tried to see who else was there. Several sharp needle-like things came together and raked his right shoulder and arm. The pain stung as if poison entered the wounds.

Darkness engulfed Lewis. The headlights narrowed and began to fade. For some reason, he couldn't stand up. One last punch to the head sent him to the asphalt.

Void...total blackness.

The back door of the bakery burst open as Francie DeWitt entered the alley with a couple of plastic bags of garbage in hand. She opened the lid of the dumpster by the door and dumped in the two bags.

The motion sensor lights flooded the alley, spotlighting on a crumpled figure of a man lying on the ground in a pool of blood. The smashed front end of the Toyota sat with its headlights broken and dangling from its socket.

Without hesitation, Francie ran to the man's aid. Slowly, she squatted and turned him over. The blazer sleeve of his right arm hung in bloody shreds. His side oozed red life's fluid. She checked his neck for a pulse.

Still alive.

Francie looked up, searching the alley to see if she could see anyone or anything connected to the attack.

Nothing!

Knowing she had to move quickly, Francie struggled to get the man to his feet. Lewis drifted in and out of consciousness. Instinctively, he leaned on her and pushed himself to his feet. Fumbling with the doorknob, she finally got the door open and she pulled the wounded man inside. The click of the lock sounded.

Unbeknownst to Francie, disembodied eyes watched from the shadows of the wall separating the alley from the house next door. After a moment, Franklin reappeared along with his BMW. As he looked in the side mirror, the whites of his eyes returned and he gasped, struggling for breath. Holding his chest with one hand, he fought to stop hyperventilating.

Inside the bakery, Francie half dragged Lewis to a nearby stool where she propped him up against a wall so she could find something to place on the wound to stop the bleeding. Grabbing clean towels from the cupboards, she wrapped some around his bloody arm then pressed a few against his wounded side.

"Come on mister. Help me out here. Press the towel against your wound so I can get you to a hospital," she whispered softly to Lewis. He obeyed.

She moved to the wall telephone, lifted the receiver and started to punch in numbers.

"NO!" Lewis gave a weak call out to her. "No police! No hospital!"

"Look, mister. You'll die if you don't let me…"

"NO!" Lewis staggered to Francie and grabbed her arm. "NO HOSPITAL! NO POLICE!"

Francie stared at him a moment. He looked like he was about to drop as he gasped. She hung up the receiver and let him lean on her.

Tonight, she wouldn't do the usual mopping and cleaning that's done when she closed at seven-thirty each evening. Instead, Francie pulled and half dragged Lewis to the propped open front door and out to her car parked in the lot in front of the building.

After stuffing him into the front seat, she went back to close and lock the front door.

As she drove, Francie tried to keep the man awake. She feared if he passed out before she could stop the bleeding, he would die.

"Hey, mister. Don't pass out on me. Talk to me. What's your name?" She nudged him when his head started to loll about. This would awaken him with a small start and he'd mutter a bit before starting the whole thing all over again.

After twenty minutes or so, Francie rolled up to a building with the words: Angels Bluff Apartments. After clicking the remote, the gate rose and allowed her to move into the parking below.

Parking the car seemed easy compared to getting the wounded man upstairs to her apartment. Francie's heart pounded in fear that he would die or that whoever attacked Lewis would find them and finish him off.

For a few minutes, she struggled to get him out of the car and up the stairs. The stairs really caused a problem. Every step felt strained, as she had to stop to adjust his weight and shake him now and again to awaken him so he could help push himself upward.

After what seemed forever, she finally got him to her apartment and into the bedroom. She made sure the door was locked. Then she bustled about getting a pan filled with water, a first aid kit, a paring knife and small needle nose pliers. Right now, as she glanced at a framed picture of herself and others outside the Dorset Nursing School, she wished she had completed her nursing qualification.

The bleeding had to be stopped first. Digging inside the first aid kit, she found two bottles with Chinese characters on them. Each contained Yunnan Paiyao, a Chinese herbal powder to stop the bleeding. After opening the bottles, she carefully pulled back the blood soaked towels from his side and ripped open his shirt. The sight of the blood and festering wound turned her stomach, but she held her breath and poured the powder into the hole in his side that was oozing red life's fluid. Instantly, the wound closed and the bleeding stopped.

Next, Francie stripped off his shirt and blazer. His right arm and shoulder looked as if claws had ripped them open. She counted three open wounds on his forearm and two on his shoulder. Again, she poured the Chinese powder into the wounds and the bleeding stopped immediately.

Now, she proceeded to wash the blood off from around the wounds, careful not to remove the powder. Since blood covered his pants, she removed them gingerly, trying not to see something she shouldn't.

Several times, she threw out the dirty, bloody water from the bowl and filled it with fresh water. Now, she had to remove the bullet, something she'd never done before. After adjusting the table lamp and switching on the ceiling light, Francie braced herself for the procedure. For a moment, Lewis rallied and grabbed her hand just as she attempted to push away the Chinese powder from the wound. Their eyes met.

"I'm not trying to hurt you, mister. I have to take out the bullet. Please let me do this. You'll die if I don't," Francie tried to hide the tremor in her voice. Her hands turned ice cold, but she steadied the knife. Lewis looked at the knife and back to her. After releasing her hand, he nodded and closed his eyes.

"This is going to hurt, but I have nothing to deaden the pain. So, hang on!" That said, Francie scraped away the power and poked the tip of the knife into the wound. Lewis let out a blood-curdling scream as he grabbed the edge of the bed and squeezed so tight his knuckles turned white.

The knife gingerly probed deeper, until the tip hit something hard. With towels under his side to catch the blood, Francie poked the knife in at an angle to go up under the bullet. In agony, Lewis gritted his teeth and moaned.

When she saw the tiny metal object sticking up through the bloody flesh, she grabbed it with the needle nose pliers and yanked it out quickly. Again, Lewis screamed as if he were dying. Face distorted in pain, he gasped for oxygen.

More powder went into the wound. The bleeding stopped instantly. The only thing she could offer for pain was over the counter pain relievers. For sure, the wounded man would cherish liquor of sorts, a good Scotch, or bourbon perhaps, but Francie had none. Therefore, she offered him ibuprofen, and water to wash it down.

Turning off the ceiling light, Francie finally got a good look at Lewis in the lamplight. His features relaxed and his breathing tried to regain a normal rhythm. Gently, she mopped his handsome face with a clean wet washcloth, as she caressed his ash blond hair and pushed a few stands from his closed eyes. Slowly her eyes and hands moved to his bare, heaving chest as it rose and fell with the rhythm of his breathing. Something made her want to kiss him, but she didn't. What came over her? Why would she feel the urge to kiss a man she didn't know, especially since he nearly bled out in the alley behind her bakery?

She added another blanket to the bed as she tucked in the sleeping man. Then she quietly went out to the kitchen with the bowl of water, the washcloth floating on top. Returning briefly to the bedroom, she gathered up the soiled clothes and put them in a garbage bag then set them in the kitchen, not sure what to do with them.

Thinking he might have a wallet with ID, Francie went back to the plastic bag, opened it, and pulled out the pants. Sure enough, she found a wallet, a keycard, and badge for Sudicorp. The badge had the picture of Lewis Avery, Chief of Safety, and Security. The wallet contained his driver's license and a few credit cards, along with fifty dollars in cash. All this, she set aside on the dresser in the bedroom. The bullet she placed in a glass jar and twisted on the lid. This she set next to the rest of his belongings on the dresser.

Sudicorp...wasn't that the name of the company Lloyd said he worked for?

As she pondered this, her cell rang. She fumbled around looking for her purse. Grabbing it off the kitchen table, she opened it and pulled out the cellphone.

"Hello," she answered softly.

"Cuz, it's me. Are you okay?" Meggie sounded off at the other end.

"Yeah, I'm okay."

"You didn't seem okay this morning. I heard you and Lloyd having words then you both ran outside. I tried to stop you guys, but things got weird. What happened?"

"What do you mean, weird? We didn't see you."

"Lloyd acted afraid of something and you took off in the car."

"Nothing happened. Sorry we disturbed you."

"Why are you whispering? Is he there?"

"No, no, Lloyd's not here. I found a shot and wounded man in the alley and I brought him home to patch him up. He's sleeping right now."

"What? You brought a strange man home? Why didn't you call the police or call an ambulance? Why bring him home?" Meggie sounded worried."He insisted on no police and no hospital," Francie tried to justify.

"And what if the one who shot him followed you? They could kill you both."

"Gee, I never thought about that. You're right, Meggie. That was stupid of me," her face distorted into a worried frown. "By the way, I need to get his car out of the back alley. Can you help me? Please, pretty please..."

"Why not? When did you want to move it?"

"Tonight, while Mr. Lewis Avery is asleep."

"Is that the name of the wounded guy, Lewis?"

"Yes, come pick me up here at my place and then we'll go to the bakery."

"It would have been a lot easier to call the cops," sighed Meggie.

As promised, Meggie picked up Francie and drove to the back alley behind the bakery.

The first thing Francie did was open the back door, pull out a garden hose, attach it to the sink in the kitchen and turn on the water. Then she flushed off all the blood from the asphalt. Once she'd finished, she turned off the water, detached the hose and tossed it under the industrial sink.

The smashed up Toyota still had the key in the ignition and Francie slid under the steering wheel and turned it. It took a moment to start, but when the engine roared, she nodded for Meggie to back out.

After Meggie did so, Francie backed out the Toyota then rolled down the window on the passenger side to talk to her cousin.

"Can I leave his car at your place? You have a two car garage and I have…" Francie started but Meggie cut her off.

"Sure, sure. I knew that was coming. I can keep it there. What happened to the front end? You think it'll make it to my place?"

"I don't know what happened and I think it'll make it. Let's go."

With that, the two cars moved in single file, the Toyota in the lead.

Now that Lewis' car rested in her garage, Meggie turned to her cousin and said, "I still want to know what you and Lloyd were having words over. You nearly gave me a heart attack. I tried calling you all day."

"I turned my cell off when I opened the bakery, and I hid in the kitchen when the time came for Lloyd to get his muffin and coffee." Francie started walking to Meggie's car. Light poles lined the small, two-lane street. Silence fell all around them.

"Come on. Details. There's a twenty-minute drive to your place. Talk to me," Meggie opened the car door and slid in under the wheel.

Francie got into the passenger side. Meggie started the car and backed out of the driveway. As they took their time getting back to Francie's, the conversation continued.

"You know how sometimes I see visions about the people I touch. You know, like I did to you a couple of times," Francie reminded her cousin.

"Like when we were kids and you started yammering about how I had a crush on my math teacher and cheated on my spelling test?" Meggie grinned with amusement.

"You didn't find it funny at the time. You wanted to strangle me," they both started laughing.

"Go on. What happened with Lloyd?"

"He touched me and I saw visions again. The prior ones were creepy enough, but this one was different." Tears welled up in Francie's eyes as the intense emotions and gory details came back to her.

"Different, how?"

"There was a castle, a village with knights, and other people dressed like in a Renaissance Fair. I saw a knight that looked like Lloyd, a bloody fight at some bridge and then when the knight returned everyone was dead and the village burnt to the ground." Francie started crying again. For a moment, she shook all over. Meggie patted her arm and tried to comfort her.

"I didn't mean to upset you. Guess I don't understand. Why are you so touched by this vision? Granted it was a terrible thing for the people, but what does that have to do with Lloyd and you?"

"My visions are never riddles or symbolic. They are what they are."

"What does that mean?"

"I think Lloyd was the knight. In the vision, I saw a woman and two children. I think they were his family."

"Not possible. Nobody lives that long. Don't be so upset. It doesn't mean anything," Meggie shrugged.

"It wasn't just a vision. I felt like I was there. The smell of the burning wood, burning flesh and blood...I could smell it. I felt all the anguish, sadness, and anger of this knight."

"Do you know how you sound? People will think you're a nut job. You didn't tell Lloyd what you saw, did you? I hope not."

"I told him. He seemed upset. I felt like my head would explode. So many emotional scenes flooded into my mind at once. I was dizzy, sick, in pain, and terrified all at the same time. I didn't want him to touch me or talk to me. I had to get away from him." Francie buried her face in her hands and wept bitterly. Meggie glanced at her cousin and shook her head in sorrow. Then she patted her on the shoulder.

"Francie, we're at your place. Don't let this vision come between you and Lloyd, or me for that matter. Maybe you should see a shrink about these crazy perceptions. They're not natural." Meggie pulled in front of Francie's apartment building.

"I have to check on my patient. Come by tomorrow and see him. I am curious as to what happened." Francie gave her cousin a hug and opened the car door.

"Take it easy, girl. If you need me, give a shout." Meggie smiled and Francie nodded then backed away from the car as her cousin drove off.

Upstairs in her apartment, Francie crept to the bedroom door and peeked in on Lewis. He seemed to be resting peacefully and comfortably. Quietly, she moved to the bathroom, closed the door, and took a shower.

Dressed in pajamas, she wrapped a light blue terrycloth robe around her and tiptoed to the sleeping man. His forehead felt like he had no body heat. He actually shivered beneath the blankets.

She said a silent prayer for God to help him recover. Then she went to the closet in the living room and pulled out sweats that used to belong to her now deceased father. She held them up and nodded. They looked like they'd fit.

Softly, she tiptoed back into the bedroom and gently pulled the blankets back. Lifting one leg at a time, she slipped the sweat pants on Lewis then struggled to pull them up. He winced once or twice when she moved him. Looking at the sweat top, she decided it would disturb him more if she tried to slip his arms into the sleeves, so she laid the top across him and pulled the blankets over him.

Moving to the kitchen, she heated water in a kettle to make peppermint tea. With the tea bag in a mug of steaming water, she tiptoed back to the bedroom and set it on the table next to the bed. Lewis still shivered. Feeling his chest and stomach, he had no body heat at all. Picking up the mug of tea, she blew on it to cool it down a bit. Then she lifted his head up and put the mug to his lips.

"Please Mr. Lewis, drink the tea. It'll help you," her soft voice said. Opening his mouth a little, he took in the minty flavored tea. The warm liquid slid down his throat. When he finished the tea, Francie placed the mug on the little table and climbed into bed next to him. Body heat from her would stimulate him to restore his own heat, so she gathered him into her arms, pulled the blankets over them and snuggled him to her.

As the heat of the tea and Francie washed over Lewis, his features relaxed and his sleep seemed restful. Something about the man seemed familiar. In the dimness of the night-light, the scent of his flesh mingled with the urge to touch his face, plagued her. Lovingly, she caressed his head and hair. She placed a soft kiss on his cheek and just held him, until she too fell asleep.

Chapter Eight
Franklin's Lab at Sudicorp

The sterile white lab hung in deathly silence, while Dr. Thomas Franklin and lab assistant Lon Jamison tinkered with the metallic gun. The dark crystal lay on the workbench.

Drake Carver stormed into the room unannounced, making Lon jump.

"Ahhh!" Screamed the young man as tools went flying in the air.

"At least let us know you're coming to visit, Drake. I'm afraid poor Mr. Jamison may have a heart attack if you don't," Franklin remarked calmly, as he replaced the dark crystal into the gun.

"Sorry Lon. I would think by now you'd be used to things here," Carver tried to smile.

"I'm afraid the shadows still unnerve Mr. Jamison. He can't get used to three-dimensional silhouettes moving about on their own," Franklin continued, looking up from his work.

Lon muttered an apology, scrambled to gather up the tools he dropped, and set them on the workbench.

"May I please be excused, Dr. Franklin?" Lon was trembling, his hands shook and his teeth chattered. Franklin chuckled and bowed his head in agreement. Lon took off toward the door, slid his keycard in the slot, and ran out as soon as the door opened.

"Did you want another lab assistant?" Carver asked with concern. "I don't want Lon to pass out or have a heart attack."

"He'll be fine. I rather like him. He can be witty and he is a bright young man."

"What the heck happened last night? Mac and Ty are dead. Found them near the overpass in the heart of L.A. on the Harbor Freeway. Lewis is missing, car and all." Carver glared at Franklin.

"Please have a seat. I am sorry about Mac and Ty. Occupational hazard. Couldn't be helped," was the cold reply.

"They were ripped to bloody pieces and I'm supposed to write this off as an occupational hazard? Admit the experiment is getting out of hand. This has to stop, NOW!" Carver, still standing, jerked the gun from Franklin and set it on the workbench.

Frank turned red as anger washed over him. "Don't ever do that again."

"Or what, Franklin? You'll set your pet shadows on me. Where is Lewis?"

"I believe he's still alive. Can't say for sure. I went back to the alley and everything was cleaned up and his car was gone."

"What the crap does that mean? The security videos show he went after you for something, but you ran and didn't talk to him. A set-up?"

"Do you think that I would set him up? Last time, you tricked him into shooting Helen. Knowing I would react violently and try to kill him. It was you who told him Helen had breached protocol and violated company policies when all the time you wanted her dead. I was the one having an affair with her," Franklin got up so fast the stool turned over.

"She was my wife and yes, I know you were having the affair with her, but Lewis was the best candidate to kill her. So, let's not bring out dirty laundry from my closet. I want to know why two men are dead and Lewis is missing," Carver took an ominous step toward Franklin.

"Lewis attacked me. He followed me into the city proper and I shot in self-defense."

"What happened to Mac and Ty?"

"I acted in self-defense."

"I don't see any marks on you. They are in bloody shreds. How is that self-defense?"

No answer.

Seeing he'd get no response to that question, Carver asked a different one, "You mentioned an alley. What alley?"

"Behind the bakery."

"Francie's bakery?"

"Should I require an attorney?"

"I don't know, should you?" Carver tossed the question back to him.

Franklin recalled acting like this before, but never because of a Sudicorp experiment. Due to the nature of the business, deaths and violence like this could not go without notice from the Office of the President. He didn't care. Franklin stood in defiance. He would admit to nothing.

Carver looked past him a moment and sighed. "We've known each other a long time, Franklin. We've been through a lot together, but you've never involved the workplace. I know you hate Lewis, but if you've killed him, I won't be able to cover it up. I don't even know how to explain the deaths of Mac and Ty."

"You're so clever, I'm sure you'll find a way." Franklin pushed past Carver and headed for the door.

Before leaving, Carver gritted his teeth and kicked one of the nearby stools, one with no shadow.

Chapter Nine
Francie's Apartment—Morning

Sunrise brought tiny rays of sun reaching their arms up and across the land, over the trees and foliage and into the slit of drapes in Francie's bedroom. Twittering birds flitted from tree to tree as the world awoke from slumber.

Lewis Avery stirred a bit and opened his eyes. For a moment, he tried to focus. When he did, he didn't recognize anything. Under the window where sunrays slipped in through the slit of the drapes, a footlocker sat with fluffy stuffed teddy bears and puppies rested on it. A dresser stood straight ahead next to the door. Bottles of perfumes, lotions and powders stretched out across it, along with Lewis' wallet, his Sudicorp badge and a glass bottle containing the bullet pulled from his side.

Suddenly, Lewis realized he was not alone in bed. Slowly, he turned his head, only to see a sleeping Francie cradling his head in her arms.

An angel, I have died and gone to heaven. A smile crept across his face as he scooted up a little, wrapped his good arm around her and pressed his lips to hers.

"Mmm," she moaned quietly. Lewis pressed his lips harder on hers then feathered kisses to her cheek and down her neck.

Startled, Francie's eyes popped open and she pushed him back. "Please stop! I'm not that kind of girl!"

His smile and bright eyes told her he meant no harm. "You are in bed with me," he grinned.

"I only meant to keep you warm. You had chills and were shivering." Francie removed her arm from under his head and tried to scoot out of bed, but Lewis caught her arm gently.

"I didn't mean to offend. You looked so beautiful and peaceful, I couldn't help myself."

"I assure you nothing happened," Francie again tried to move, but Lewis wouldn't let go of her arm.

"That's too bad. I was hoping to have some new, fond memories to keep me company on future cold nights." He released her and Francie quickly scooted out of bed. She had her pajamas on under her bathrobe, so the poor man had to use his imagination.

"Looks like you're feeling better. You're flirting," finally she smiled. "My name is Francie, Francie DeWitt."

"Thank you for saving my life, Francie DeWitt. For a while, I thought I was going to die."

"I did too, but you are alive and hopefully getting well. Are you hungry? I can warm up some beef stew or if you want eggs and bacon, I can fix that too," she offered.

"Beef stew sounds good if it's not too much trouble. By the way, my name is Lewis."

"I know. I removed your clothes and took the liberty to set your wallet and Sudicorp badge on the dresser," she pointed. "I peeked at your ID, Mr. Avery."

"Lewis. Mr. Avery is too formal. Did you happen to peek at anything else?" He grinned.

"Lewis! Please!" red faced, Francie turned quickly, grabbed the doorknob and opened the door. However, before she could zip out, Lewis called out, "I'm only teasing you."

She smiled and said nothing as she headed for the kitchen.

Lewis grimaced as he pushed himself up. The zip up top of the sweat suit lay across him. Noticing his right arm in bandages as well as his side, he was taken aback at the great job the woman had done.

Amid the quiet rustle of pots, pans and dishes from the kitchen, he could hear Francie softly humming. The song fell from her lips and found its way to the man's ears and to his heart. It was an old Stephen Bishop song, It Might Be You.

"Time, I've been passing time watching trains go by, all of my life. Lying on the sand, watching seabirds fly. Wishing there would be someone waiting home for me. Something's telling me it might be you; yes, it's telling me it might be you, all of my life." Francie moved about, taking the leftover beef stew out of the refrigerator and putting it in the microwave to heat.

By now, Lewis stood in the doorway holding his side, with the top of the sweats over his injured shoulder.

At first, Francie didn't see him and went on singing. "Looking back as lovers go walking past, all of my life, wondering how they met and what makes it last. If I found the place, would I recognize the face? Something's telling me it might be you."

Finally, she stopped singing. She looked up and saw Lewis standing at the end of the counter where the dishes were set in the basket to dry.

Fearing that he had taken a turn for the worse, she moved to him and looked up into his face. "Are you all right, Lewis? Did my singing disturb you?"

Without another thought, he took her in his arms and crushed his lips to hers. He held her so tight, Francie almost couldn't breathe, but his body felt good as she wrapped her arms around his neck and he pressed his bare chest to her. Oddly enough, she saw blossoms of light bursting in her mind's eye.

They held each other for so long until Francie had to break the kiss. They stood for a moment, their gaze locked. "I've never kissed anyone and seen fireworks," Lewis kissed her face and pulled her to his bare chest.

"Neither have I, but I always knew that fireworks came from true love," Francie sighed with a silly smile on her face as she laid her head against his chest.

"Did you see them too?" He asked in surprise.

"I did. You were wonderful!" She sighed with delight, like a child savoring its favorite candy. Once again, their lips met and they melted in each other's arms until the bell from the microwave went "ding."

Francie again broke the kiss, "Oh, the beef stew!" Gently she pushed him back, moved to the microwave and pulled out the container of food.

With a big ear-to-ear grin, Lewis shook his head. "Fireworks? Seriously?"

"You saw them too. You admitted it." Francie placed the food in a bowl for Lewis and one for herself. Then she helped him put on the sweat top and zipped it up.

As they sat around the small table in the kitchen, she offered him warm biscuits in a basket. A pitcher of orange juice sat in the middle of the table along with a couple of glasses.

"Don't think I've ever had beef stew for breakfast, but it's delicious," said Lewis as he quickly shoveled the food into his mouth. After the fourth biscuit, he mopped up the last bit of gravy from the bowl and popped it into his mouth. Francie tried to keep up with him, but she could only eat half her food and half a biscuit.

"That was delicious. Best I've ever eaten," Lewis said as he took the pitcher and poured orange juice in each of the two glasses. After draining his glass, he looked to Francie as she shyly stared at him with a lopsided smile.

"I'm so glad you feel better." She said.

"Your song earlier, it was mesmerizing. Have you always sung like that?" Lewis asked.

"What? Something's Telling Me It Might Be You? That's an old Stephen Bishop song. I just sing for fun and I like the song," Francie took another bite of stew.

"But you do know that it's not just the song. When I heard you sing it made me…a…I don't know how to say this politely…hot for you," Lewis hoped he hadn't offended her.

"What? You're kidding, right?" Suddenly, she remembered the last time she sang at the karaoke bar where Lloyd came to her rescue from the men mobbing the stage when she had started singing.

"Seriously. I've never felt like that before. I hope I wasn't too aggressive. You don't seem to be the kind of woman who has a habit of kissing strangers," Lewis studied her carefully. "However, you were in bed with me this morning," he grinned.

Francie blushed again, and smiled.

"I'm not offended. I'm attracted to you, too. I may be in love, at least that's what fireworks during a kiss means to me," she still felt shy in talking to a stranger like this, but something compelled her to look into his sleepy blue eyes.

Poor Lewis couldn't resist and again he pulled her to him, chair and all. Their lips pressed hard against one another and great blossoms of white and multicolored lights burst into sight once again. The heat of two bodies pressing against each other brought a tingle through their entire being. This time, Lewis broke the kiss.

"You're right; this has to be true love. Or else, I'm really dead and in heaven, kissing my guardian angel," he smiled, holding her close and feeling her warm breath tickle his face.

"You're not dead and I think we're moving too fast." Francie pushed him back gently. "Come and sit on the sofa." She stood up and caressed his good arm. The man didn't need any coaxing. He got up and followed her to the sofa. Francie grabbed a blanket lying across the back of the sofa and spread it out for him to sit on.

"Is there anyone you want to call? Wife, girlfriend, mother…"

"Stop! Trying to find out if I'm married or committed to someone, right?"

"Guilty."

"Well, I'm not married or committed. And you?"

"Same. Footloose and fancy free," she smiled.

"You come and sit with me. I'm still a sick man and need attention," Lewis took her hand in his.

"Let me get my first aid kit. I need to check your wounds. We also need to talk about what happened to you?" she squeezed his hand and he released hers.

In a moment, Francie came bouncing back with the first aid kit and some rubbing alcohol.

"If you don't mind, I need to remove your top," gingerly, she motioned to the zipper. Lewis took her hand in his, brought it to his lips and kissed it.

"You can touch me and undress whenever you'd like," he grinned.

"I hope you don't mean what I'd have to kill you for if you meant it," she gave a wry smile as she reclaimed her hand and unzipped the top.

Helping him remove it, she heard him wince in pain and his face distorted in anguish.

"Sorry, but I have to change the bandages. I don't want your wounds to get infected."

This time, he said nothing. He just watched Francie remove the bandages from his side. With a clean cloth, she soaked the tip in alcohol and dabbed it on the flesh that was all wrinkled and red with the caked up Chinese powder crusted over it.

Lewis grimaced each time she touched the cloth to the skin around and on the wound. Then Francie spread some sort of ointment over the puckered flesh, before placing a gauze pad over it and wrapping the gauze around his body as well as over the pad to keep it in place.

As she placed a piece of adhesive tape on the tail end of the gauze, Lewis gently lifted her chin up to him and leaned in to kiss her again. Francie dropped the roll of gauze and reached for him. A flash of light brought a vision into her mind, similar to the ones she'd seen when Franklin touched her.

The image unfolded as Lewis' car chased a BMW through the streets at night, weaving in and out among other cars and down a dark alley. The only lights appeared to come from the headlights of the two cars.

When the BMW stopped, the car behind smashed into the rear. A man that looked like Lloyd jumped from the BMW with gun drawn and started firing at the man that emerged from the damaged car at the rear of his. This man looked like Lewis Avery. There was an exchange of gunfire. The bullets coming toward Lloyd seemed to melt into the darkness enveloping him. The ones coming at Lewis made him duck, but he cried out in pain when hit. He crumbled a little and dropped his gun. Lloyd's magazine was empty. He tossed the gun and lunged for Lewis. The two men struggled and both sent punches to the face and head of the other.

Shadows danced like demons in the dimming headlights as a loud ripping sound rang throughout the darkness. Again and again the ripping sound came. Lewis screamed and dropped to the ground. Lloyd raised back to give him once last blow to the head, then the vision faded...

With a gasp, Francie broke the kiss. Startled, Lewis asked, "Did I do something wrong?"

"Do you know who did this to you?" Francie nodded to the wound in his side.

"Yes. What's wrong?"

Removing the bandages from his right arm, the long, deep slices of skin were revealed. The puckered, red flesh had the same crusty powder over it. Francie looked Lewis in the eyes.

"Do you know what did this?"

"Oh my God! No! I don't," Lewis attempted to touch the claw marks, but Francie stopped him.

"Let me attend these as well," Francie said as she proceeded to clean the crust from the sliced flesh. After applying the ointment, she wrapped them in clean bandages.

"They look like claw marks," Lewis finally spoke. "I remember feeling the bullet burn its way into my side, but I don't recall the claws. Seemed like I hurt all over."

"Why were you fighting in the alley?"

Lewis narrowed his eyes at her. "How do you know I was fighting? Did you hear something?"

"You were lying in the alley behind my bakery in a pool of blood when I found you. Who were you fighting?"

"Did you see anyone?"

"If I'd seen anyone else I would have said so. I only saw you and your car."

"It was pitch black out there. I could only see shadows in the headlights and Franklin, the man I was fighting." Lewis said.

"Pitch black? The lights work with motion sensors. Movement activates the light. It couldn't be pitch black. Who's Franklin?"

"Motion sensors? The alley had no lights. I couldn't see my hand before me if it hadn't been for the headlights. Franklin works at Sudicorp, where I work."

"Sudicorp, huh? This is the second time I've heard that name. I know someone who works there. He says he's head of the research and experiments." Francie puzzled at Lewis' account of what happened. It seemed to coincide with her vision, but she didn't want to tell him this yet. She didn't want to sound loopy to a man she'd just met and might possibly be in love with.

"That's Franklin. Thomas Franklin, the man I was fighting," Lewis replied.

"No, the man I know is Lloyd Maxwell."

"I'm Chief of Safety and Security and I know everyone who works there. We don't have anyone named Lloyd Maxwell."

A strange feeling of discomfort washed over Francie. Lloyd had never lied to her, at least as far as she knew. What did this and her visions mean?

"What does Franklin look like?" Francie had to know.

"He's about average height and weight. He's got light brown hair, blue eyes..."

Francie finished his sentence, "and a British accent..."

"That's him."

"He seems a little wound too tight, edgy?" Francie continued.

"You got it. Dr. Thomas Franklin."

For a moment, Francie said nothing. Had the man she'd dated for nearly two years lied to her all this time? All the visions were unquestionably true. Who was the man she knew as Lloyd Maxwell? What was his real name?

"Francie, are you okay? Franklin is the man you know, isn't he? I remember now. He's got your picture on his workbench and claims you're going to marry him." Lewis recalled.

"I am so not marrying him and I know him as Lloyd Maxwell. What's going on? Why would he be fighting you?"

Lewis sighed as if relieved when she said she had no intension of marrying Franklin.

"I don't know why he's lying about his name. Why did he attack me? I guess he didn't want to answer my questions. That's all I was trying to do, ask him some questions, when he ran. Then he started shooting at me and something killed the two men with me." Lewis tried to explain.

"When you were fighting, there was no one else there; only some shadows in the headlights."

"Wait! What? When did you come out of the bakery? Did you see Franklin fighting with me?"

"It's hard to explain. I didn't actually see him fighting with you. I just have these…never mind. You're going to think I'm crazy."

Francie started putting the roll of gauze into the first aid kit, but Lewis gently took her hand in his. "Please tell me what's going on? You witnessed the fight?"

"It's complicated. I'm not sure how to explain. When I touch certain people, I see things, visions, what's inside of them. I experience the event physically and emotionally. Occasionally, I hear sounds. With you, I can see the fight as you experienced it. I see the darkness you described. For you, the lights did not come on at all, regardless of the motion sensors. You're freaked out, right? I sound like a nut job, don't I?" Francie tried to get up, but Lewis pulled her back.

"I'm not freaked out and you don't sound like a nut job. I just want to understand. We have many unique experiments at Sudicorp. Can you do this, reading a person-thing, at will? I mean can you turn it off and on?"

"No. It comes when it comes. I have no control over it. Most of the time, I can read men. Once I read my cousin, Meggie, but that was rare to read a woman. All these visions are taken at face value. They are not symbolic or riddles, they are what they are."

"How do you know Franklin?"

"I used to go out with him. I guess off and on for about two years. And I am not going to marry him. I am not seeing him anymore. He knows that. I'm confused. Let's not talk about this now." Francie packed up the first aid kit and got up.

Lewis motioned for her. "Come here. I'm not freaked out. I still feel what I felt before; fireworks and love for you."

She smiled. "Thanks for that. One other thing, I know this sounds old fashioned, but I want to be married to the man I am with, you know, I want marriage, not a hook up."

Lewis looked at her thoughtfully. "That means you and Franklin…?"

"No, we didn't, not that he doesn't want to, but I told him the same thing. If this is a problem with you, then break my heart now and make it quick and clean." Francie feared he would bail on her, but to her surprise, he agreed.

"I respect that and I accept your terms. I know you say we're moving too fast, but you are the only person that has ever saved my life and made me see fireworks with a kiss. How could I let you go?" He reached out and caught her arm. Pulling her down on his lap, he wrapped his arms around her, wincing in doing so. "You know when you save somebody's life, that life is yours. You're responsible for it forever. No exceptions."

"You mean you will wait for...you know what?" Francie asked in surprise.

"I mean, I've already made up my mind to marry you. I just haven't had a chance to ask, since I've been trying to heal and all. You couldn't get rid of me if you wanted to," Lewis gave her that silly grin of his and again he claimed her lips. Not only did Francie throw her arms around his neck, but she kissed him back so hard that he broke the kiss, gasping.

"Fireworks?" She beamed with happiness.

"No, oxygen...lack of," gasped Lewis in a comical way. Then they both laughed.

Chapter Ten
Downtown Los Angeles—Day—Corner Coffee Shop

Inside a local coffee shop, the usual lunch crowd scattered themselves about, some in booths or at tables, and a few at the counter.

As she poured coffee, the waitress, a mature woman they called Dee Dee, jerked her head around at the flicker she caught from the corner of her eye. Since the place seemed pretty full, it could have been anyone. Yet, it didn't look like anybody could move that fast. It didn't seem important, so Dee Dee shrugged and moved out from around the counter and on to the booths.

There it was again, that flicker of something in the corner of her eye. This time, she set the coffee pot down on an empty table and spun around in search of whatever kept whizzing by. No one else noticed. The chatter from the guests continued and the clang of tables being cleared of dishes and silverware rang out.

Fellow employee, Miranda, a dark haired lady who looked like she'd been around a while, peered at Dee Dee over her horn-rimmed glasses. "Hey, Dee, what's up? You look spooked."

"Twice I thought I saw something run past me. I just caught it out of the corner of my eye, but when I turned to look, nothing. Nobody moves that fast."

"Maybe it's one of the kids. There're a couple of them back in the corner. Don't let 'em get to you," Miranda said.

"Did you see that flicker of movement?" She asked as she jerked her head around.

Dee Dee picked the coffee pot up from the table. "Looks like you saw it too. You've got that look."

A bell "dinged" in the background.

"Oh, shush! It's nothing." Miranda dismissed the subject and moved quickly to pick up her next order. When she reached the kitchen, the orders were set on the pick-up counter, but she couldn't see any of the two cooks. The essence of a black, smoky mist swirled around the stove and sink.

"Pablo! Armando!" Miranda called out.

No answer.

"Pablo! Armando! Where are you? I need more gravy on this order," Miranda called out again.

No answer.

Annoyed, she picked up the plate of food and moved to the swinging doors to the kitchen.

"Hey you guys. I'm not kidding. I need more gravy on this order. Come on. Answer me." Miranda cautiously moved farther into the kitchen to the greater part of where the smoky mist gathered.

After making the rounds to refill coffee cups, Dee Dee rounded the counter, set the coffee pot down and looked up at the pick-up counter. No orders.

"Hey, Pedro! Armando! Anybody, where are my orders?" Dee Dee called out.

No answer.

Exasperated, Dee Dee turned on her heels and pushed open the swinging doors of the kitchen. The clatter and chatter from the coffee shop echoed in the silence of the kitchen. Dee Dee narrowed her eyes and looked around gingerly.

Where has everybody gone? She wondered. As she turned around, a black silhouette rose up behind her. It clearly had the shape of a man, moving toward her at a frightening speed.

"AHHH!" she screamed, and then she was gone.

Chapter Eleven
Movie Theatre—Downtown Los Angeles—Twilight

Sunset crept slowly over Los Angeles as a crowd of people of various ages stood in line for the latest blockbuster movie. The weather couldn't have been better; blue skies, lots of sunshine and temperatures in the mid-seventies.

With the queue as long and thick as it was, how could anyone feel the push of a dark mist trailed by several silhouettes as they entered the building?

The posters in the lobby hailed the latest attraction: "Zombies from Outer Space."

With their excitement over feature films like this, no one noticed the black streams of mist crawling across the floor of the lobby and into the various theatres within.

Dr. Thomas Franklin stood near the entrance, watching the unsuspecting movie-goers pile into the building. In moments, his eyes flashed to solid black as a bolt of power like high voltage electricity surged through his body. As soon as the line decreased outside and the line at the concession stands dwindled, he stretched out his arms and looked up to the heavens, crying out, "Veniat me, tenebrae. Tenebrae meum servábit. 'Let me into the dark. Darkness is my command.'"

The mist across the floor thickened and soon the entire lobby filled up with the roiling black clouds until light diffused.

All that was left was a void. And silence, a crypt-like silence.

Chapter Twelve
On the Beach—Day

Seagulls filled the skies over the sandy beaches of Ventura, California. The hot sand warmed the feet of the few people strolling along the shore, including Lewis Avery and Francie DeWitt. The sun would be up for a couple more hours and they wanted to make the most of it.

It had been a long time since Lewis felt this happy and stress free. His wounds were healing and he had no thought to contact Drake Carver about his status or whereabouts. He didn't even care if he lost his job. Now, all he cared about was holding hands with the woman he loved as they walked along the beach squishing sand between their toes.

"I've been tied to the office for so long that I've forgotten what it felt like to just look out over the ocean and feel the breeze on my face. For the last few days, I haven't even thought about work or my boss." Lewis squeezed Francie's hand and looked at her lovingly.

When Francie reached for him, he leaned down and their lips met. After the kiss broke, Lewis smiled and held her close.

"I really never believed a kiss could bring actual fireworks. You are amazing!"

"No, *you* are amazing. I wish we could be like this forever; always in love and together eternally." Francie tightened her embrace.

"You are a hopeless romantic, aren't you? But after knowing you, I am too."

"Who was Helen?" Francie's question soured the mood.

Lewis' demeanor changed and his smile faded. "Helen? Why do you ask me about Helen? Are you reading me again?"

"No, this is part of what I saw the other day. Helen and Lillian...what were they to you?"

"Do we have to talk about this now? I don't want to spoil the mood." He released her, took her hand in his, and started walking.

"Okay."

"I can't keep anything from you, can I?" He looked into Francie's pretty face.

"Eventually I'll find out, but I can understand if you don't want to talk about it. Just like not calling in to your job," she remarked. Lewis just looked off into space.

"I don't feel like answering questions, when I know I won't get any answers of my own."

"If you know Lloyd tried to kill you, why don't you tell the police? Or your boss, what's his name?"

"Yes, what's-his-name." Lewis didn't want to be serious. Many things swirled around in his mind. Even though he never liked Franklin, he couldn't understand why the man would deliberately try to kill him. Carver had to know this. Wasn't he the one who called him to question Franklin in the first place?

"Penny for your thoughts," Francie squeezed his hand.

"Is that all my thoughts are worth?" Lewis tried to make a joke. "How about giving me another kiss for my thoughts?" With this, he scooped her up. She threw her arms around his neck. First, she feathered kisses over his neck and face before slowly moving to his lips. Lewis always had a bright, positive attitude, no matter what the subject.

After a few deeper, passionate kisses, Lewis carried his lady to a nearby food stand that had chairs and tables in front. He sat down with Francie on his lap.

"Did Franklin ever take you out here?" Lewis wanted to know.

"If I answer your questions, will you answer mine?" Francie snuggled up against his chest and kissed his neck again.

"Why not? Helen was married to my boss, Drake Carver. She worked at Sudicorp, helping Franklin with much of the research."

As Lewis recalled the events, a vision flashed before Francie:

In one of the cold sterile labs of Sudicorp, the semi-lit room revealed a handsome woman of forty-something standing over a stack of papers, some she shoved into an open briefcase, while others she fed into a paper shredder.

Lewis entered the scene, gun drawn and pointed at the woman. The peroxide blonde quickly snatched a gun off the table and turned, firing a couple of shots at him.

Since this vision also came without audio, Lewis' lips moved without a sound. Again, the woman fired at him. He returned the fire and dropped the blonde where she stood.

Red fluid seeped from her lifeless body and formed a pool around it.

Suddenly Franklin appeared, wild-eyed and crazed, running to the dead woman. He mouthed some words and then collected the woman's gun and started firing at Lewis.

Without a return of fire, Lewis dropped to the floor and rolled over a couple of times, out of the line of fire. The repeated click of the trigger assured him the doctor's gun was empty.

Franklin dropped the gun and fell to his knees, weeping over his slain lover.

The vision faded as Lewis concluded, "I had no choice but to shoot in self-defense. I didn't know until that night that she and Franklin were having an affair. He and I were never friends, but after this, the tension got worse."

"So, Franklin, Lloyd, was having an affair with Helen who was married to your boss, what's-his-name?"

"Drake Carver. Yes. Sounds sorted, doesn't it?"

"Sounds like a fricken' soap. I'm so sorry this happened. You think Lloyd was trying to kill you because of that?" Francie slid her hand down the front of his shirt and began caressing his chest. For a moment, he didn't answer. Closing his eyes, he savored the sensual feel of her hand on his bare skin.

"Lewis, you okay?"

He claimed her lips again and said, "Just enjoying you, my dear. I don't know why he was trying to kill me. Now, to answer your other question; Lillian is Carver's daughter. She and I used to be together. That was a long time ago. And since you'll find out anyway, I should tell you she had a son for me, but I've never seen him."

No answer. Francie seemed deep in thought. Lovingly, Lewis caressed her face.

"Penny for your thoughts," he tried to smile, hoping the truth of his past wouldn't turn her away from him.

"So, you had an affair with your boss' daughter and Franklin had an affair with his wife? You guys ever seen General Hospital or All My Children? You'd fit right in." Francie grinned and shook her head.

"Are you disappointed in me? I haven't changed. I thought I loved Lillian, but she was a user like her mother. When she's done with you, she'll toss you like a dirty towel." Lewis tightened his embrace on Francie.

"Do you still love her?"

"No! That was a long time ago. She went on to Berkley and became some kind of teacher in San Francisco."

Francie adjusted herself in his lap then laid her head on his shoulders. "Don't ever leave me, Lewis Avery. I've never been happier in my life. Please say that you will always love me and that we'll always be together."

"Now I'm asking. Francie DeWitt, will you marry me?" Lewis made her look at him.

"Are you serious?" Her eyes lit up and her face brightened.

"I couldn't be any more serious. You saved my life in more than one way. I am yours, forever, so will you marry me, that we may be together and in love eternally?"

With eyes half closed and lips pursed, Francie answered, "Yes, Mr. Avery, I will marry you." His mouth covered hers and once again, the proverbial bloom of lights exploded, like those over Sleeping Beauty's Castle in Disneyland.

Chapter Thirteen
Francie's Apartment

Nearly a week and a half had passed since Francie found Lewis in the alley. He grew stronger each day, even if he still wore bandages and had to be careful how he moved, but walking around and helping Francie with things in the apartment made time go quickly.

His wounds didn't feel as sore and they actually itched a little; a good sign of healing in progress. Francie only went to the bakery when she knew Lloyd wouldn't be there and she had Meggie lock up for her.

Currently, Lewis sat on the sofa watching the local news while Francie puttered about in the kitchen.

The camera came back to a newscaster on the television and he began a new report: "Our next story takes us to Arnie's Coffee Shop in downtown Los Angeles, where the customers say the cooks and waitresses have disappeared. A black mist is blamed for the mysterious claims. None of the witnesses would agree to be interviewed on camera. They said they feared for their safety.

"We will now go live to Arnie's Coffee Shop where P. J. Andrews is reporting."

The scene shifted to a corner building where a long shot showed the name on the building as Arnie's Coffee Shop.

Police officers were on hand to speak to Andrews. With the microphone to his lips, Sergeant Romero answered the reporter's questions.

Andrews asked, "Sergeant Romero, tell us what happened here. Eyewitnesses say four employees of Arnie's Coffee Shop disappeared in a puff of smoke. Is that what happened?"

"No, Mr. Andrews, that's not true. The fact is that we are still investigating the situation."

"Where are the employees? I understand there were two cooks and two waitresses who are missing."

"We are looking into that. Nothing has been confirmed and we cannot release the name of employees until we are sure what happened," Romero tried to move past the reporter, but Andrews kept the microphone in the man's face.

"What is the black mist that the eyewitnesses spoke of? I understand the kitchen became so thick with it..." but before the reporter could finish, the officer pushed past him and out of camera range.

Lewis puzzled and turned the volume down. "Francie, did you hear that?"

"Heard it. That's weird. Black mist? What's up with that?" Francie stopped tinkering around to talk to Lewis.

"Did Franklin ever talk to you about any of the experiments at Sudicorp?"

"Are you kidding? If he couldn't give me his real name, why would he tell me about his job?"

"True. Just wondering."

"Why? Do you think the news story has something to do with a Sudicorp experiment?"

"Maybe." Lewis picked up the newspaper from the coffee table in front of him. "There's a similar article that says the same thing happened at a local movie theatre. A bunch of people in the individual theatres vanished. No names were released until they can confirm details. Witnesses say a black mist crept across the floor and then started filling up the building." He tossed the paper back on to the table.

"Do you think it's the same thing Lloyd had with him the night you and he fought in the alley. You know the darkness and shadows?"

"That's what I'm thinking. Need to find out what's going on." Lewis picked up his cellphone from the coffee table and started pressing buttons.

Lewis covered the mouthpiece of the cell and said, "Baby, don't say anything. I'm calling my boss." Francie nodded an acknowledgment.

The cell rang several times until a female voice answered on the other end. "Thank you for calling Sudicorp Research. My name is Jess. How may I direct your call?"

"Hey Jess! It's Lewis Avery. How are you?" Lewis tried to sound cheerful.

"Mr. Avery, are you all right? We've all been so worried about you. Where have you been?" asked the woman on the other end of the call.

"Just a little R & R. Put me through to Drake Carver, please." Lewis tried to avoid too many questions.

"Right away, Mr. Avery." After a brief dialing sound, Drake Carver picked up.

"Carver here," came the voice on the other end.

"Carver, it's Lewis."

"Where the heck are you? What happened? Are you okay?" Carver asked with concern. The quiver in his voice almost convinced Lewis that he truly cared for his well-being.

"I'm alive. Did you ask Franklin what happened?"

"Yes, but you can imagine the answers he gave me."

"Did you even look for me?"

"Where would I look? Your cell was off for days. Where are you?"

"What am I seeing on the news about black mist and people vanishing?"

"Oh, you saw that. I know what it sounds like, but I'm sure there's a good explanation for what happened."

"Like what? Maybe Franklin's experiment?"

"When are you coming in? We need to talk."

"We are talking."

"I mean in person."

"Did you call me on the night I disappeared and tell me to question Franklin?"

"Just come in and let's talk. Things are pretty crazy without you here." Carver's voice still quavered a little.

"I'll let you know," Lewis finished and broke the connection.

For a moment, he didn't say anything. He just held the cellphone and stared off into space. Part of him wanted to return to Sudicorp and find out why Franklin wanted him dead. The other part just wanted to run away with Francie and hide.

"What's wrong, honey? What did your boss say?" Francie rounded the kitchen counter and moved to the man she loved. Gently she caressed his hair as he reached for her and pulled her down on his lap.

"I have to go to Sudicorp. I'm not getting any answers. Those news reports are disturbing and Franklin trying to kill me is more than disturbing. I just don't want to leave you here alone."

"I can go with you."

"I don't want Franklin to know we're together, at least not yet. Maybe you could stay in the lobby, or did you want to go to the bakery?" Lewis wrapped his arms around the young woman and held her close. The warmth of her body filled him with such peace and love, like nothing he had ever known. He buried his face in her neck and closed his eyes.

"I'll do whatever you want. I've never dealt with anything like this before."

"I have, but I was alone. I had no one to protect and nobody to worry about. Go to the bakery, then. Stay there until I come for you. Where did you say my car was?" Lewis looked into her pretty face and his eyes pleaded for a kiss. Smiling, Francie leaned in and their lips pressed together.

Gently, Francie broke the kiss. "Your car's at my cousin Meggie's. She has a two-car garage. You should take my car. Yours is pretty beat up."

"Just like the guy who owns it," Lewis grinned. "Come on, laugh. It's better than crying." They both laughed in unison.

Francie had been letting Annalisa open the bakery. When she knew Franklin wouldn't be around, she'd allow the girl to go home early. Later, Meggie would swing by and close, so Francie wouldn't have to deal with Franklin in the evening. Only today, Annalisa had a doctor's appointment and couldn't open, so Francie had to step in.

"I'm ready. Just drop me at the bakery and pick me up when you're done." Francie wrapped her arms around Lewis' waist.

He kissed the top of her head and smiled. "My dear, you never told me why you chose to take me home and care for me, instead of calling the police or an ambulance."

"You told me not to call the police or take you to the hospital. Besides, whoever hurt you could have found you."

"Well, they could have followed you and killed us both," Lewis remarked. He made her look at him and then he leaned down and claimed her sweet, soft lips.

Francie broke the kiss gently. "I have to go. You have my number in your cell, right?"

"Right."

With that, she kissed him once more before they left the apartment.

By seven thirty that morning, the usual crowd stormed the bakery for their regular fix of their favorite drink and pastry. Like the famous geyser, Old Faithful, Franklin appeared in the doorway. A lustful smile crept across his lips at the sight of the woman he loved.

Since Annalisa had gone to her doctor's appointment, Miguel and Pedro, the bakers, had to take turns helping Francie behind the counter, serving customers.

Francie froze at the sight of Franklin. *What do I call him, Lloyd or Franklin?* She thought to herself. *Hang! What do I say to him?* With a slight tremor to her hands, she rang up the next customer and gave them their pastry and drink.

"Good Morning, Miss Francie," Franklin lovingly looked her up and down. Finally, his eyes rested on her face. "I was worried about you. You haven't been here for a few days. Is everything all right?"

"Everything's just great," she forced a smile as she packed up a blueberry muffin in a little bag and poured him some coffee. After putting a lid on the coffee, she scooted it over to him and smiled, "It's on the house."

"Thank you, but you don't have to do that. I didn't come in for free pastry. I came to see you." Franklin gently touched her hand.

Quickly she pulled away and said, "Can't talk to you now. Busy!"

"I apologize for the inconvenience. If you are free for lunch, I'll swing by and pick you up. I'd like to talk to you. Please…" He looked at her with those beautiful pleading eyes.

Taking a deep breath, she agreed, just to get him to leave. More people crowded in and Marco couldn't handle it alone. Franklin nodded and flashed those pearly whites. Then he picked up the coffee and pastry and left.

Francie fanned herself with her hand then breathed a sigh of relief. A thought came to mind. *What am I going to say to you at lunch? What do I call you, Lloyd or Franklin?* She again thought to herself.

Chapter Fourteen
Sudicorp—Office of Drake Carver

Carver stood at the door, reaching for the doorknob just as the door burst open and Lewis Avery barged in.

"Good morning to you, too. Aren't you the one who is always complaining about people who don't knock before entering," Carver glared.

"I'm here. Now, how about some answers?" Lewis glanced about the room as if looking for something.

"Come in or back out. Don't just stand in the doorway," growled Carver.

"How can I be sure you and Franklin won't try something?" Lewis took a step back. Carver grabbed his arm, yanked him inside the office and slammed the door.

"Be careful what you say. What are you talking about? I'm not trying to do anything. Let's talk to Franklin and confront him."

"Are you nuts? The guy tried to turn me into hamburger and you want us to talk to him? Why can't we just report this to the cops like normal people?" Lewis jerked his arm away from Carver.

"Did you or did you not call me that night and tell me to question Franklin about something missing in one of the labs?" Lewis stood defiant before his boss.

"I did not call you. I thought I told you that. Whatever happened was all Franklin's doing. Moreover, we can't involve the police. This is a government project, remember?"

No answer. Carver motioned to the door.

"Not yet. What about the talk of black mist on the news? Missing people, black mist, and nobody wanting to be interviewed on camera. I can see one person, but everybody? Now, don't tell me this isn't as a result of Franklin's experiment," Lewis crossed his arms and glared at Carver.

"You are absolutely right, but I can't control Franklin. I thought I knew him, but I guess I was wrong."

"What's with you two anyway? I get you are friends or something like that, but you two act as if you're hiding something. Enlighten me?"

"No! Move! We need to talk to Franklin first." Carver shoved Lewis aside, opened the door and left the office.

Franklin's lab hung in crypt-like-silence as he and Lon struggled with the dark crystal in the metallic gun.

"Mr. Jamison, will you please not hold on to the crystal so tightly. It causes the mechanism in the little stand to grip it tighter." Franklin spoke quietly.

"Sorry, Dr. Franklin. I just didn't want to drop it," Lon replied, shifting his eyes from side to side, his teeth chattered a bit and his hands trembled.

"Are you cold or has something frightened you, Mr. Jamison? You're shaking like a leaf." Franklin took one last turn of the screwdriver and set it down on the workbench. Then he held up the gun and looked into the sight, just as Lewis came through the door with Carver in tow.

He lowered the gun as the men drew closer.

"Up to your old tricks, Franklin?" Lewis shoved the gun aside.

"What tricks might that be, Lewis?" Franklin eyed him suspiciously. "You look well."

"All things considered. Let's talk about the night you led me down an alley and tried to kill me."

"What do you mean?" Franklin handed the gun to Lon, who then placed it in a case that auto locked.

Lewis narrowed his eyes at him. Then he pulled off his jacket and rolled up the sleeve of his right arm to reveal the claw wounds. They didn't look as red as before and the skin seemed to be knitting back together.

"Nasty gashes you've got there. Nice job of healing. Who's your doctor?" Franklin asked nonchalantly.

"You bastard! I got a call about something missing from one of the labs. I approached you in the Sudicorp parking lot to ask you some questions. Why did you run?" Lewis raised his voice as he moved closer to Franklin.

Rising from the stool, Franklin moved away and turned to Carver. "Why have you brought him here? I have nothing to say." Then he looked at Lewis. "I will have to ask you to leave my lab. You're disrupting the experiment."

"While we're on the subject of experiment, tell me about the missing people and the black mist that's all over the news," Lewis stood his ground and fired off his questions. His hands flexed with the itch to draw his gun and shoot the doctor.

Franklin said nothing. Looking from Carver to Lewis, he repeated his request for them to leave.

"I have nothing to say. My work here is almost finished. I have a luncheon appointment. If you will excuse me, I have a few more things to do before that time. I trust you can find your way out?" Franklin glared at Lewis.

"I will not stoop to your crude and petty accusations. Your questions will eventually be answered." Franklin finished.

Carver nervously drew his handkerchief from his pocket and mopped his brow.

"I'm not leaving until I get some answers. I want to know why you tried to kill me. This is twice, now," Lewis shook a little and drew his gun from the shoulder holster.

Carver knocked the gun hand to one side and raised his voice, "You can't shoot him. Calm down!"

"Why the heck can't I shoot him? If you'd found me dead in the alley, would you still let him go?"

Even though Lewis had not addressed him, Franklin stoically replied, "You would have never been found."

If was all Carver could do to hold back an angry Lewis. Straining against his strength, Carver finally pushed Lewis back.

"Give me the gun. Officially, you should be on a medical leave. That means you shouldn't be in possession of a gun and shouldn't be in the building. I thought the two of you would talk."

"Why on God's green earth should I talk to Lewis? There is nothing to say." Franklin then turned to Lon.

"Please leave us for now. I will need your assistance in half an hour." Lon nodded in response and practically flew out of the room had he not stopped to run his badge through the slot for the door to open.

With Lon out of the room, Franklin menacingly turned to Lewis, who was still being held back by Carver.

"Do not come here again unless requested to do so. If you disobey, there will be hell to pay." Something about his eyes made both men back down. The whites seemed to melt away, but before they could change any further, Carver pulled hard on Lewis' arm, literally dragging him to the door. Then, he ran his badge through the slot. The door slid open and Carver pulled an angry Lewis out of the room. By now, his face had turned beet red and he raised the gun again, but the door closed.

The men out of sight, Franklin's eyes turned solid black and his face contorted with the stress of immense power.

Chapter Fifteen
Francie's Bakery at Noon

Noon came and Lewis hadn't returned or even called. Francie really didn't want to go with Franklin, but when he drove up in the BMW, she couldn't refuse. She feared he'd make a scene and ruin her business.

Annalisa smiled. "Go on. Make the guy happy. It's only lunch."

"To Lloyd, lunch is a commitment." Francie removed her apron and adjusted her hair. How do I look?"

"Beautiful! Now go out there and knock him dead," smiled Annalisa.

"Don't tempt me," Francie mumbled under her breath as she rounded the display cases filled with pastries, cookies and cakes.

Francie walked outside before Franklin could make it into the building. "Miss Francie," he bowed like a Victorian gentleman. However, when he tried to take her hand in his, Francie sidestepped to avoid his touch. Giving a faint smile, though he looked hurt, he opened the door for her. She slid into the passenger seat and he closed it.

Inside the BMW, Franklin drove and tried to make small talk on the way to the restaurant.

"I hope nothing disastrous kept you from the bakery. You look well." Franklin said.

"I'm okay and yourself?" was her cold reply. Looking out the window, Francie tried not to think about who was driving. Her hands quietly fidgeted with the handle of her purse.

"I hope nothing happened at the bakery to keep you away."

"Lloyd, if you want to know something, just ask. Don't beat around the bush." Francie snapped.

"I wasn't beating around the bush. I was being tactful." Franklin snapped back.

"What do you want to know?"

"Have I offended you?"

"Why do you ask?"

"Because of your rudeness."

Silence.

"We haven't spoken since the night you ran away from me." He looked from the road to her.

Biting her bottom lip, Francie decided she owed him an explanation of why she ran from him. However, she shuddered at the thought of reliving the horror of the vision she'd seen when he touched her.

"I guess I owe you an explanation for that night. I have the ability to see a person for what they really are. At selected times I get these visions when certain people touch me. I broke up with you twice because of such visions, darkness, and some creepy shadows. I don't know what it means, except it is what it is.

"The night in question was different. More intense. I think I told you this, but I'll tell you again. I saw a medieval castle, a village, and people dressed like in a Renaissance Faire. The knights dressed in chain mail armor. The lead knight had a wife and two children. I saw a lot that night. So much flashed before me I thought my brain would pop. The emotions and everything that happened, the battle at the bridge, the village massacred and burnt to the ground. The castle destroyed." Francie paused, buried her face in her hands and wept for a few minutes. Franklin took out his handkerchief and offered it to her. Reluctantly, she accepted and dabbed her eyes daintily.

She continued, "At first I thought the leader of the knights looked like you. However, he didn't just look like you, he was you. Granted his hair was longer and disheveled, but he was you. Same face, same sad blue eyes.

"For a moment, I felt like I was transported there. I witnessed the entire bloody scene. Body parts scatted all over the place. The stench of burning wood, burning flesh and blood made me gag. You as the knight cried out in such…anguish at the sight of the remains of your family. Should I go on?" Finally, Francie looked at him as they reached the restaurant.

"I beg you to stop! I assume you saw much more," Franklin stopped the car as a valet came to take it and handed him a claim check.

"I did," Francie replied. The valet opened the door for her and she got out of the car, walked to the entrance and waited for Franklin.

Inside Chez Pierre, white tablecloths covered the myriad round tables scattered about the room. A podium stood in the center of the walkway, where a tall young man wearing a dark suit waited.

Franklin walked up to him and said, "Dr. Thomas Franklin, reservations for two."

The young man looked down at his reservation sheet. "Ah, yes. This way please, Dr. Franklin." The young man picked up a couple of menus and led the way to a table by the window. Setting the menus on the table, he pulled out a chair for Francie. When she sat down, he gently pushed the chair under the table. Franklin seated himself. The young man handed them the menus. "Your waiter will be with you momentarily. May I get you a beverage?"

"Water with lemon, please," said Francie. She tried not to look the man in the face due to her eyes being red from crying.

"Scotch straight up." Franklin ordered. The young man bowed and left.

Turning to Francie, Franklin asked in a quiet voice, "Did your visions take you to another period of time?"

Francie closed her eyes and fought to keep the visions from returning. She didn't want to relive the horror, but Franklin placed his hand over hers and the visions returned.

A flicker of white light flashed in her mind and there before her stood Franklin in the dress of a gentleman in Victorian England. Wild-eyed, he was in hot pursuit of a young woman, whose tear-stained face was distorted in terror. She stumbled and fell to the floor. Franklin grabbed her by the hair of her head and jerked her up violently. Forcing her to stand, he drew back with one hand and slapped her face repeatedly. Then, he dashed her to the floor and brutally clawed at her clothes.

The vision vanished as Franklin's voice brought Francie back to the present. Her eyes jerked open in terror, gasping for breath as if she had been the woman assaulted by Franklin.

"Are you all right? Another vision?" He asked quietly.

"You asked me if I'd seen visions from another time. Just now, I saw you beating and violating women. This is all you, isn't it? There were many others. Men you murdered as well. I can't bear to watch anymore. So many visions…so many emotions…my head is about to explode." Distressed at what she had just seen, Francie fought back her sobs again.

"You saw all of that. Yes, it was I. All of the visions are of me. Originally, I was born in the 1100's, destined to become a knight, Sir Gregory of Cornwall. I assume your mind is not accustomed to reading the soul of one as old as I am. This would account for the feeling that your head is going to explode. I do apologize, but unfortunately, I do not control that," he tried to touch her again, but she pulled her hand away.

"How is it possible for you to be here? How have you lived this long?"

"I shall eventually answer that question. When the male population reacted to your singing, I thought you might be a siren. This confirms it. You have the ability to read souls, meaning to see their past and future, with all the empathy, sense, and sight as if transported to wherever that soul takes you. Therefore, my love, you know what I am. You are correct. The visions are what they are. They are neither symbolic nor riddles." Franklin paused as the waiter brought his drink and Francie's water.

"I'll have the pecan encrusted chicken salad," said Francie. "I don't understand how this all fits. Part of me detests you and the other part…"

"The soup of the day," ordered Franklin. The waiter bowed and left.

"The other part, what? Still loves me? I did what I did out of vengeance." Franklin said as he glared at her.

Beautiful sunlight shone through the ceiling to floor windows that were draped with delicate pastel curtains which were bunched in the middle and pulled aside.

The young woman couldn't bear to look at her luncheon companion. Her heart pounded like a trip-hammer. It was all she could do to keep from hyperventilating.

"Breathe, Francie. Take a deep breath and then exhale." Surprisingly, Franklin's voice calmed her. She took a deep breath and then slowly exhaled. Weak and tired, she fell back in her chair.

"Better?" Franklin again leaned over to touch her hand, but she pulled it away.

"Don't touch me!" she said coldly.

"Francie, I'm only trying to help," Franklin tried to touch her again, but she scooted her chair away.

"Don't touch me!"

"I know these feelings are quite disturbing, but I can't make them go away. However, you can learn to control them."

"What kind of monster are you? You enjoyed the murder and torture. I don't know why I even agreed to lunch."

With a long sigh, Franklin pulled back and grabbed the tumbler of Scotch. He threw it back as if it was water. Then he raised his glass to signal the waiter for a refill.

No one said a word for a while. The food came though neither felt like eating. The waiter brought a refill of Scotch and took away the empty glass.

"Did you say I was a siren? What are you talking about?" His statement finally soaked in. "Reading souls?" questioned Francie, as she picked at her food.

"Those possessing the Song of the Lorelei have the ability to read souls. To see the past and future of a person," Franklin stared out into space. "You are the second siren I've known."

"Don't tell me, Arianna was the first," Francie looked his way.

"She was. Even after reading my soul, she loved me unconditionally. Why can't you?" Franklin turned to Francie.

"She didn't see what I've seen."

"No, I suppose she didn't. However, she did tell me to release the darkness before it consumes me."

"When did she tell you that, before or after she died?" Francie needled him to keep from remembering the terrifying visions.

Franklin gave a long, exasperated sigh, "Before and after. I heard you speak in her voice just before you ran away from me that night. Then, you turned into her."

"I so did not. You wigged out and I saw my chance to get away and took it." She replied defiantly.

Franklin threw back the Scotch. Francie narrowed her eyes and her brows knitted together. "You've drunk too much. I'm going to call a taxi back to the bakery."

"Blast you woman! Must you nag about everything? Don't curse, don't swear, don't drink too much and God forbid, don't touch me. Bloody hell, aren't you ever satisfied? I'm in pain and all you're worried about is if I'm bleeding drunk!" Franklin blurted out, unceremoniously.

The sudden outburst made Francie flinch and scoot her chair farther away. She'd never seen him like this. There had been times she'd said or done something that displeased him, but never had he raised his voice, or deliberately used profanity. It seemed as if he did so to challenge her.

"I don't feel like eating." Francie pushed her food away.

Franklin signaled the waiter. When the waiter arrived, Franklin asked him to prepare the food to go and ordered another Scotch. The waiter bowed and took the food back to the kitchen.

Inside the BMW, Franklin drove, while Francie reluctantly rode as a passenger.

Franklin stared ahead at the traffic. "I killed to avenge the death of my family. Those I killed were the descendants of the man who led the attack on the village."

"So this was all about revenge? The people you murdered didn't kill your family. They were innocent. How can you think killing them was okay?

"You don't like being told you're wrong. I can see it in your face." Francie continued.

"I should like to speak with you alone, not in a public place. I know you won't invite me to your new apartment, therefore, I'd like to ask you to dine with me at my home this evening," Franklin appeared to hold back something.

"NO! And you're right; I won't invite you to my place. That was the reason I moved, to keep you from hanging around." Francie didn't like being rude, but the visions scared her more than her feelings for Franklin.

The parking lot to the bakery loomed up. Franklin pulled in and parked. Without looking at her, he said, "I'll be at the karaoke bar at 8 pm. I'd like you to be there, however it's your choice. Before you go, please sing something for me. Sing that cowboy song about 'how many arms have held you.' It makes me believe you care." He wouldn't look at her and she shivered, but too afraid to refuse, she sang;

"How many arms have held you and hated to let you go. How many, how many I wonder, but I really don't want to know. How many lips have kissed you and set your soul aglow. How many, how many I wonder, but I really don't want to know. So always, make me wonder and always make me guess. Even if I ask you, darling, don't confess. Just let it remain your secret. For darling I love you so. No wonder, no wonder, I wonder, but I really don't want to know." Though Francie had sung more out of fear for his temper than any real desire to do so, she also felt suddenly sad. This was one of the moments that made her remember the times spent with Franklin, the times she felt love and caring for a man who worshipped her.

Without looking her way, Franklin sat gripping the steering wheel with both hands. His eyes closed tightly, a thin stream of tears trickled from the corners of his eyes.

"Thank you for that. Just go. I can't bear to look at you." Franklin said.

For an instant, Francie felt sorry for him, even after all she'd seen. No one knew him better than she did, and yet somehow, she didn't know him at all.

Sadly, but with relief, she opened the car door and slid out. Franklin pushed the bag containing the food toward her. She picked it up and shut the door. He drove off without a word.

Inside the bakery, Annalisa smiled with excitement to hear how lunch went. A few people milled around, but nothing like the morning rush.

"Well, how did it go?" Annalisa beamed, watching her friend and boss shuffle across the floor. Francie tossed the bag of food on the little table behind the display cases of pastry.

"Here's the lunch. Pecan encrusted chicken salad."

"What? You didn't eat?" Annalisa puzzled as she opened the bag.

"Lloyd's soup is there, too. Enjoy!"

"Wait! What happened? Nobody ate?"

"Nobody ate." Francie walked away.

Chapter Sixteen
Sudicorp—Carver's Office

Carver pulled Lewis into the office and closed the door quietly. Lewis still had the gun drawn and his hand shook with anger.

"You shouldn't have charged him like that. You just make him mad." Carver motioned for him to sit down, but Lewis ignored him.

"I can't talk to Franklin anymore. He won't listen to me and I can't pull the plug on this experiment without your help. In the past, I could control him, to a point, but now, it's impossible."

"What is it with him and you? What are you hiding? This stinking experiment was not to leave Sudicorp, but we've got people disappearing and black mist sightings. Franklin's violated the company policy and the approvals for the experiment. None of this should have happened. Not to mention he tried to kill me twice," Lewis finally holstered his gun and sat down.

"No, he only tried to kill you once. That was in the alley the other night." Carver sat in the chair next to Lewis. He wanted to stay on his level. Reaching for a pen, he rolled it repeatedly between his fingers.

"What about when I shot Helen?"

"He was reacting. I set her up for you to shoot. You were supposed to nail him as well," Carver stopped rolling the pen and looked Lewis in the eye to see his reaction.

"You what! You set them up for me to kill. Are you crazy?" A knot formed in Lewis' stomach and his mind reeled with the realization of what actually happened.

"Helen wanted everything if I divorced her. I knew Franklin was headed the way he is now. Using you to take out both of them would have made things easier, safer. So, blame me and not Franklin."

"Well that was a revelation! You miserable bastard! I can't believe you," Lewis jumped up and headed for the door, but Carver rose up quickly and caught his arm.

"We've got worse problems than what I did years ago. Franklin is out of control. The black mist and disappearing people never should have happened, but it has. We need to stop him, but I don't know how." Carver sounded worried and his hands shook a little.

"So, now you come to me. You used me to kill Helen and since I failed to kill Franklin, you want me to finish the job. NO! Do it yourself!" Lewis jerked away from him.

Carver called out, "He'll take Francie away from you."

Lewis jerked around and glared at Carver. "Don't bring her into this"

"I have to. She is the only thing that has meaning to him besides controlling darkness and shadows. We need the gun. I've asked Lon Jamison, Franklin's lab assistant to get it for us this evening. Franklin should be out of here by seven-fifteen this evening. We need someone to distract him from returning. He does that sometimes. Goes out for a while and then returns here to work on the experiment."

"Are you asking me to have Francie keep him busy? She saved my life. I won't do it. He'll hurt her," refused Lewis, his face flushed crimson and his blood boiled.

"She is the one person he won't hurt. Here, let me show you his notes," Carver finished and rushed to his desk. After pulling a key from his pocket, he opened one of the drawers and drew out a ringed binder. Gesturing for Lewis to come over, he flipped through the pages, until he found the right one.

"Look here. This is a rough schematic of the gun and here are the settings. We need to help each other. Franklin is a keg of gunpowder with a lit fuse. What do you say?" Carver seemed more desperate than sincere.

Lewis took the binder from him and examined it carefully, reading over the notes.

A portion of the notes read: *The settings are simple. The change from laser to electricity is done by the flip of a switch in Exhibit C. The laser is only used to temporarily stun the shadows, but it does make them volatile. Avoid this method if possible.*

The trick to traveling through the darkness was easier than I thought, but the power of my mind is not always strong enough to hold the portal open for me to travel through. I've had to use the gun to boost the energy, but sometimes, this takes a toll on my body.

The next phase was to teleport a living person from one dimension to another. This I have done without the gun, with success. However, bringing them back has been a problem. I am still working on the settings of the gun to assist. For some reason, my mind alone is not strong enough to bring them back.

Lewis finished reading. For a moment he toggled his attention from the schematic, then back to the notes.

"According to this, I can short circuit his brain, which may cause everything to reset. But he hasn't tested that theory. If this fails, two things could happen, the people never return, or Franklin's brain is fried. What kind of odds are these? This is why I didn't want to approve this stupid thing." Lewis tossed the binder on the desk and turned away.

Carver appealed to his love for Francie. "If you don't help me, what will happen to Francie? We can only imagine the kind of power he now possesses even if he isn't at his peak of strength. You and Francie cannot hide from him. The shadows can and will track you down."

Lewis turned back to Carver. "Did you say the shadows will track us down? They are capable of that?"

"They communicate with each other. Franklin has EVP recordings as proof. They now have a mind of their own and Franklin is the only one who can control them."

"EVP recordings? I thought that was only used to record ghosts."

"In a way, shadows are much like spirits; they are detached from their living, or non-living object, just as a ghost is separated from the mortal body. This is why they have become three-dimensional."

"Not good. I'll go along with your suggestion for now, only because I have no other plan. I'll tell Francie tonight." Lewis drew his gun. "If I have to, I'll use this to stop him."

Chapter Seventeen

Francie's Apartment—Later That Day

The bright light over the little kitchen table made a great place to read over Franklin's notes. Lewis flipped through the pages, pausing now and then to refer back to the schematic. Francie kissed his cheek gently and patted his back.

"I need to ask you something, dear. Carver wants to get the gun away from Franklin, but he needs to make sure he's distracted and doesn't return to his lab." Lewis set down the notes and gathered Francie up into his arms. Her warm body felt good against him. She pulled his head to her breast and hugged him.

"You want me to distract him, don't you?"

"I don't want to ask, but what else can we do?"

"Carver's the boss; can't he just ask for the gun?"

"He should, but he says he can't. That's why I have to ask for your help. I know
Franklin's been a pain, but just one more time."

"I really don't want to see him again. He was at the bakery at seven-thirty this morning as usual, and then I had to have lunch with him to keep him from causing a scene."

"You had lunch with him?"

"You didn't call and I didn't feel I should interrupt you."

"You can call me at any time. Did he hurt you?" Lewis looked into her eyes.

"No, but I hurt him. I think he knows you are here with me. I didn't tell him, but it was the way he acted. I explained about the visions and why I ran from him. Needless to say, I lost my appetite and Lloyd drank his lunch."

"Drank his lunch?"

"Scotch, straight up."

"That's a broken heart drink.""Then he yelled at me. This was the first time he'd ever raised his voice and deliberately used profanity. He scared me. Now, he wants to meet at the karaoke bar at eight o'clock tonight. I so don't want to see him again."

"We have to stall him."

"How about a two-by-four upside the head?" Francie looked serious, but Lewis had to smile.

"A two-by-four? Seriously?" Lewis grinned and made her laugh.

"Okay, maybe not. I'm not good at things like this. How can I distract him?"

"You used to sing together. Do a few duets with him."

"You don't know what you're asking."

"I'll be there. He won't see me and I'm packing." He nodded to the holster and gun hanging from a hook on the wall with some keys next to them.

"We'll all be packing up to leave town if he finds out I'm using him. Besides, you had a gun the last time you two tangled and how did that work out for you?"

Lewis fell silent. His gun hadn't helped at all.

"You don't know what he's like nowadays. Please don't make me do this," she threw her arms around his neck and hugged him tight. The scent of his flesh intoxicated her. He turned her over and claimed her lips. Both of them melted into each other's kiss.

Finally, she broke the kiss. "If you want me to do this, let's go. I've got to close the bakery and then meet him." Reluctantly, they separated. Lewis grabbed his holster and strapped it on, before slipping on a jacket that had belonged to Francie's father.

She went into the bedroom and changed into a pretty black dress with a plunging neckline and black-strapped pumps.

"You sure you want to wear that? I said distract him, not seduce him."

"I generally wear black when I sing and this is the only thing I could find in a hurry. Let's do this thing," and with that, Francie grabbed her purse and sweater.

~ * ~

At the karaoke bar, Franklin sat at the same table where he'd met Francie and Meggie the last time he was there; the table that was at the front, nearest the stage. The DJ took his time to set up his karaoke machine and the monitor for the words display.

Lewis pulled a cap down over his face and sat in the far back in the dimmest part of the room. Francie froze when she saw Franklin's back. She looked at Lewis and he kissed her lips tenderly, shooing her onward. Shaking her head, she hugged Lewis tight. After holding her a moment, he kissed her again and pushed her toward Franklin.

With a long sigh, Francie bounced over to the man. He looked quite dashing in a white open collared shirt with the sleeves rolled up and jeans. When he saw her, he stood up like a gentleman and pulled out the chair next to his. She sat down and he pushed the chair under the table.

"I'm sorry about what happened at lunch," Francie apologized. Franklin sat down and scooted his chair up. An intoxicating fragrance wafted around her and tickled the man's senses.

Leaning into her, he whispered, "You look so beautiful tonight, and the fragrance…"

"…your favorite, Channel 19. It was the last Christmas present you gave me." Francie smiled faintly as she turned to look him in the eye.

He eyed her lovingly. "I remember. We enjoyed the holiday together with your family."

"Like I was saying, I'm sorry about the way I acted at lunch," Francie tried to sound sincere. His closeness worried her, yet he did ignite a flame of passion within the soul. Part of her struggled against the darkness she'd seen. However, surprisingly enough, another part of her wanted to be with him.

"I thought we may sing some of the duets we did before. Since your solos drive men to distraction, I suggest that I interact with you to counter the effect." His eyes pleaded for her affection.

From the farthest part of the round table, Franklin slid a list of songs to her. "We could do, 'I've had the Time of My Life,' from Dirty Dancing. Remember when we worked in the 'lift' at the end of the song," he chuckled a little. Soon they both laughed.

"You dropped me the first few times we tried rehearsing, remember that? I guess you liked having me on top," she teased.

"No offense, but there was nothing romantic, or sensual, about how I fell backward and dropped you on top of me. I hit my head and, together with your weight, I was nearly knocked out. As you would say, 'that was so not fun'." His eyes brightened at the memory and his laughter sounded hearty.

For a moment, they both laughed and exchanged their version of how they perfected the 'lift' at the end of the song. The 'lift' was a nod to the final musical number at the end of the film, Dirty Dancing, where Patrick Swayze caught Jennifer Grey and lifted her up over his head.

"You look happy this evening," Francie caressed his face. He placed his hand on hers and kissed first the palm and then the back of her hand.

"I am happy you're here with me."

"I never asked what name you wanted me to call you. I know you as Lloyd Maxwell. Sudicorp calls you Dr. Thomas Franklin, and lastly, you hailed as Sir Gregory of Cornwall," Francie asked as he brought her hand to his lips. She heard his breathing grow a bit ragged.

After a brief pause, he whispered in her ear, "What's in a name? That which we call a rose by any other name would smell as sweet."

"Oh, I know this. It's…Shakespeare. Isn't it?" Francie laughed and bounced up and down like a child.

"You're right, my love. Which play?" He chuckled again.

"Oh, I know this one, too. Romeo and Juliet."

"Right again. Who's speaking?"

"Juliet. 'Tis but thy name that is my enemy. Thou art thyself, though not a Montague.What's Montague? It is nor hand, nor foot, nor arm, nor face, nor any other partbelonging to a man. O, be some other name! What's in a name? That which we call a roseby any other name would smell as sweet…' You taught me that."

He took her head in both hands and pulled her to him that he might taste her lips once more. So many kisses from a man this passionate for her made Francie's head spin. No fireworks, but the heat from his touch and kiss scorched her very soul.

Breaking the kiss, Franklin grinned, "I can't believe you remembered that speech. Did you enjoy Shakespeare after I explained the play to you?"

"Yes, I did. Your explanation was better than what I got in school. I had to do extra credit to get a decent grade for Romeo and Juliet. Too bad you weren't there..." then she caught herself. The glow in Franklin's face confirmed that she'd said too much.

"Had I known, I would have been at your side. Even now, I am your humble servant." Again, he brought her hand to his lips. He didn't speak like this all the time, but now she understood why he sounded like a chivalrous knight or someone from the Renaissance era on selected occasions.

From the table at the rear of the room, Lewis Avery watched all the laughter and affection displayed between the woman he loved and the man he hated. His eyebrows knitted together as he narrowed his eyes at the scene.

Wasn't there any other way a woman could distract a man besides kissing and touching him? For a moment, he considered using the two-by-four on Franklin as Francie had suggested earlier. No one to blame but himself for the way she and Franklin were acting.

Time passed quickly and before he knew it, Francie and Franklin got up on stage for the first performance of the evening. More people had started filling the bar by nine o'clock.

The DJ stood at the rear of the stage in the midst of his karaoke machine where he could slip the CD's in and out. The monitor displaying the song faced the audience at Franklin's request. He and Francie stood on stage with microphones in hand.

"Good evening ladies and gentlemen. Welcome to karaoke night at the Auswicke Paradise. My name is Anatole and I will be your DJ this evening. The first performance will be from our good friends, Lloyd and Francie. Glad to see you back. It's been a while." Anatole nodded to the couple. Franklin smiled and returned the nod. Francie looked out into the audience searching for Lewis.

"Their first number is, 'I've Had the Time of My Life.' I hope they will do the 'lift' for us as they did the last time. That was a real treat. Ladies and gentlemen, Lloyd and Francie." The DJ finished and slid the CD in place. The musical intro began. Franklin beamed like a glowing ball of sunshine.

He moved to the music and began on the musical cue, "Now I've had the time of my life, now I never felt like this before, yes I swear it's the truth, and I owe it all to you."

Francie picked up the next lines, "Cause I've had the time of my life and I owe it all to you."

As they continued singing, Carver slipped into the bar with a cap pulled down over his face and slid into a chair at Lewis' table.

"Could you be less conspicuous?" Lewis grinned and shook his head.

"It's the best I could do at the last minute. Look at you. What's…?"

"Shoo," Lewis put a finger to his lips and pointed to the performers. "Franklin is singing. Then he and Francie are going to do the 'lift'."

Carver jerked his head around to the stage. His eyes widened and he whispered to Lewis, "The lift? Huh?" Then he turned his attention to the stage. "I didn't know Franklin could sing."

"I didn't know he could dance. Watch him." Lewis nodded toward the stage.

"He's pretty good. He and Francie make a great couple..." Carver caught himself. Lewis narrowed his eyes at him.

At the musical interlude, Franklin leapt off the stage and moved in rhythm to the music, mike still in hand. Then he turned to the stage and smiled at Francie.

At that moment, she felt happy, just as she had before she'd read his soul.

Together they continued, "So I'll tell you something this could be love because I've had the time of my life. No I never felt like this before. Yes I swear, it's the truth, and I owe it all to you."

Even though the movie had the 'lift' a little sooner, Franklin and Francie arranged for the 'lift' after the last line of the song. Some of the men from the audience gracefully lifted Francie up off the stage and on to the floor. She handed the mike to one of the men and then turned her attention to Franklin. Quickly, he set the mike on a nearby table. Most of the audience were singing along with the music or cheering.

Throwing her head back and laughing with love in her eyes, Francie looked Franklin in the face. His smile and bright eyes gave her the courage to take that running start. He bent his knees just as she approached him. Then he caught her sides with both hands and lifted her up over his head. At the same time, Francie spread out her arms and arched her back. In perfect balance, Franklin gracefully held her over his head. Then, he gently let her down, slowly, sensually sliding her down the front of his body, her face to his, as they took in each other's breath.

Together they moved to the remainder of the music as the audience, going wild with excitement, stood and gave them a standing ovation. Even Lewis and Carver had to join in. Though they weren't Patrick and Jennifer, Franklin and Francie had given an outstanding performance and had truly had the time of their lives.

Carver's cell rang. He barely heard it over the applause and roar of the crowd. Covering one ear he put the cell to the other as he got up and moved to the door, away from the cheering audience.

"Carver here." He said into the cell.

"It's Lon Jamison, sir. I've opened the box that had two passcodes, but there is another box within it. This one needs a key, a physical key. Looks like it's a molded shape; like a bunch of blocks." Lon said from the other end of the cellphone.

"I don't have any keys for this experiment. That means Franklin has it." Carver thought aloud.

"Yes, sir. It's on the key ring he carries with him all the time. Mr. Carver, these shadows are…are really scary. I have the blow torch, but they still creep up close."

"Get out of there and wait for me in the hall by the lab. I'll bring you the key." Carver hung up and moved to Lewis.

The applause had died down and there was another person singing on stage. Carver claimed his seat at the table and leaned toward Lewis Avery, whispering, "We need the key to the second box that houses the prototype. The key is in his pocket."

"The key is in his pocket? Are you telling me you want Francie to get the key?"

"Well I can't get it from him and neither can you. She's the logical choice," Carver spoke with a voice of authority, even though it quivered a little.

Lewis didn't answer. At that moment, they saw Francie get up from the table and bounce towards them, the ladies' room was in their direction.

Quickly, Lewis grabbed her arm and directed her into a dim corner of the room.

"You looked and sounded great out there." He pulled her to him and kissed her gently. Poor Francie was feeling a little used and confused with all the kisses from her favorite men.

"I hate to ask, but we need you to get the keys from his pocket. One of them is for the second box that contains the gun. Can you do this for me? Please?" Lewis looked at her with those seductive bedroom eyes.

"Key? You want me to get a key from his pocket. The only way I can get the key without him knowing it is to have him take off his jeans, and that's not happening." Francie sounded resolved. Shuddering at the thought of how to get the key, Francie bit her bottom lip.

"I'm not telling you to get him out of his jeans. Just see if you can pull the key ring out of his pocket without him knowing it. Either Carver or I will pass by and you can toss one of us the keys. We'll remove the right one. You don't have to be a pickpocket to do that." Lewis tried to sound like he knew what he was talking about.

"Why don't you or Carver pull the key ring out of his pocket?" Francie retorted. "He's wearing jeans. Jeans are tight. How can I get the keys without him knowing? My job sucks," and with that she disappeared into the restroom.

Carver heard everything. He looked to Lewis who said nothing.

"She'll be fine. I promise he won't hurt her." Carver attempted a smile. Lewis still said nothing.

In a few minutes, Francie emerged from the restroom and returned to Franklin, without even looking at Lewis or Carver.

Franklin arose when she approached the table and pulled out the chair for her. Then he pushed it in when she sat down.

"Do you remember our trip to Hawaii?" Francie asked as she threw her arms around his neck. His eyes widened and he swallowed.

"Of course, I remember. How could I forget? It was the first time I'd ever seen you in a swimsuit. I also recall you slapping my face when I became too aggressive." The words barely got out of his mouth when Francie pressed her lips hard against his. Her hand moved across his chest, down to his stomach and across to his pocket. His body quivered and flushed hot. A low moan slipped out from his lips.

After a few minutes of digging in the man's pocket, she couldn't move any deeper due to the tightness of the denim. Moreover, what would she do with Franklin, whom she had now led down a most awkward and lustful road?

Francie broke the kiss and laid her head on his chest. He panted, his entire being felt hot. Looking down at his pocket, she saw that nothing bulged from it. Rolling her eyes, she realized she'd been searching the wrong one. With the other hand, she rubbed his side and moved down to the other pocket. Something bulged and it felt like metal keys.

Francie kicked off her shoes and moved to sit on his lap. Without warning, she again pressed her lips hard against his, as she pushed her hand down into the other pocket. When he stirred from her probing, she stuck her tongue into his mouth, hoping to take his mind off what her hand was doing.

His hands roamed her back and arms.

From a distance, Lewis watched in painful disgust at the flagrant display of affection. "Happy now? The woman I love is making out with the man who tried to kill me."

"I'm sorry, Lewis. I'm sure it pains her to do it." Carver made a poor attempt to comfort him.

"She doesn't look like she's in pain to me." Lewis looked daggers at the couple.

"Well, I'm sure Franklin's in pain."

"Not the kind I want to give him. I should rethink why I didn't kill him the night I shot Helen. Next time, I won't hesitate."

Francie's hand held up the keys, as she motioned for someone to come and get them. Seeing his cue, Carver jumped up and pushed his way through a sea of crowded tables.

Quickly and quietly, he took the keys without Franklin acknowledging his presence. In the dimness of the bar's light, Carver found the odd shaped key that looked like several different sizes of squares smooshed together. Removing it quickly, he put the other keys back in Francie's hand. She and Franklin hadn't even come up for air.

Returning to Lewis, Carver held up the key. "Got it! I'm going back to Sudicorp to bring Lon the key. Get her out of here as soon as you can."

Lewis said nothing. Carver left without another word.

At last, Francie broke the kiss. Franklin panted and gasped like a puppy in the dead of summer heat.

"You okay, Lloyd?" She rubbed both hands over his chest.

"My God, woman! You could give a man a heart attack. I didn't know you French kissed like that," Franklin said between gasps.

"My first time. How did I do?"

"As I said, you nearly gave me a heart attack," he tightened his grip on her. "Was this a sample of what the rest of the evening will be like?"

"Maybe." She said playfully, as she broke his hold and slid off his lap. Teasing the man seemed cruel and heartless, but at the moment, she didn't have a choice. Reaching down, she picked up her shoes and put them on. Franklin watched her as if he were a hungry beast.

In the blink of an eye, the crowded tables, the stage and DJ all faded away and melted into an eerie dimness. Franklin had Francie by the hand. She flinched when she realized they no longer sat in the karaoke bar.

"Where are we?" she gasped. She felt his hand squeeze hers. When she looked up, she could only see his silhouette. Gut wrenching terror shot up her spine and she shook from it.

"We are wherever you want to be. I can give you anything you desire," said Franklin, as the dimness changed to an island paradise of palm trees and sandy ocean shores, with blue skies as a backdrop.

"I know Lewis is at the karaoke bar. Tell him the gun won't do him any good." Franklin continued.

"You knew…" Francie's voice trailed.

"When you reached into my pockets I knew you wanted the key. I let you do it, because I liked the way you touched me. Pushing your tongue in my mouth was a delightful sensation. Nevertheless, you used me."

She could hear the sadness in his voice.

"Please don't take offense, my love. I'm not complaining. I am at your service. Use me whenever and wherever you wish. Only tell Lewis it's not over yet."

He turned to her and made her look at him in the reflected light of the tropical scene. "You are the only one that can cure or kill me. I command the darkness and the shadows. Do you comprehend the power it takes to do that? There is nothing that I can't give you. Now, let's return to the bar before we're missed."

"Wait! Lloyd, why are you doing this? What is this darkness?"

"What do you think it is? Twice Arianna told me to release the darkness before it consumes me. The veiled woman looking into a bowl, the one you saw me talking to, the oracle, told me the same thing..." His voice trailed.

"You can't release the darkness, because you are the darkness." Francie realized.

In a moment, she found herself with Franklin back in the karaoke bar, sitting at the same table they'd been at all evening. Beside her, Franklin sputtered and gasped for air. Holding his chest, panic seized him as he struggled desperately to breathe. She really thought he would die.

Gathering the man into her arms, Francie held his head to her breast, caressing his face and hair, she quietly whispered, "Take a deep breath and then exhale slowly."

The sweet instructions calmed the man as he sucked in a deep breath of air and let it out slowly. Desperately clutching her, the panic left him as he closed his eyes while the woman he loved held him to her breast.

Chapter Eighteen
Outside of the Karaoke Bar

Lewis rolled up in front of the bar with Francie's car just as she emerged from the building. Quickly, she got in and waved for Lewis to go.

"Are you okay? I couldn't find you for a few minutes and then you were back. Restroom?" Lewis asked as he drove. He directed his look from the road to Francie, her face was expressionless but she fidgeted with her purse handle and wouldn't look at him.

"No. I think a brief visit to Hades is more like it." She blinked back the tiny pearls of water welling up in her eyes. "Go before he recovers. He's in the bar acting like he can't breathe. It's the only way I could get out."

"What are you talking about? Did he hurt you?" Lewis tried to keep his eyes on the road, but his heart ached for the pain he had made Francie experience.

"No, he didn't hurt me. I hurt him."

"What happened? You know that Hades is not a place, but a person."

"For heaven sakes, Lewis! Don't get technical with me. Lloyd knew you were in the bar. He knew I took the keys for you. He told me to tell you the gun wouldn't do any good and it's not over yet." Francie wouldn't look at him. Lewis wasn't sure what to say when she acted aloof.

"I'm sorry I put you through this. I know you didn't want to go there tonight. Tell me where he took you."

"Still looking to complete a Sudicorp experiment, aren't you? I DON'T KNOW WHERE HE FREAKIN' TOOK ME! It was somewhere in darkness. One minute we were at the table and the next we were standing in an eerie, dimly lit place. Then he made the scene of an ocean and a beach. It looked like the one he and I stayed at in Hawaii. I really don't know where we were. He didn't say. When he brought us back, he started gasping for breath and clutching his chest. I calmed him down and then left. It looks like whatever he's doing is killing him. This evening has been a nightmare. I don't like teasing him or leading him on. I know he tried to kill you, but do I have to be the one to put the proverbial knife in him?" Finally, she turned to Lewis.

"I don't know what to say. It hurt me to see you with him, but it was all my fault." Lewis turned a corner and slowly rolled to the gate that protected the underground parking. He pressed the remote and it rolled up. Then the car moved slowly into the parking area.

Upstairs in Francie's apartment, Lewis laid the prototype on the kitchen table, drew the copies of Franklin's notes from the inside of his jacket pocket, and tossed them next to everything else. Turning to Francie, he gathered her up into his arms. His entire body ached for what he'd done to the woman he loved. Regardless of that, the warmth of holding her close seemed to calm both of them.

Still holding on to Lewis, Francie said, "Next time you get the keys from Lloyd." They both smiled. He leaned into her and their lips met. After a minute or so, Lewis broke the kiss.

"This isn't the way you kissed Franklin." Lewis teased.

"Want me to get your keys?" Francie tried to smile. Then they both laughed.

"Come my dear. Let's see what this gun looks like."

After releasing Francie, he turned the light on over the table and sat down. For a few minutes, he fiddled around with the gun. Francie sat down across from him, watching attentively.

Sliding open the little door of a compartment at the top of the gun, Lewis motioned for her to come around and look. She obeyed and he started to explain what she was looking at.

"The gun is off. See, that light should be on and this thing should be humming. This means Franklin is no longer connected to the computer chip. He's using his own energy. That's why he's gasping for air each time he exerts extra energy. I saw it happen to him when he gave me a demonstration of his command over the shadows. Afterwards, he ended up gasping and holding his chest like you said he did tonight." Lewis looked up the gun.

"So, is this good or bad for us?"

"This power drain may be temporary. The experiment is still in progress. If he had been connected to the computer, he wouldn't be struggling for oxygen. This means, he wasn't connected to the computer when I saw the demo, or he had to increase the power of the gun afterwards. The prototype has two settings, laser, and straight electricity. Not sure what would happen if I shot him with either one. It could kill him or could make him stronger if he is able to absorb the energy, especially the electricity."

"So we're back to square one. I really hope you don't have to kill him. I mean…"

"I know. Even if he tried to kill me, I shouldn't hold it against him." Lewis looked her in the eye. His heart sank at the thought that she still loved the man who tried to take his life.

"That's not what I mean. Good heavens! I don't know what I mean. You have every right to want him dead, but…"

"You still love the guy, don't you?"

Francie hesitated, but finally replied, "I just want to stop hurting him. Me…I'm talking about me. I don't want to be with him, but I don't want to hurt him, either. On the other hand, I don't want him to hurt you." She tenderly caressed Lewis' short ash blonde hair.

"I know we haven't spent much time together, not like you and Franklin, but I love you more than anything in the world. I'm afraid I'm losing you." He pulled her to him and buried his face in her neck. Warm tears moistened his eyes.

Lewis felt like Francie loved him. The tenderness of his touch and the softness of his voice appeared to make her quiver, but was that with joy?

"I love you no matter what. I want to be with you. Nothing will make me leave. Trust me." She said softly. Then she made him look at her. This time, she sat on his lap and kissed him long and hard the way she had Franklin. She even slipped her tongue into his mouth, which surprised him, but he enjoyed it and accepted it happily. This made him warm all over and when he broke the kiss, like Franklin, he panted and gasped for air.

"Oh my! I didn't expect you to do that. You make me crazy!" He held on to her so tightly, she couldn't move.

"Could that give a man a heart attack?" She smiled, rubbing her hand over his chest.

"Definitely!" He replied, still panting.

"Should I call an ambulance? You'll need some serious oxygen when I'm done with you." She smiled and kissed him long and hard again.

This time, she broke the kiss. A shuffling noise outside got her attention. Lewis heard it, too. Gently, he slid Francie off his lap, went into the bedroom, and looked out the window overlooking the street. Beneath a streetlight, Franklin stood, looking up into the two-story window. Black mist crept along the sidewalk, swirling around its master, as three-dimensional shadows danced about like imps from the inferno. Lewis couldn't be sure, but he thought that Franklin's eyes had turned solid black.

With a shudder, and wide-eyed, Lewis quickly went back to the kitchen. "He's out there under the light. Let's go. He's coming for me."

Francie swallowed hard. She ran to the bedroom and looked out the same window. Gasping in horror, she jumped back. Running to Lewis, she helped him gather up the notes.

"He's got that black mist with him like I saw in the visions," Francie had a tremor in her voice.

"That's his experiment, to control the darkness and the shadows. Hurry! Let's go. I think he tracked us by the shadows." Lewis slung the strap of the gun over his shoulder and caught Francie's hand.

"I need to change my shoes. Can't run in heels," she sputtered.

"No time," Lewis practically dragged her from the apartment.

Like mice seeking escape, the two tiptoed into the underground parking, but first Lewis peeked through the rollup gate. Franklin stood adjacent from it, only a few yards away.

Quietly, Lewis motioned for Francie to move back. There had to be another way out.

Francie pointed across the parked cars. Another door beckoned to them at the far end. They hurried to it and pushed it open carefully. A slight creak groaned from the rusty door. Lewis stopped and listened to see if Franklin or any of the shadow minions heard it.

Silence.

Lewis tried again. The door still made a sound, but not as loud as the first one. He got it open just enough so they could squeeze through. From here, they took off through backyards and in between houses, trying to stay away from the light.

After a few minutes of stealing through alleys and climbing over fences, Lewis bumped into something as he helped Francie over a chain link fence. In the dark of someone's backyard, he could see silhouettes scampering about like rats. They seemed to dwindle in size until ready to attack. The one he'd bumped into stood about his height, six feet. With the butt of the gun, he hit the thing in the head. Shockingly, the shadow seemed pretty solid, not the thin, web-like material he'd felt in the early stages of the experiment.

In the darkness, Lewis quickly switched it to laser. Then he aimed and fired as the shadow lunged toward him. A laser beam shot out of the barrel and knocked the shadow to the ground. Seeing that it didn't get up, the others scampered away.

Without a word, Lewis gently pushed Francie to move on. By now, she was shaking from actually seeing a shadow acting on its own. Heels were not meant for running or climbing over fences. She felt so helpless and like such a burden to Lewis.

As they scurried past more houses and ducked in and out among trees and bushes, a street light loomed ahead and there they saw Franklin standing beneath it with roiling black clouds hovering around him. Black mist crawled along the ground as the shadows roamed the areas that were absent of light.

This time they stood close enough to see that his eyes *had* turned solid black. Stretching out his arms, Franklin said something neither Lewis nor Francie understood. Then one by one, the streetlights winked out as they had the night he chased Francie through the streets of Los Angeles.

"He did this when he chased me downtown. Let's go. I'm scared." Francie whispered.

Lewis didn't respond right away. Silently, he scanned the area for an escape route. So far, there wasn't anywhere they could go without being seen. The fences were too tall for Francie, especially in a dress and heels.

Then it dawned on him, if he could stun a shadow with the laser, maybe he could do the same with Franklin. He didn't know how long he'd be unconscious if it affected him at all, but hopefully they would have time to move from here.

What happens to the shadows with no one to command them? Lewis wondered, but that was a risk he'd have to take. Quietly, he held up the gun and aimed. With Franklin in his sights, he started to pull the trigger, but something sharp raked across his still injured right arm. The pain stung him so badly he dropped the gun and grabbed his arm. Francie reached out for Lewis, but she too felt the searing sting of something sharp tearing into her flesh. A warm, sticky wetness ran down the injured limb.

Lewis managed to pick up the gun with a hand full of the sticky wetness, but too late. Franklin jerked his head around in their direction. Those eyes, like tiny black coals, emitted an eerie illumination, akin to dying embers. His features distorted with the power of darkness, he shouted out commands in Latin. Lewis didn't know what he said, but he had an idea when the black mist swirled his way.

"Go! Now!" He pushed Francie. They moved fast. Franklin had already seen them, so shooting across the street in front of him didn't matter anymore.

By now, the neighborhood seemed like a void, no streetlights and barely a glimmer from inside homes, or from a distance. Stars winked out as the roiling clouds of darkness grew dense.

Lewis kept feeling for Francie in the blackness. Now and again, he had to shoot out a laser beam. He could hear the skittering and scampering of things moving over sidewalks and grass.

"Francie, are you okay?" Lewis turned and reached out for her.

"No," she whimpered.

In the pitch black he couldn't see her arm, but he felt it covered in sticky wetness.

"Oh my God! You're hurt."

"Get me out of here. I'll live," came the weak reply.

Lewis put one arm around her and pulled out his cellphone with the other hand. Flipping it open, the light shot out and illuminated the immediate area of their faces. For now, he couldn't worry about Franklin seeing it. He had to have help. Instinctively, he pressed a button that dialed Carver's phone.

The line picked up and the voice on the other end answered, "Carver here."

"It's Lewis. We need help. Franklin's tracking us with shadows. We can't get out of Francie's neighborhood."

"Are you on foot? Can you get to Spring Street? I know she's not far from there," replied the voice at the end of the cell.

"We can't see our hands before us. All the lights are gone, everywhere."

"Do you have the gun with you?"

"Yes."

"Set it on 'laser' and aim anywhere. Hopefully, no one's in your way. Then fire. Keep firing until you see light. Then run toward the light. Try to get to Spring Street. I'll be there."

"Hey, how do you know where Francie lives? You said you know she's not far from Spring Street."

"Move it!" Carver ignored the question and disconnected the call.

Lewis pressed his lips to Francie's. Releasing her, he painfully lifted the gun and pointed it into the darkness. Pulling the trigger, he held it back, forcing a steady laser beam to plow into the void. After a few minutes, a glimmer of the real world peeked through. Streetlights from a distant neighborhood came into view. With the hole big enough for them to get through, Lewis ceased firing and helped Francie to the other side.

Another fence loomed up before them. Francie groaned when she saw it, but Lewis grabbed her up and pushed her up and then over the chain link. He followed close behind. The hem of her dress caught on the tip of some of the jagged points on top of the fence. Lewis had to rip off a chunk of dress to release it, as Francie fumbled to free herself.

Lewis felt mounting agony since the first wounds hadn't healed. His arms and side ached until he had to grit his teeth to keep from crying out.

A rustle from behind reminded them that Franklin and his shadow minions were not far away.

Removing her shoes, Francie held on to Lewis' hand as they scurried downhill toward the major part of the streetlights, where they knew Spring Street was.

As they reached the bottom of the small hill, they looked back to see Franklin elevated above the fence, arms out stretched, still chanting commands in Latin. As he slowly descended, he reached down and claimed the scrap of Francie's dress from the fence. Upon reaching the ground, he found her shoes.

Lewis pulled Francie on. "Don't look back. Keep running," he urged.

Stray shadows danced like fireflies in and around the streetlights, confusing any observer. Shadowy hands grabbed at them as they passed. A low murmur pierced the silence when another laser beam shot out from the prototype.

The screech of tires ripped open the night as Carver's steel gray Toyota wheeled around the corner.

SPRING STREET read the street sign on the corner.

Carver saw them running, firing a laser beam now and again. He pushed open the doors of the passenger side. Francie slid into the seat and slammed the door. Lewis scrambled to get into the back, but something jerked him back hard and yanked him to the ground. He let out a howl, as he flailed the air to fight off his misty black attacker.

Carver leapt from the car and ran around to help Lewis. The gun had rolled into a ditch. Carver picked it up and pulled the trigger. Laser beams fired repeatedly into the creeping, black mist crawling over the ground, wrapping itself around Lewis. Finally, the mist retracted and released its victim.

Carver helped Lewis up and pushed him into the car. Then he ran around to the driver's side, set the gun next to Francie and slid under the steering wheel. Barely slamming the door, he took off as if his shirt were on fire.

Chapter Nineteen
Inside Carver's Toyota

As Carver drove, he glanced over at Francie; her head lolled back and her arms were streaked with blood and dirt. The hem of her pretty black dressed hung in tatters with a large chunk ripped out. Dirt and blood covered her bare feet and legs.

A glance in the back seat found Lewis holding himself, his face distorted in agony. His clothes were also in tatters and warm, sticky fluid covered him.

"Are you guys okay? I got there as soon as I could." Carver tried to break the silence.

Francie groaned and Lewis grunted a response.

"What happened? Why did he come after you? He seemed in a good mood at the bar," Carver pressed harder on the accelerator, as he looked around for any peace officers seeking to give out traffic tickets.

"That was before he noticed Lewis was there and that I was after the key for him. Next time, do your own dirty work," Francie sputtered venomously.

"I'm sorry I put you two in danger," Carver tried to apologize.

"Just drive," Lewis moaned.

"I'm taking you to my home. You will be safe there," Carver remarked as he turned a corner.

Trying to calm his throbbing arm and side, Lewis closed his eyes and lay back against the seat. Then he realized that strange lights lined the windows and ran around the body of the car.

"What's with the lights, Carver?" Lewis asked as he winced in pain.

"Simulated sunlight. My home has the same inside and out. I had them created and installed for such an occasion," Carver replied.

"Simulated sunlight? Why you miserable..." Lewis started.

"No name calling. I didn't know for sure if Franklin would get out of control, or I would have told you. That's my home at the end of the cul-de-sac," Carver said as he slowed down and rolled up into the driveway that was lit with the same lights decorating the Toyota.

Inside the house, contemporary furniture scattered about the entryway and living room with dark blue accents throughout.

Trudging through the door, Francie flopped down on the dark blue sofa with matching pillows. Lewis staggered in and plopped himself down on the overstuffed chair, holding his blood-streaked arm with the tattered sleeve.

Carver entered, closed the door, and locked it. A large, middle-aged Latin woman with her dark hair drawn up into a bun emerged from the kitchen wearing an apron.

"Ah, Señor Carver, why are you so late? The little one is asleep," the woman took Carver's coat and put it in the closet by the door.

"I apologize. Dominga, these are my friends, Lewis and Francie. Please help me see to their wounds and get some fresh clothes for them."

Then he turned to the two bedraggled people and said, "Dominga is my housekeeper and nanny. Feel free to ask her for whatever you need.

"Come into the kitchen, Lewis. I'll see what I can do for you." Carver helped Lewis up and led him to the kitchen.

In a few moments, Dominga returned to the living room and helped Francie to the bathroom. Dominga tried to make idle chatter, but Francie said nothing as the woman helped her out of the tattered dress. Lifting each of her arms, Dominga washed off the blood. The claw marks weren't very deep but some wet, sticky red ooze seeped from the wounds. From a first aid kit, Dominga pulled out a gauze pad and a roll of gauze. Now and again Francie winced as the housekeeper dabbed on some antibiotic ointment and bound up the wounds on both arms. Her bare feet needed attention.

In the kitchen, Carver did the same for Lewis, but a little more talk came from the two.

A shirtless Lewis sat at a small table. He winced and grimaced as Carver applied ointment to the clean wounds and wrapped them in a gauze pad and gauze.

"What else are you not telling me? You and Franklin used to be close, but now you say you can't control him. What's going on?" Lewis grumbled and looked at his friend and boss.

"I'll tell you some things in a minute. Francie needs to hear what I have to say, too." Carver replied. From a distance, the faint sound of a child's voice drifted into the kitchen.

As Lewis and Carver came into the living room, Francie sat on the sofa wearing one of Carver's shirts. She had rolled up the sleeves and tied the ends at her waist. A blanket covered the rest of her. Dominga handed Lewis a shirt.

"Hope it fits, Señor Lewis," the housekeeper smiled. Lewis returned the smile and took the shirt.

Again, a child's voice called out, "Daddy, Daddy, is that you?" In a moment, a little towheaded boy walked out in his pajamas, rubbing his eyes with both hands.

With a loving smile, Carver knelt down and hugged the child. "Did I wake you up? I talk too loud, huh?"

"No, I don't sleep good when you aren't home." The little boy clung to Carver.

"Big guy, you've been calling me daddy, but remember, I'm Grandpa," Carver gently pushed the child back and looked into his little face.

"Grandpa wants you to meet your real daddy. Daniel, this is Lewis Avery. He's your real father." Carver turned the boy around to face the man.

When he heard this, Lewis abandoned the buttons on his shirt and nearly fainted. Trying to blink back the tears, he slowly bent down and picked up the boy.

"He's mine?" He asked in a quavering voice.

"Yes. This is Daniel. He's been with me since birth," Carver stood up and moved to another overstuffed chair where he sat.

"Why didn't you tell me? Last I knew, Lillian took him and wouldn't allow me to see him. I tried to get custody, but…" Lewis' voice trailed.

"I know. I've had custody for the last ten years."

"Hey, fella," Lewis patted and hugged his son. "How is my little man?"

"Daddy…" the boy started, but Carver corrected.

"Grandpa. Lewis is your daddy."

"Grandpa calls me big guy. I'm not little," Daniel continued.

"Okay, big guy, how are you?"

"Fine."

"Did you go to school today?"

"Yes."

"Did you have homework?"

"Yes. Did it all," the boy yawned and rubbed his eyes again. Lewis took him over to a worn out Francie. With a half-smile, she patted his little hand.

"I'm Francie. Nice to meet you, Daniel. How old are you?" She tried to sound cheery.

"Ten. How old are you?" asked the boy innocently.

Lewis smiled and hugged his son. "It's not polite to ask a lady how old she is."

"Sorry," apologized the sleepy child.

"Lewis, his bedroom is around the corner. You tuck him in," said Carver.

With that, Lewis told his son, "Say good-night."

"Good-night," Daniel repeated then he yawned again. The boy still in his arms, Lewis disappeared around the corner to the child's bedroom.

Carver looked to Francie. "You don't remember me, do you?"

Wearily, she shook her head and lay back with eyes closed.

"I'll take off my glasses." Carver removed the glasses. Francie forced her eyes open. Then she blinked rapidly to get the sleepiness from them.

Squinting, she replied, "You look like my chemistry teacher in college, but that can't be." Closing her eyes again, she let her head fall back on a pillow."

"It is me. Look again."

Opening her eyes and lifting her head, "Mr. Bradshaw? Marion Bradshaw?" Then she sat up. "It is you. Why are you at Sudicorp and why use a different name?"

"I'll answer that eventually. It's nice to see you again. I didn't know you and Franklin were together, until I saw your picture on his workbench." Carver searched her face for a reaction.

"I am so not with him, and why do you call him Franklin? I know him as Lloyd Maxwell. Why did you guys change your names?" Curiosity demanded answers.

Carver had just opened his mouth to reply when Lewis emerged from the other room.

"Why didn't you tell me you had Daniel? Why wouldn't you let me see him?" Lewis stood before his boss without a smile.

"Because of Franklin. You know why he's trying to kill you, right?" The answer came matter-of-factly.

"Educate me."

"Have a seat. We need to talk." Carver motioned to the sofa. Francie moved over to allow Lewis room to sit. He put an arm around her and she laid her head on his chest.

"He wants to kill all of the descendants of the man who killed his family," Francie said wearily.

Lewis puzzled and made her look at him. "How do you know this?"

"Lloyd told me. You are a descendant of the man who led the massacre," Francie looked at his face. Reaching up, she kissed him tenderly.

Lewis broke the kiss.

"She's right, but how…" Carver began but Francie cut him off.

"Lloyd said I was a soul-reading siren. Go figure."

"You're a siren? Then you know what he is?" Carver acted surprised. Lewis looked from Francie to his boss.

"What's going on? Francie told me about the soul-reading thing and that Franklin was a twelfth century knight? What's up with that?"

"Both of you know who he is?" Carver didn't know what to do. "All these years Franklin's and my identities never saw the light of day. Now, all of a sudden, the cat's out of the bag."

"Why didn't you tell me this? Sudicorp researches nothing but strange things. Nothing could have surprised me, except you and Franklin should have been the subjects of research and experiment. I can't believe you kept my son from me all these years."

"The boy is my grandson and I didn't want him killed. Up until now, I didn't know that Franklin's family was massacred. He never talked about it," Carver replaced his glasses and leaned back in the chair.

"The reason doesn't matter. The fact that he's trying to wipeout me and my bloodline is problem enough. He needs to be put down like a rabid dog!" Lewis' voice rang with hatred and vengeance. Francie looked at him with widened eyes.

"Put him down like a rabid dog? I understand what you feel, but he deserves a fair trial. Lloyd thought he was doing the right thing. Crazy as it sounds, he did." Francie stood up for Franklin.

Carver studied her carefully. "Are you in love with him?"

"No!"

"I think you are, at least a part of you is. I saw the way you kissed him," Lewis looked away sadly.

"Lewis, that's not true. I love you," she tried to make him look at her.

"He nearly killed both of us and you can't see it in your heart to kill him. Why? If you hadn't found me in the alley, he would have killed me." Finally, he looked at her.

"But I did find you and saved you. Please believe me. I don't love Lloyd or Franklin or whatever you call him. What's up with that anyway? Why do you guys use two different names anyway?" Francie clung to Lewis as she turned the subject.

Carver coughed and squirmed in his seat. "Forget about petty jealousy and help me stop Franklin while we can. We need to bring back the people who disappeared and put the shadows back where they belong. Listen to me, both of you. If Franklin reaches the point where he absorbs energy, the laser and electricity may not stop him, then we only have one option, Francie." He looked to her and said, "Remember, the Song of the Lorelei was never meant to fire a man's passion or stimulate his libido. It was meant to drive him to self-destruction."

Chapter Twenty
Sudicorp—Carver's Office

At the door of Carver's office, he and Lewis argued about how to handle Franklin.

"I won't let you use Francie. She's not part of this." Lewis said as he tried to get past Carver.

"She was involved before she met you. Listen to me; we can catch him off guard. Right now, he's in his office and won't suspect anything." Carver tried to sound convincing, but his wide-eyed look and trembling hands said differently.

Lewis looked around the admin's area. "Where are Francie and your secretary?"

"They're called administrative assistants now. I had Sierra take her to the cafeteria."

"Sierra, the crazy administrative assistant who has the hots for Franklin?" Lewis flushed with anger and pushed past Carver.

The two moved down the hall to the cafeteria, only to find most of the women standing around listening to Francie singing, Never Knew Love like This.

"I never knew love like this before, now I'm lonely never more, since you came into my life. You are my love-light, this I know and I'll never let you go. You're my all, you're part of me. Once I was lost and now I'm found, then you turned my world around. When I need you, I call your name. Cause I never knew love like this before. Opened my eyes, cause I never knew love like this before. What a surprise," Francie sang, not realizing that Franklin stood back against some vending machines, trying not to be seen. Sadness and desire washed over him, but he bit his lip to keep from succumbing to the primitive cries within.

Carver and Lewis stood in the doorway, mesmerized by a siren's voice.

At that moment, Francie didn't see any of the men. The women cheered and danced. Music and song offered a welcomed distraction. Sierra, Carver's admin assistant, a Latin beauty with coal black hair and dark flashing eyes, danced and cheered with the music, but with ever a wary eye on Dr. Thomas Franklin. Still moving with the music, she made her way to him.

"Hola Tomás," Sierra smiled seductively and tried to put her hands on him. Franklin moved back, away from her grasp.

Not looking at her, he said quietly, "Sierra, please act like a lady and remember your place."

The woman huffed and stormed away. No one ever accepted rejection well.

Francie continued, "Cause I never knew love like this before. This feeling's so deep inside of me, such a tender fantasy. You're the one I'm living for. You are my sunlight and my rain. And time could never change what we share forever more… Ooooh-whooooa

I never knew love like this before. Now I'm lonely never more. Since you came into my life

Cause I never knew love like this before. Opened my eyes, cause I never knew love like this before. What a surprise!"

Lewis couldn't hold back. He ran to Francie, gathered her up in his arms and kissed her with such fiery passion that both bodies broke into a sweat. The proverbial fireworks exploded again. For a moment, they seemed to melt away into a world of only two.

Seeing the entire display of affection, Franklin's eyes turned solid black. He trembled with rage and in seconds, he had vanished.

When the kiss broke, Carver stood next to them. "No time for that. Francie, I can't believe you'd sing solo. You know what that does to men."

"It didn't seem to affect you." Francie eyed him suspiciously.

"Massive self-control. Now, come on. Both of you," he said, pulling the wax earplugs from his ears as he pulled Lewis and Francie on, pushing past the ladies that wanted an encore.

Hurrying down the hallway toward them, Lon Jamison looked more frightened and panicky than usual. His blond hair disheveled, he sputtered, "There's no time. He's turned. He's angry that I helped you get the prototype." The lad paled and tiny pearls of perspiration broke out on his forehead.

Carver's heart raced and he felt his stomach draw up in knots. "Hurry, the elevator!"

The elevator doors opened. Lon stepped in with Lewis close behind, but before the others could enter, something pushed the "close door" button and another thing yanked Francie back.

The doors closed quickly. Carver pushed the down button repeatedly, but to no avail.

The display over the elevator doors lit up as it descended, but then suddenly jolted with a loud "banging" sound. The noise of the motor died. No movement.

Pushing the buttons didn't do anything. The entire elevator, stuck between floors, hung in tomb-like silence.

Pulling out his cellphone, Carver called for help from Lewis' department. Francie screamed and pounded on the closed doors.

Three men from Safety and Security came up in the second elevator.

"Lewis! Honey! Can you hear me?" Francie called out. A muffled, distant sound certified that her sweetheart heard her, a good sign of him being alive.

In the excitement, no one saw Franklin appear behind them. All attention centered on trying to pry the doors open. Without a word, he moved closer to Francie. Wrapping his arms around her, they both disappeared. Carver jerked about.

Gone. No one there.

"Francie, where are you?" He started pacing then called aloud. Where are you?"

No reply.

The three men from Safety and Security finally pried the door open with what resembled giant pliers. The tallest of the three secured a cable to his waist, and the other end to the next tallest man. Then the tallest man lowered himself down on top of the elevator.

Taken by surprise, Francie struggled for oxygen, and to free herself from the arms around her waist. A mass of black void engulfed her. Nothing registered in her mind as it kept spinning around like a top. With breathing now difficult, she lost consciousness and fell limp in the arms that held her.

When she came to, she found herself in a brightly lit room filled with a mix of Victorian and Regency style furniture. Arms still held her, but not as tightly.

Franklin looked pale and drawn as he forced in a lung full of air and exhaled it slowly. When he acted like this, she knew he had turned back to himself and suffered from an energy drain. Trying to pull herself up, she had to place an arm around his neck for support. He helped her sit up on his lap.

"Feeling better, my lady?" Lovingly, he caressed her hair.

Surprisingly, Francie felt drained. Dizzy, she fell back in his arms.

"Take care, my love. Your strength will return momentarily. We traveled a distance together and that exerts more energy than usual." Franklin tried to explain.

"Where…where are we?" She asked weakly.

"My home, the one I designed for you," he kissed her forehead and adjusted her in his arms.

"Lewis, where is he?"

"Not here. Don't talk so much. Save your strength." Franklin held her to his chest. To Francie the room swayed back and forth. Instinctively, she threw both arms around his neck and clung to him.

After a few minutes, the room stopped swaying and her breathing calmed to normal.

"Lloyd, why am I here? Lewis…"

Tenderly, he cut her off by pressing his lips against hers. She didn't resist. The void of darkness haunted her, but the soft, warm lips of the man she knew as Lloyd Maxwell took her away from that and sent her into a surreal realm all his own.

Gently, she pushed him back, breaking the kiss. She tried to get up, but he held her fast.

"Take it easy. Don't try moving too quickly. You'll get dizzy again." His voice sounded gentle, yet weak. Looking into his face, he seemed melancholy.

"I brought you here to keep you safe. Don't worry about Lewis. Please, just let me talk to you, alone. The way we used to."

"You tried to kill us last night." Francie pushed him back, shuddering at the thought of his dark display.

"I wouldn't have hurt you," was his sad reply. "I would never hurt you. I came for Lewis. He made you deceive me. With that, among other things, I chose to deal with him that night."

Kissing her face and hair, he released her. Arising from his lap, Francie steadied herself and gazed about the room.

"You were going to kill him."

"I would have, had you not been there. One way or another you keep saving his life." Franklin blurted out in disgust.

A fireplace stood before Francie as she turned to the right of the sofa. A coffee table was placed off to the side, with another sofa facing the one she and Franklin sat on. A sliding glass door gleamed back at her from the rear of the room. Two doors separated by a portrait of Franklin in the clothes of Victorian England.

The foyer led to the front door and to its left a spiral staircase led upward.

Slowly, she turned back to Franklin, who now stood close to her. The color returned to his face and his breathing went back to normal.

"I want to go home." Francie moved away a little farther.

"You are home. I designed it for you. You say you love Lewis, but you cannot deny the heat of passion fueling our kisses."

She didn't know what to say. The ordeal of running from him weakened her. The bottoms of her feet still ached. Nevertheless, he spoke truly; she did feel the heat from his touch and kiss. With Lewis, she saw fireworks, with Franklin, she felt heat. Which one is true love?

"Would you like to see the rest of the house? Then, I'll show you the gardens." Franklin motioned toward the door at the left of the portrait.

Pausing at the painting, Francie asked, "Is this you?"

"Yes. Back then, I was called Lord Wilfred Benfield of Canterbury."

"Nice pic, but it doesn't do you justice. You are better looking in person," she smiled, trying not to make him angry.

"That's quite a compliment. All things considered. Thank you."

"Before we tour the house, may I ask some historical questions?"

"Of course, by all means," replied Franklin as he and Francie paused at the door to the library.

"Where you anywhere near Whitechapel during the time of Jack the Ripper?"

"Jack the Ripper?"

"He was English."

"Seriously, Francie? Jack the Ripper? Has this anything to do with reading my soul and witnessing the vengeance I wreaked upon my enemy's bloodline? You'd have to ask me about a serial killer?" He almost laughed.

"I'm sorry. Didn't mean to insult you. I just thought if you were in that area when Jack was there, you might have seen or heard something differently or more than history states."

"Curious about his identity? Did you think it was me?"

"No! Of course not. Just…just…never mind. How about dragons?"

For a moment, he paused and gave a blank stare. Holding back the laughter, he finally answered, "Dragons? Now it's dragons?"

"Well, you were a knight. Did you ever fight a dragon?" Innocently, she defended her question.

"Depends upon your perspective. I've seen creatures that defy logic of the modern world, but if you are talking about the ones seen in films, no. I have not seen a flying, fire-breathing dragon. They did not terrorize towns and villages. There were no sacrifices to a live creature such as that. However, there were virginal sacrifices to the gods of choice for prosperity at certain times of the year. Does that answer your question?"

She swallowed hard. "Virginal sacrifices?"

"Yes. I've witnessed those. Ghastly ritual! Should I go into detail?

"No, I'll pass."

"Good. Any other historical questions?" Franklin had to bite his bottom lip to keep from laughing.

"How about the Knights Templar?"

"What about them? Did I meet them or was I one of them?" This time he couldn't contain the laughter. A chuckle escaped him.

"Both, and did they find the Holy Grail?"

"The Holy Grail? Now it's the Holy Grail. Which one? The one in Indiana Jones and the Last Crusade, or the one from the Da Vinci Code?" By now, Franklin struggled to hold in the laughter.

"You're making fun of me."

"Depends upon your perspective. No, we did not find the chalice of Christ and no, we did not find the remains of Mary Magdalene. Must all of your questions be based upon a film or a song?" Franklin could not hold back any longer, so he let out a hearty laugh.

"You think I'm funny. You're making fun of my questions." A smile crept across her face.

"Depends upon your perspective. I could be laughing with you." By now, he was laughing so hard, he had to catch his breath. "No matter how I feel, you can always make me laugh."

Francie laughed with him. She really didn't mean to ask humorous questions, they just seemed to come out that way. Watching him closely, she did feel sorry for his loss and loneliness. No matter what he'd done, good or bad, she felt for the man, making it difficult to hate him.

"One last question, please," she begged.

"All right, one last historical question. Not a movie question."

"Not a movie question. Did you fight in the Revolutionary War?"

"You mean the one here in America? Yes, I did."

"Whose side did you fight on?" She asked innocently.

Again, he gave her a blank stare without a word. He pursed his lips together to keep from laughing. Then he replied, "I was born in England. Which side do you think I fought on?" A chuckle slipped out again.

"I don't know. Maybe you were a double spy for America."

"You mean a double agent. A spy? Don't make movie references. I was not a spy. I fought as a soldier aiding my country, to claim the first thirteen colonies, which called itself the United States, English colonies. No ruler wishes to lose control of its people. Independence was unheard of. Does this make sense to you?" He gave a lopsided smile.

"I guess. How do you feel about that now?"

"If we were in a British colony at this moment, then Lewis would have been shot and you would be my wife. Any other questions?"

"No. That's it. You don't have to shout." She half smiled. They used to have friendly banters like this in the past. It felt good to see him happy.

"No more for now, anyway." He chuckled.

Finally, Franklin opened the door to a beautiful library, with a huge oak desk sitting to their right and a comfy-looking stuffed swivel chair behind it. The rest of the room had scattered tables and chairs, with a door leading to the room next to it, the trophy room.

With wide-eyed fascination, Francie sauntered in, amazed at all the books from ceiling to floor and from wall to wall. Gingerly, she ran her fingers along a line of books, which all had something to do with physics. Another shelf held books on mathematics and equations.

"These are all physics and math. You've read all these books?" She turned to him.

Franklin gave a faint smile. "Yes, I have read all of them."

"So you really have a Ph.D. in Physics?"

"I wouldn't lie about that."

Francie looked up at the books near the ceiling. "What kind of books are they?"

"I have a rolling ladder. Would you like to climb up and see what they are?"

"Way up there? No thanks. It'd be my luck that I'd fall off the stupid ladder."

"I'd catch you," he smiled.

"Ah, no. I'm good." Francie wandered around to another wall of books. "Politics, huh? Don't you read for pleasure?"

"Of course I do. Come here," he motioned for her to see the wall opposite the desk. The shelf eye level to him held a row of books that began with Dracula and ended with Edgar Allan Poe.

No longer swelling up with fear, Francie felt much more like her old self and gave a lopsided smile. "Dracula? Seriously? Light reading before bed?"

"Everybody's different. Sometimes a good scare makes a person sleep well. Besides, this is a first addition Dracula. Bram even signed it," Franklin grinned.

Francie pulled out the copy of Dracula and opened it. The title page read: *To my good friend Wilfred Benfield, signed Abraham (Bram) Stoker.*

"Wow! The authentic autograph of Bram Stoker. That's a keeper. Was Wilfred Benfield you, like in the painting?"

"Yes, it was. I was Lord Wilfred Benfield."

"Lord Wilfred Benfield, huh? Interesting! If I read Dracula before going to bed, I wouldn't be able to sleep. Edgar Allen Poe?" Francie replaced Dracula and pulled out a periodical similar to a magazine and began reading, "Once upon a midnight dreary, while I pondered weak and weary, Over many a quaint and curious volume of forgotten lore, while I nodded, nearly napping, suddenly there came a tapping, As of someone gently rapping, rapping at my chamber door. 'Tis some visitor, I muttered, tapping at my chamber door - only this, and nothing more." She stopped as Franklin applauded.

"Well done my love. Well done. Please read on." Franklin took a seat behind the oak desk. Francie flipped to another work of Poe and turned to Franklin and began to read, "It was many and many a year ago, in a kingdom by the sea; that a maiden there lived whom you may know by the name of Annabel Lee. And this maiden she lived with no other thought than to love and be loved by me. I was a child and she was a child, in this kingdom by the sea. But we loved with a love that was more than love - I and my Annabel Lee; with a love that the winged seraphs of heaven coveted her and me."

"That is one of my favorites. You read it very well, my love. Please continue," Franklin looked off into space.

"No, it saddens you, my darling. I shouldn't like to see you sad," Francie's speech pattern changed and a lilting British accent seeped through, which made Franklin sit up and take notice.

"What did you say?"

"Since the children and I left, sadness prevails in your life. Take a wife and leave the past where it is," Francie no longer spoke as herself. "It breaks our hearts to see you like this, my beloved Gregory."

"Arianna!" Franklin jumped up from the chair and stumbled around the desk to reach Francie. By the time he got to her, she'd snapped out of the possession and looked at him as if he'd gone mad.

"What's wrong? Why are you coming at me like that? You look like you've seen a ghost." Francie closed the periodical and backed away from him.

"I have seen a ghost. You don't remember what you just said?" Franklin grabbed her shoulders with both hands and stared her in the face.

"What did I say?"

"You said you shouldn't like to see me sad and that it prevails in my life. You sounded like her. It was her voice." Franklin leaned in to her face to see if he could find any traces of his dear, dead Arianna.

Francie tried to shrug off his hands that gripped her shoulders. "I didn't say that. Let me go. You're hurting me." Instantly, the hands released her.

"This is the second time you've spoken in Arianna's voice and not remembered it. What is she trying to tell me? She said take a wife and leave the past where it is. Does that mean anything to you?" asked Franklin.

"Sounds like it is what it is. You've been grieving all these years. Maybe you need to move on."

"Move on? I know you've read my soul and no one knows how I feel any better than you do. However, have you ever lost a loved one to violence? Have you ever lost everything you valued in life in a matter of minutes?"

Francie shook her head no.

"I thought not. You comprehend, yet you don't. What you see and feel when you read a soul is what that soul experienced. Certainly, it pains and chokes you until you almost can't breathe, but in truth, it's the fear you react to, not the sadness, the loss, or loneliness." He trembled when he spoke, but his voice cut her like a double-edged sword.

"You believe I've gone mad? Be truthful. Have I taken leave of my senses?" Franklin never looked away from her.

"No one would call you crazy to your face." She replaced the periodical of Poe and tried to turn the subject as she moved to another section of books.

"All things considered, seeing a ghost just added to the weirdness of our entire relationship." Franklin looked away as he referred to the night he saw Arianna his murdered wife.

"The Olympians? Greek mythology? Why is it under theology?"

"It's not mythology. It's a religion."

As she ran her fingers along the spines of books, she noticed that "Hades" and "The Underworld" were in the titles a number of times.

"Hades? The Underworld? I thought you were a man of science. What's up with that?""Did you know what the purpose of my experiment at Sudicorp was?"

"Learning to control shadows and darkness?"

"That's rather a simplistic explanation. Think of the power one can possess should they learn the secret of controlling shadows and summoning darkness. Through the darkness, one can travel to wherever they desired, even the Underworld."

To this Francie said nothing. Her blank stare told Franklin she didn't understand or know what to say.

He continued, "I've been searching for the path through darkness that leads to the

Underworld. I'm trying to release Arianna and the children."

"If it were possible to bring them back, then they would be alive. Is that right?" Francie finally spoke.

"Yes."

"Then supposing that's true, wouldn't you have your family and wouldn't need me?"

"Why not you? We could learn to live together."

Francie paused a moment. Again, he began to frighten her. Nothing he said made sense, but then the ravings of a madman never do.

"Weren't you raised a Christian?" Francie tried to understand him.

"Your point?

"The Underworld and Hades is not a part of Christianity."

"Again, what is your point?"

"What makes you think your family is in the Underworld?"

"Because I fought with Hades and won. He has shown me the path to the Underworld. Now, I must free them."

Shaking her head, Francie sat down on the nearest chair. "You fought Hades? I don't like playing the devil's advocate here, but how do you know you fought Hades?"

"The gods are able to assume the forms of fouls, beasts and humans. The creature I engaged battle with was half bull and half man."

"A Minotaur? The one allegedly killed by Theseus."

"Not the same one, but similar. Once I thrust it through with a sword, the Minotaur faded and turned into Hades in human form. Winning the contest of the Minotaur, he officially bestowed upon me the right to travel through the darkness, where I discovered the Underworld."

"I'm sure you fought something, but I have to tell you there is no Hades or Underworld as described in Greek mythology. Yes, I said mythology. Now, don't get upset with me, but you cannot believe in Christianity and Greek Olympians at the same time. The beliefs counter each other. Christianity believes in one god. The Olympians believe in many gods." Francie tried to appeal to his logical, scientific side. A mix of fear, anxiety and compassion washed over her. How could she make him see the error of his thinking?

"What do my religious teachings have to do with my battle with Hades and the right of passage to the Underworld?"

"And you thought my dragon question was strange. Are you listening to yourself?"

"Christians believe in Hell, which is the same as the Underworld."

"Okay, what makes you think your family is in Hell? Did Hades tell you that?"

"No. I dreamt it on several occasions. I have visions or dreams as well as you. I've seen them in a dark place filled with doom and dread."

"Maybe reading all those scary books before going to bed is affecting your dreams. There is no Underworld."

"I've seen it. I needed to find out if I could transport people from one dimension to another and I did it."

"Are you responsible for making the people in the coffee shop and the movie theatre disappear?"

"Not disappear, but rather transported from this dimension to the Underworld."

"This is not science. Sounds like hocus-pocus. The world of science does not open up doors to the Underworld."

"There is a fine line between science and theology. Let's continue this conversation another time. I feel you are bored. Come with me, my love. Let's explore the trophy room." With that, Franklin motioned for her to follow him as he walked to a door at the back of the room, between bookcases, which led to another chamber.

Chapter Twenty-one
Sudicorp—Inside the Elevator

Inside the elevator, two human shadows backed Lewis and Lon into a corner. The only thing keeping them at bay was the flame from a lighter Lewis held. Taking off the jacket he borrowed from Francie, he lit it and pushed it toward the animated shades.

From the exterior, the muffled whirring of an acetylene torch sounded. Lon cowered in the corner with his arms over his head, shivering like a leaf on a windy day. Lewis examined the walls and ceiling, looking for a way out. Punching buttons did nothing. The panel didn't light up and the phone didn't work. From time to time, Lewis picked it up and tapped the switch hook several times, to no avail. He tried his cellphone, but that didn't work either.

No reception.

"Lon, help me look for an emergency exit. These elevators have to have them. I made sure of it, but for some reason, I can't find it." With his foot, Lewis moved the burning jacket closer to the shadows. The flames grew and the smoke nearly choked the men.

Lon coughed and tried to get up, but the movement opposite him from the black masses waiting to attack made him hide his head again.

Lewis pulled him up by the arms and forced him to climb up on his shoulders and push on the ceiling. Nothing gave way and no door or exit could be found.

"Are you sure? I inspected both elevators before allowing the installation. I know there was an exit." Lewis insisted, his eyebrows knitted together and his eyes narrowed as Lon continued pushing the ceiling with both hands.

At last, the shaken Lon looked down at Lewis and said, "Please let me down. I don't do well with heights and I'm getting dizzy." Carefully, Lewis helped him down.

From the opposite corner, a shadow diminished in size until it nearly vanished, except for the small dot running across the wall, to escape the flames.

The muffled voice of Drake Carver pierced the walls and alerted the men that efforts to open the elevator were still in progress.

"I hear you, Carver, but there is no emergency exit and nothing on the panel works." Lewis called out. Normally, trapped in an elevator shouldn't take long to resolve. Generally, Lewis wouldn't feel a slight panic in the core of his being.

"Try to roll the door open," was Carver's muffled request.

"I tried that, but I'll try again. How is Francie?" Lewis asked as he moved to the doors. Positioning his hands on them, the power shut down just as he tried to pull them open. "Carver can you hear me? How is Francie?"

"Come on, Lon. Stop sniveling and give me a hand." Lewis said. Reluctantly, Lon moved to the doors as he nervously glanced at the shadow in the corner. From the flames of the burning jacket, he realized one was missing.

"Mr. Avery, weren't there two?" Lon nodded to the dim silhouette standing in the opposite corner.

Lewis turned to Lon. The blazing fire illuminated one side of his face while the other stayed shadowed. "Two of what?" Lewis squinted and turned to see what Lon referred to. When he saw the lone shadow, it dawned on him.

"Oh, Lord! The other shadow! Where is it?" He looked about in the dimness, his heart pounding rapidly. It felt like the night he and Franklin fought in the alley. This he didn't want to repeat.

The muffled sound of Carver's voice urged him to try forcing the doors open. Just then, something skittered across the wall next to them. Lewis pushed Lon back. The smoke swirled around the small compartment and tickled their noses. Both men began to cough and fan the smoke away. A dark spot slid across the doors and down to the floor. Slowly it grew to its full height, turning to them without a face. Lewis backed away, careful not to excite the thing. Slowly, he reached down for the burning jacket and held it up to the shadow minion. Quickly, it backed away, dwindled to a speck, and slithered across the floor before disappearing into the crack that separated the doors.

The increasing smoke made the tiny compartment hazy and breathing became an issue. Lon coughed and coughed until he had to cover his face with his lab coat. Lewis tried to coax him into helping him force the doors apart, but the smoke choked him again and he continued coughing and gasping for oxygen.

Chapter Twenty-two
Exterior of Elevator

Down in the elevator shaft, the three men from Safety and Security worked diligently to get the elevator opened. Cables and open toolboxes cluttered the floor before the opened doors.

Carver tried to recall if anything in Franklin's notes related similar conditions to this. Hearing the low familiar murmur, he knew the shadows were inside the elevator.

No one could figure out why nothing could crack the doors open. It seemed like something had hermetically sealed it. He knew he'd have to get them out soon, or they'd run out of air. The fire that had been started with Lewis' jacket obviously created more urgency than he knew. If they didn't suffocate from the lack of oxygen, they would die of smoke inhalation or death by shadows.

Carver's cellphone rang. Pulling it from his jacket pocket, he saw it was from Francie.

"Hello, Francie? Are you all right? Where are you?" Carver worried that Franklin had kidnapped her.

The voice on the other end replied, "I'm good. I'm with Lloyd, err, Franklin. I don't know what to call him. He hasn't hurt me. How is Lewis? Did you get him out?"

"No. Nothing penetrates the metal. It's as if something has sealed it. Shadows are inside and I don't know what to do." Carver talked into the phone as he watched the men set small charges of C4 to blow a hole in the top of the elevator. "The air is shut off in the elevator and we can't turn it back on. We have to get them out soon or they'll die."

"No air and shadows? Are you sure?" asked Francie, almost in tears at the other end of the cellphone.

"I can hear the low murmuring. Do you think you could talk to Franklin? Maybe he'd help," Carver suggested. He knew he put her on the spot, but what else could he do.

"I'll try," she replied, almost in tears as she hung up.

"Francie, wait!" Carver shouted into the cellphone, but dead air assured him she'd hung up.

Black masses darted in and out of the elevator. The three men trying to open it didn't say anything. Assuming their eyes played tricks on them, they continued their work, but Carver shivered. He knew what they were. A chill ran up his spine.

Chapter Twenty-three
Franklin's Home—Trophy Room

The trophy room contained the stuffed heads of rhinos, lions, boars and other animals mounted on the walls, scattered throughout the room. Display cases of various preserved animal body parts and relics from a variety of regions from Africa and Egypt were lined up against the walls and some in the center of the room. More than anything, it resembled a stuffy museum.

Francie disconnected the cellphone and looked in horror at Franklin. He looked at her knowingly and grinned. For a moment, they just stared at each other without a word.

"You did this," Francie's eyes welled up with tears. "The elevator is sealed up with shadows in it. The power is shut down. They'll die."

Franklin just looked at her and said nothing. Quickly, she moved to him and looked up into his face, pleading. "Please Lloyd, please don't kill Lewis. Please let him go."

"What makes you think I can help him?"

"Nothing can crack the elevator open and shadows are in there. The air is shut off. Please, please Lloyd. They'll die. Lon, your lab assistant is with Lewis. Please, don't let them die." Francie reached for him.

Franklin acted cool, as if he didn't care, but he pulled her to him and asked, "What do you offer in return for my services?"

"What?" Surprised that he'd even suggest that she'd give him something in return and cheapen his feelings for her, she felt humiliated and feared what he'd planned.

He tightened his hold and made her look at him. "How much is the life of Lewis Avery worth to you? What will you give me to save his life?"

Shocked, she stared at him blankly. What could she say? Warm wet beads of watery fluid streamed down her face.

"You still have feelings for him, don't you? Trapping him in the elevator was meant to kill him. Why should I reconsider?" Franklin asked with coldness in his voice.

"God have mercy! You haven't changed. Nothing I've said has made a difference. You're still a cold blooded murderer!"

"Murderer? How is vengeance murder? It's justice. Lon Jamison betrayed me and Lewis is unfortunately related to a sadistic monster," Franklin showed no emotion, and no conscience.

Francie struggled for freedom, but Franklin held fast. A low murmuring hummed along the baseboards about the room. His ears perked up. Releasing his grip, he grabbed Francie's wrist and pulled her around the room with him, saying commands in Latin.

"Venite ad me. Sustine me mandato. 'Come to me. Wait for my command'," Franklin ordered. Trembling, Francie struggled for a deep breath, fearing what she'd see at his command.

The room fell silent. However, nothing came forth. A flush of anger washed over him. Tightening his grip on Francie's wrist, he repeated the order, "Venite ad me. Sustine me mandato."

Finally, something stirred and black masses skittered from the baseboards into the middle of the floor and took form of two human shadows. Francie gasped aloud then jumped back, but Franklin wouldn't let go, and pulled her back to him.

"From time to time they try to defy me. In the end, I am the victor." Franklin said quietly, turning to the woman he loved. "Somehow, you can still make me feel…you know…"

"…guilty." Francie finished his thought.

"Thank you. Guilty. It was so much easier when I didn't have someone constantly reminding me that taking a life is wrong." Then he said something to the shadows, which sounded almost inaudible. The shades sank into the floor and vanished.

"What did you say to them?" Francie trembled from his cruelty and tears still streaked her pretty face. She struggled to free herself from his grasp, to no avail.

"Does it matter? As long as you get what you want. Just remember, there is always a cost for what we ask." Having said that, he fell silent and moved to the door that led back to the living room.

Chapter Twenty-four
Sudicorp—Inside the Elevator

The flames from the burning jacket died down, allowing smoke to fill up the small enclosure. Lewis coughed and gasped for air as he lay on the floor, trying to keep Lon from passing out. Blinking his eyes rapidly, he kept shaking Lon and calling out to him. Both men began to see the tiny embers dwindle into a circle of void, easing their vision.

Just then, the wall rolled up, like a door, allowing the air to suck out the smoke. The men began to rally. The lights came on and at the opening stood a human silhouette.

Lon scrambled to get up with Lewis' help, but before he knew it, something hit him and claw marks raked across both arms.

"Ahhh! Ahhh!" screamed Lon, holding his arms up before his face. Red, sticky body fluid squirted out like ketchup from a squeeze bottle.

Lewis tried to get up, but something dark pulled him down to the floor. Fingers wrapped around his throat and tightened, regardless of how much he clawed at the shadowy hands. A horrible, sinking feeling hit him in the pit of his stomach, when he realized how close he was to dying. Once again, his vision blurred as his oxygen shut down and hands slowly crushed his throat.

With blood soaked arms, Lon Jamison managed to move and pull a cigarette lighter from his lab coat. He flicked it and stuck it up in front of the faceless mass that strangled Lewis. It released its victim and backed away. Gasping and coughing, Lewis held his throat as Lon grabbed his arm and pulled him to his feet.

Holding the flaming lighter up before him, Lon scared away the shade guarding the dark doorway, as he pulled the sputtering, gasping Lewis behind him. Together, they disappeared into the darkness. The portal rolled down and vanished, leaving the elevator sealed and empty.

Chapter Twenty-five
Franklin's Home-Dining Room

At the head of a long table covered with a white tablecloth, Franklin sat, and at his left was Francie, dressed in dark slacks and a pastel print blouse. A covered serving dish containing asparagus with hollandaise sauce was set in the center of the table. The plates before them had roast lamb and herb roasted, new potatoes. Francie picked at the food on her plate. Crying always upset her stomach. Not understanding what Franklin meant about a price coming with whatever we ask for had added to her upset. She really did love Lewis. He made her feel happy and secure. Never in her wildest dreams did she ever think Franklin would be so cruel and heartless.

"Are you going to be this way all evening?" Franklin barked. "Your dinner is getting cold. The lamb will be ruined."

"I'm not hungry." Francie pushed away her plate.

"Not hungry. Why? Still worried about your beloved Lewis? He and Lon are not dead."

Her countenance brightened. "You mean it? They're okay?"

"Yes, they are alive. Did you think for one minute that I would refuse your request?"

This made her feel like eating, so she pulled the plate back, picked up the knife and cut up the lamb into bite-sized pieces. Finished with his meal, Franklin watched her eat.

Once finished with her dinner, Francie pushed the plate back and dabbed her mouth with the napkin on her lap. "It was delicious. Thank you."

"I shall give your compliments to the chef." Franklin answered coldly.

"May I call Carver again, please?"

"Of course you may. You're not a prisoner."

Francie didn't need any more encouragement. Quickly, she drew the cellphone from her pocket and pressed a button. The cell rang a few times before pick up.

The voice on the other end answered, "Carver here."

"It's Francie. How are Lewis and Lon?"

"I'm glad you called. They're no longer in the elevator."

"What do you mean?"

"There's a dead silence within. Nobody answers me and it is considerably lighter."

"Lighter?"

"We have the elevator set to give temperature control, vitals and weight. The elevator is empty and there are no vital signs. I don't know how they got out or where they are. We're looking for them now. If you can shed any light on this, please tell me." Carver sounded confused, and his voice seemed hesitant.

"Empty? Thanks," she replied, as she puzzled at what he meant. Snapping the cellphone closed, she looked to Franklin who stared at her with interest.

"The elevator is empty. How can that be?" Francie wanted to know.

"How can that be, indeed. Come, let us go into the parlor, and err, rather the living room." He started to rise from the chair, but Francie got up and moved to him.

"You didn't kill them, did you?" She searched his face for an expression of emotion.

"I told you they are *not* dead. I am a man of honor." He pulled her down on his lap. They looked into each other's eyes. Francie gingerly touched his face and flinched as a vision unfolded.

Franklin stood with arms outstretched, eyes solid black, emanating with an eerie, red-black pulsing illumination, not akin to light, as we know it. His face distorted with the energy pulsating from within, he mouthed something inaudible. Behind him, a portal of darkness opened like a gaping maw.

Francie blinked rapidly, dispersing the vision, and tried to push away, but Franklin held her fast. In wild-eyed panic, she struggled against him.

Quietly, Franklin asked her, "What did you see? Stop trying to get away."

Everything swirled around in her mind. She knew he had turned into what she'd seen in the vision, but why did she see it again? How many times must she see the same thing in this man's soul?

"Let me go," her struggling calmed and she became still. Tears streamed down her face. "Please, let me go. I can't bear to see anymore."

"Francie, what did you see?" Franklin became concerned about what she'd envisioned in his soul.

"I saw you exactly like you turned the night you came after me and Lewis. Your eyes turned solid black and some sort of energy surged through your body! Feeling...it's...please, let me go!" She trembled and her hands turned ice cold. Wrapping his arms around her, he held her to his chest, and cupped his hands over hers to warm them.

"It's all right. I know," he tried to comfort her. His voice sounded softer and more caring. What caused the mood swings?

"It's not all right. You're changing. Whatever is in your soul terrifies me. Even when I talk to you, you're emotionally hot and cold."

Franklin loosened his hold and she pushed up and looked at him. "One minute you're laughing and talking like the Lloyd I used to know. The one...the one..." she faltered.

"The one, what?" He made her look at him. "Say it, Francie. The one you fell in love with."

Still trembling, she closed her eyes and repeated the words, "The one I fell in love with."

"That's what I wanted to hear." Lovingly, he caressed her face and hair.

"You aren't listening to me. I don't know whether you love me or if you'll kill me. I keep seeing the same vision, only now it's worse. Do you realize you keep changing?"

Silence.

Franklin seemed to ignore her words, as he continued to caress her face and hair, looking at her lovingly. Suddenly, Francie caught something dark out of the corner of her eye. Jerking her head around, she gasped and pushed Franklin hard to get away.

His head jerked around to follow her gaze. A human shadow moved closer then stopped at the other side of the table.

"What is that? Let me go!" Francie blanched white and now her feet turned as cold as her hands.

"It's only my shadow," said Franklin nonchalantly.

The thing scared her so badly that she clung to him, since he wouldn't release her.

"Y…your shadow?" She looked around him and the chair he sat on. He didn't cast a shadow and she hadn't noticed. Then she looked back at the stationary shadow, standing, waiting for a command.

"Didn't you notice? I separated it from myself days ago," he gave a half smile.

"Why?"

"Because I could. It wants to clear the table. With your permission," he said, almost mockingly.

"Whatever."

He looked to the shadow and gave it a command in Latin, "Aufer a ipsum. Duc eos ad culina. 'Remove the dishes. Take them to the kitchen'." Immediately, the shadow began stacking the dishes and after gathering them up, took them to the kitchen.

Then Franklin looked back at Francie. "Don't be afraid of the shadows. I command them." He said, but the words didn't comfort her.

Finally, he released his hold and she slid off his lap. "That's what I'm afraid of," she mumbled.

Franklin arose and led her to the living room. "Please sit with me awhile. Sing for me."

"Sing for you. After telling me I'm a soul-reading siren, you ask me to sing. Why?" She feared everything he said and did, but something in her just wouldn't keep quiet.

"I should like to you sing, Crazy for You, the Madonna song." He made her sit next to him on the sofa.

"You said I'm not a prisoner. I want to go back to my apartment," she protested.

"You refuse my request?' The way he replied, she wasn't sure if he was upset or didn't care.

A tingle of fear edged her very core, but she pressed the issue anyway. "I refuse."

Silence.

In the background, the clang of the shadow placing the dishes in the kitchen sounded.

"I really must find a way to tell that bloody shadow not to make so much noise." Franklin said coolly. Then he arose and motioned for her to follow him. He led her upstairs and opened the door to the second room in the corridor.

The décor appeared simple and a king sized bed covered with a floral comforter lay before them as Franklin flipped on the light. The bathroom stood to their left, with a dresser and red padded bench next to it.

"This is your room for now. If you need anything, I am at your service," Franklin made a slight bow and closed the door. Quickly, Francie locked and braced herself against it. Her heart pounded like it would pop out of her chest. For a moment, she hyperventilated. Taking a deep breath, she calmed herself.

Pulling the cellphone from her pocket, she pressed the icon for Carver. This time the cellphone rang until it went to voice mail. She closed the phone. Why wouldn't he answer? She really didn't want to leave a message.

Nothing made sense. Nevertheless, she was tired and a good hot shower would make her feel better. Having a closet filled with your size of clothes and shoes would be every woman's dream, but this felt weird. She opened it and found it filled with clothes and shoes in the colors, size and style she liked, but she hadn't picked out any of them. Franklin had. On many levels, this creeped her out.

After kicking off her shoes and removing her clothes, she wrapped a towel around her body. Then, she grabbed a tank top and a pair of rayon shorts and went into the bathroom to shower. The warm water felt good and refreshing. All she wanted to do was call Carver once more before going to sleep.

When Francie turned off the water, she thought she heard the door to the room open. With little movement, she cocked her head from side to side, listening.

Fay E. Simon

Silence.

Sometimes running water plays tricks on the ears and makes one think they hear bells ringing or other noises. Francie figured as much and got out of the shower, pulled a towel from the bar and dried off. After slipping on the tank top and rayon shorts, she dried her hair with a fresh one. Since the mirror had steamed up from the hot shower, she opened the bathroom door a little to let out the steam.

On a Plexiglas shelf near the fogged up mirror, she found her favorite body lotion. Smiling, she picked up the bottle, tipped it upside down and squeezed out a little in her hand. Then she cocked her left leg up and placed her foot on the toilet seat as she massaged the lotion in to her leg. She was repeating the action on her right leg when she felt a draft, as if the door might be opened wider.

Looking up, she gasped and flinched when her eyes met those of Franklin's. He stood in the doorway of the bathroom, eyeing her wantonly. The white shirt he wore at dinner was now opened half way down to his navel, exposing a lot of his bare chest. The button at the top of the zipper of the jeans was not buttoned. Only the zipper closed them, and his hands rested on the pockets.

"Lloyd, what're you doing here? Get out! I'm not dressed," she put her foot down. Franklin said nothing. He kept eying her like a hungry beast, while a wicked smile inched across his face.

Francie looked around for a bathrobe, but remembered she hadn't brought one into the bathroom. Gesturing, she said, "Lloyd, please move. My bathrobe is in the bedroom. Please let me pass."

He neither spoke nor moved. This unnerved her more than if he'd said anything.

Looking around the bathroom, she couldn't find anything to cover herself with, even if she didn't show that much skin, she felt naked. After all, she only had on clothes she would sleep in. By the way he looked at her, she knew what he wanted. It felt as if he literally undressed her with his eyes.

Francie's hands and feet grew cold with fear. Her heart raced and tears began to well up in her eyes. Cautiously, she moved toward him, hoping he'd move so she could pass.

143

When she got closer, he moved back a little and for a brief moment she thought he would let her go, but as soon as she turned sideways and tried to slip by, he grabbed her shoulders with both hands and slammed her against the frame of the door. Her head jerked forward and back as in a whiplash. The sudden jolt of pain in her neck and head sent shockwaves throughout her body. Immediately, he pressed himself against her and tried to pin her to the doorway. Quickly, he wrapped his arms around her, forcing his lips on to hers.

In the past, heated passion came from such kisses, but not this time. Even though he looked like the Lloyd Maxwell she'd fallen in love with, this man was a demon that only wanted to violate her. His kisses were fiery and feral.

All her struggling against him proved futile. His breath felt hot and filled with aggression as he pulled at the top, as if to rip it off her. With tears streaming down her face, she begged, "Please, Lloyd, don't do this. Please, don't! This is not you."

Forcing his kisses on her, he menacingly whispered in her ear, "Oh, but it is me! You will give me what I want, what I've been craving for ever since we met nearly three years ago."

One arm wrapped around her waist, while the other held her about the throat. She pushed as hard as she could against his chest, but he pressed himself against her all the harder. The fingers tightened around her throat as the other hand began tugging at the shorts.

Her heart sank and her head ached from being jerked around. Could this really be the man she once loved? As the fingers tightened around her throat, the world around her grew dim and a void enveloped her. All the gasping couldn't suck in enough oxygen. The panic and terror that she would die this night washed over her and all she could think of was, "God have mercy on me!"

Without warning, Franklin loosened his grip. Faltering backward, he gasped and cried out, "Arianna!"

A figure of a woman now stood between him and his prey. Dressed in a linen pendent sleeved dress with a silk over veil, the woman with raven hair stared into Franklin's face. Her eyes appeared like shafts of flames burning into his soul.

"Release the darkness before it consumes you!" said the woman.

"Arianna! I've missed you so," Franklin gasped. His hands shook and the cruelty seemed to drain from his body.

Once again, Francie saw her chance to escape. Without hesitation, she slapped his chest with both hands, grabbed his collar and brought him to her as she rammed her knee into his crotch as hard as she could. Franklin grunted and doubled over in excruciating pain.

Gasping and panting, Francie fled through the open door and downstairs as fast as she could. When she reached the living room, she looked around for a place to hide or escape. The door upstairs rattled and banged against the wall. Wild-eyed, she darted into the dining room, taking in the austere chamber and the table upon which they'd recently eaten as she searched desperately for an escape.

Franklin burst into the door moments behind her. Forcing his lungs to suck in oxygen, he stared around the room with solid black eyes. The crackling sound similar to electricity danced all around him. Face distorted in rage, he ripped the chairs from their place and tossed them in every direction. Then, he yanked the tablecloth from the table and stood back, as if he expected to find Francie beneath it.

Nothing.

He slammed both fists on the table and bellowed, "Ahh! Francie come out! Don't be stupid. I don't want to hurt you, but I will if I have to."

No reply. Nothing stirred.

Knowing there was only one entrance, he marched to the drapes. The other small decorative tables scattered about had no tablecloth, so no one could hide under them.

Moving to the drapes, he grabbed each panel with both hands and jerked down hard. He found nothing. However, when he reached the last panel, he paused. It seemed perfectly still, except for an occasional, very slight movement.

With both hands, he grabbed the panel and violently ripped it from the rods at the top that were screwed into the wall. With a tear-stained face, Francie cowered, and again, begged, "Please, Lloyd, don't do this. You said you loved me. If you love me, you don't want to hurt me," but the words barely left her lips when he lunged for her. Instinctively, she kicked him in the shins as hard as she could and ran, as he doubled over in pain.

Out of the door and into the living room, she bumped into the coffee table then into the overstuffed chair, before reaching the library door. Behind her, the crashing of chairs and the cursing of an angry man echoed from the dining room.

When she hit the door, she clutched the knob and twisted hard. The door flung open, she ran in and slammed it behind her. Looking around, she found a chair that she pushed against the door, jamming it under the knob to prevent it from turning. Then she looked for an exit. When she heard rustling from the trophy room, she tried hard to catch her breath as she recalled the two rooms connected with the door at the end of the library.

In a panic, she tried to remove the chair she'd jammed under the knob, but it was too late. Franklin kicked open the door leading from the trophy room into the library and now charged her like a raging bull. The force of his weight hit her so hard she slammed into the chair, stumbling back against part of the door. The distress of the body slam shot charges of misery throughout her. Dazed by the contact, she barely felt the hand around her throat.

Franklin wrapped the fingers of his right hand around her throat and with the other hand, swiped the oak desk clean of clutter, so he could throw her down on it. The jolt of her head meeting the desk added to the torment. The room spun around like a dizzy rollercoaster ride. The pressure of the man's body pinned her to the desk as Franklin forced feverish kisses over her face and neck. His hands groped her soft body, but the material of the shorts provoked him and he tried to tear them away.

"Please, Lloyd, please don't do this. I don't want to die," she pleaded repeatedly, but the darkness within seemed to drive him so that her cries fell on deaf ears.

Through all of this misery and trauma, Francie's hand felt for something to hit him with. She struggled hard, trying to keep her legs together to keep him from pulling down her shorts.

Finally, her fingers touched something hard and round; a paperweight. It looked translucent with a rose inside. With the will to survive, she wrapped her fingers around the paperweight and brought it down hard on Franklin's head. It rattled him, but he continued trying to strip her. Again, the paperweight made contact with his head and he dropped on top of her like a sack of potatoes.

Quickly, she pushed hard and finally rolled him off her. She scrambled up from the desk and pulled the chair away from the door. She flung it open and ran for the sliding glass door to her left.

Without looking back, Francie ran as fast as she could into the night. From a distance, the crackling of leaves and twigs sounded. The grunting and groaning that followed warned that Franklin was nearly upon her.

How does he recover so fast? She wondered. *From the kick in the shin and the thump on the head, maybe, but the knee in the crotch, no.*

To her horror, two strong hands caught her shoulders and pushed her to the ground. Again, she pleaded with him, amid the throbbing of her own head and aches in her body. Fueled by lust and cruel intent, Franklin rolled her over and pressed his weight down on top of her even harder, as with both hands he tore open the top. Francie tried to cover herself, but he slapped her hands away. The torn top didn't fully expose her nakedness, but enough of her full bosoms to make the man bury his face into her bruised neck and kiss his way down to her cleavage. The warmth she used to feel from him had fled. Now, only cold, raw wantonness drove his sick passion.

As his strong hands roughly roamed her body, he forcibly covered her mouth with his. Again, her hands felt for something with which to hit him. After a few moments of pushing and struggling against the man, her fingers touched a hard, wooden item. Amid the laboring and fighting, Francie wrapped her fingers around the piece of wood and clubbed Franklin in the head as hard as she could. He collapsed on top of her once again. She pushed and strained to push him off her.

Finally free of the dead weight, she scrambled to get up and limped back toward the lights of the house she could see from the dark gardens.

As soon as she hit the glass sliding door, she could hear footsteps in the distance, behind her. She slid open the door and staggered in. Turning she tried to slide the door shut, but Franklin caught it and yanked it sideways hard.

Panic filled her. By now, her breathing was labored and her mind spun.

How does he recover so fast? He's unstoppable! The thought repeated in her mind. There in the opening of the glass doors stood Franklin, panting like an animal. Blood ran from a split on his head and down his face. His eyes, still solid black, blazed with a tiny glow, akin to embers. Slowly, she backed away from him, stumbling back on the ottoman and then the coffee table, and finally she turned to run.

She felt something grab her hair and rip her scalp back. The painful jerk sent her head whipping like another whiplash. This time his arms caught her around the waist from behind. His face buried in her neck, his hot breath sent heart-stopping terror up and down her spine. The hands roamed her body, pulling the torn top open, so he could force more kisses down to her cleavage.

"Why are you doing this? Please don't," she begged and struggled between sobs. He held her arms down, to keep her from fighting and escaping.

"Your body feels so good next to mine. I have to punish you for teasing me so. I will make you pay for all the times you made me want you and wouldn't surrender to me," he whispered ominously in her ear. Then, he cursed and slammed her face forward into the nearest wall. Literally, Francie saw stars as her head collided with the hard surface. Pinning her against the panel with his weight, his hands roamed her sides and rear as he tugged at her shorts.

She kept telling herself she had to survive. She couldn't let this man violate her. She relaxed her torso and limbs to give the false perception of capitulation, causing Franklin to stop pressing his weight against her. The moment she felt the slightest ease of pressure, she pushed hard against the wall and back kicked with as great a force as she could, scraping her heal down the front of the leg, allowing her full weight to come down on his foot.

"Ahh!" screamed Franklin as he backed up to grab his foot. Francie shot out and disappeared into the kitchen.

The dark of the kitchen took a moment for her eyes to adjust. She ran into a chair, and then stumbled into a counter. Her hands ran over pots and bowls. Panting and dizzy, she cautiously felt her way around the kitchen to the stove. Her fingers traced the burners and over to a wooden block.

Gingerly, running her hands over the block, she recognized the handles of knives.

Violently, the swinging doors banged open, allowing dim rays of light from the living room and corridor to break the void. The silhouette of a man hesitated before stepping inside the pitch black of the kitchen.

Francie put a hand over her mouth so he couldn't hear her panting. Cowering at the edge of the stove, near the block of knives, she made herself quiet and still. Footsteps moved softly around the kitchen as the doors swung back into place. She thought to move quietly to the doors and make a run for it.

Softly, she shuffled a little to one side, scooting sideways toward the door. In a moment, the silhouette of a man popped up before her. She said nothing. The dim light from the small windows in the swinging doors glinted on the blade in her hand.

Franklin laughed out loud. "You stupid little bitch! You won't use it. You're too scared. Drop it, before you hurt yourself," he said cruelly. Francie held the grip of the knife so tightly, her knuckles turned white. He moved closer to her.

When he lunged for her, she rammed the knife into his inner thigh as hard and fast as she could. A blood-curdling scream arose from the figure now crumpled on the floor.

Then she yanked it out and raised back to strike again, when she heard Franklin's voice, pleading for her not to kill him.

Sidestepping him in the dark, she found the light switch and flipped it on. There on the floor near the stove and block of knives, lay Franklin holding his bleeding leg. With her arms and legs covered in dirt and blood, Francie moved slowly toward him raising the knife dripping with his own blood. His eyes had turned back to normal and his face now distorted in agony.

"Francie, please don't kill me. I never meant to hurt you," he begged, holding up one hand as if to block the knife, the other holding the wounded limb. His eyes held so much distress and fear as she stared at him with a vacant look.

Drops of his blood dripped a little at a time from the blade on to the hand he held up. At first, she said nothing. With rumpled and ripped sleepwear, she glared at him as if contemplating whether she should kill him.

"Please don't kill me. If you do, there will be no one to command the shadows and they will kill everything, including Lewis." Franklin said as he held his chest, gasping and panting. The change looked as if it drained him of energy, but his gasping and struggle for breath didn't seem to be as severe.

"Lewis? Okay." Francie whispered. Turning the point of the knife away, she helped him to the small kitchen table.

"First aid kit?" she asked.

Gesturing, Franklin replied, "In that cupboard, at the right." Francie moved to the cupboard and opened it. Finding the kit, she pulled it out and brought it to the table. Setting the knife down on the table out of his reach, she opened the metal box.

Finding a pair of scissors, she looked him square in the eye and said, "I'm going to split open your jeans, since I don't want you to remove them." He nodded an agreement and she proceeded to cut open the leg of the jeans. That done, she found some towels and had him place them over the wound and press down hard. Looking into the kit, she found the same bottle of powder with Chinese characters on it.

She held it up. "This stops the bleeding, right?" She asked.

"Yes. I believe I gave you some for emergencies a few years ago." Franklin recalled.

Pushing away his hand, she removed the towels and poured some of the powder into the bleeding wound. Instantly, the blood stopped. After soaking some cotton balls with alcohol, she cleaned off the blood and placed a gauze pad over it. Then she wrapped it, cut it from the roll, and tied off the ends.

"You do that very well. We could have used you on the battlefields. What patient wouldn't heal with such a skillful, beautiful nurse," Franklin tried to sound pleasant and kind. Francie said nothing. After the bandaging, she stood up, put everything back into the kit and closed the lid.

"Please help me to the sofa. I can't make it upstairs," he looked at her. Without a word, Francie allowed him to lean on her while hobbling out of the kitchen and to the sofa in the living room.

Franklin settled on the sofa and she turned to leave the room.

"Francie, where are you going?" he asked. "Really, I didn't want to hurt you. Please forgive me. Please..."

"I'm going upstairs to clean up and get dressed. I'll be back to see if you need anything." She answered coldly.

"Please forgive me. I never meant to hurt you. I tried to control myself, but I couldn't. Something compelled me."

Francie said nothing. Turning away, she returned to the kitchen and came out with the knife. However, she didn't go to him. Instead, she went upstairs.

In the bedroom, she looked around her. The door looked a little dented from Franklin's tantrum. Closing it, she turned the lock and jammed a chair under the knob.

Once again, she undressed and took a shower. Every part of her body ached; even the souls of her feet.

Out of the shower, she dressed in a pale, blue sweater and dark slacks. Then she slipped on a pair of flats. Taking the knife into the bathroom, she ran the blade under some running water and dried it off. Then she wrapped it in a clean towel and walked downstairs.

Chapter Twenty-six
Through the Darkness

The portal Lon Jamison and Lewis Avery walked through led them into a passageway that was absent of light, as we know it. Instead, a strange, creepy glow illuminated the way as the men moved farther and farther into the darkness, away from the elevator that had trapped them.

For a moment, they paused as a bright light popped up before them like a screen that displayed movies. *A tropical scene revealed itself, with swaying palm trees, a sandy shore, and a beautiful, clear ocean. Seagulls squawked as they flew overhead in the azure skies. A catamaran with a rainbow colored sail floated in the distance.*

A closer view of the catamaran revealed Franklin, in swim trunks, jumping into the ocean, as Francie in a one-piece swimsuit giggled and laughed on deck. She leaned over and waved at Franklin as he bobbed up from the water.

Laughingly, he beckoned to her. She shook her head. He reached up for her. Dodging him, she waved again. Clearly, he was trying to coax her into swimming with him. Finally, he climbed up on the boat, and grabbed her about the waist as they both went into the water.

In a moment, they bobbed up, laughing and playfully splashing water at each other. The movement of the ocean seemed to push them together. They cuddled up into each other's arms and pressed their lips together in fiery passion. Franklin's hands started to roam past her waist, suddenly the expression on her face changed to an indignant one. Francie broke the kiss and slapped his face hard.

Anger washed over him. Francie swam away and climbed up on the catamaran. Franklin remained in the water with a look that could kill.

Scene faded.

"What was that?" asked Lon, as Lewis finished tearing up the lab coat to make bandages for Lon's arms.

"Don't know. I think Francie and Franklin went to Hawaii at one time. I'm guessing this was part of that trip, but I don't know why we're watching it." Lewis padded each arm with some of the material and wrapped strips around it to hold the padding in place. "That should stop the bleeding for now. Thanks for saving me back there."

"No problem. This place is weird. Where are we?" Lon's voice was still shaky as he asked, staring at the blank, lit up screen.

Lewis moved to it and put out his hand. "I don't feel anything. Let's keep moving. Hopefully, this leads to somewhere back in the real world."

The two started walking through the strangely illuminated darkness. With the screen gone, they could barely see the outline of things like rocks and shrubs. Evidently, they walked along a path that should have been outdoors, but outdoors where?

Occasionally, they stopped to listen. Something skittered behind them in the darkness and a muttering caught their ears.

"What is that? Sounds like somebody talking real low." Lewis drew out the lighter from his pocket and flicked it on. A loud skittering sounded behind them. He whirled around and flashed it behind him, but the only thing they saw were dark, shapeless things melting into the darkness, making the sound like fairly good-sized insects moving across the floor.

"I think it's those shadows," Lon interjected. "They communicate with each other in sounds like that. You need an EVP recorder to capture what they're saying."

"They're also trying to sneak up on us in the dark. I recall Carver saying something about EVP's. Speaking of Carver, do you think our cellphones will work here?" Lewis pulled out his cell and pressed a button to bring it back to life. Lon watched him press an icon to dial Carver. The cell started ringing then went straight to voice mail. Lewis hung up and tried Francie's cell number. It did the same thing.

"Well, guess that answered my question. Is this part of Franklin's experiment?"

"Yeah, you are supposed to be able to travel through the darkness to get to wherever you want to go, even to the Underworld where Hades resides." Lon squinted in the dark, trying to make out images.

"The Underworld and Hades? What are you talking about? They aren't real. They're myths." Lewis said as he noticed a pinpoint brightness getting closer.

"They are real, Mr. Avery. They are quite real."

"Call me Lewis and what do you mean they're real?"

"The people who disappeared were shifted into the Underworld, with the permission of Hades. Dr. Franklin talked to him."

"When did Franklin talk to someone named Hades?"

"Shortly before the disappearances. Look! That light is getting brighter. Do you think we're seeing sunshine?"

"I hope so." The conversation waned as the men ran toward the light.

The faster they ran, the closer the light grew and soon they came to the end of the passageway and into the light of the outside world.

Stepping out of the passageway, they found themselves on the sidewalk in front of the Sudicorp building. Sunlight shone everywhere. Lewis looked at his watch. It read nine am.

The dark passageway rolled up to nothing. Not a trace left.

Lewis tried Francie's cell, but she still didn't answer, and again, it went straight to voice mail.

Then he called Carver. This time, someone answered.

"It's me, Lewis. Lon and I are on the sidewalk in front of Sudicorp." Lewis looked around. Nothing seemed out of order, but his entire mind spun in circles for an instant. He knew things were not right for Francie.

"Are you okay? How did you get out there?" Carver sounded concerned but relieved.

"Don't know, but Lon needs medical attention and I need to find Francie."

"Francie's with Franklin."

"What?" He didn't want to hear that Francie rested in Franklin's care. A nightmare in and of itself came to the mind of Lewis Avery.

By now, Carver stood before them talking into his cell. Then he hung up and motioned for Lon to come with him.

"Let's get you some medical attention. Wait for me and I will go with you, Lewis." Carver said.

"I'm not waiting. If he's hurt her, I'll kill him," Lewis said as he put away his cell and pulled out his gun and checked it.

"What happened to your throat?" Carver moved closer and pulled Lewis' collar aside. His neck had distinct bruises.

"Shadow tried to strangle me. Lon saved my life."

"Shadows can now strangle?"

"Go get help for Lon. Where does Franklin live? I'll meet you there."

"No, wait! I'll go with you," and with that, Carver turned quickly and ushered Lon into the building. Lewis made a face and followed. He really didn't want to wait. Something told him that Francie needed rescuing and he wanted to be her hero.

Chapter Twenty-seven
Franklin's Living Room

Franklin threw back two-fingers of Scotch as he sat on the sofa with a decanter of spirits in front of him and a plate of tacos. A bottle of extra hot sauce was set next to the plate. Francie sang along with a country and western song playing on the radio.

Watching him down Scotch and eat tacos with the fiery hot sauce made Francie stop singing and turn the music down. "You sure you want to keep drinking that stuff, especially with hot sauce? It's ten o'clock in the morning."

Franklin didn't reply and he glared at her as he ate his taco.

"Okay, do whatever. Just promise me you won't kill Lewis and you'll stop trying." Francie continued.

"Agreed. I promise not to kill Lewis." Franklin said as he threw back another Scotch.

"And you'll apologize for trying to kill him."

"Do I have to?" He shook out more hot sauce and took another bite of taco.

"You will apologize," Francie patted the towel containing the knife. Franklin's eyes grew big.

"All right, I'll apologize."

She turned the music up and changed the channel to the song 'Keep Your Hands to Yourself' by the Georgia Satellites. Then she sang along.

Franklin interrupted, "Is this another cowboy song for me to hate?"

"Yes, another one for you to absolutely detest."

"It's painful to listen to."

"You mean the dialect. It's the way some people talk in certain parts of the US." Francie didn't want to talk to him, but she didn't want to be rude.

"I know, but they sing like that, too?" He downed another Scotch. Then he muttered, "Keep your hands to yourself."

At that moment, a rustling and banging noise sounded at the sliding glass doors. Lewis hit the glass and slid it open. Francie limped to him and threw her arms around his neck as their lips pressed together passionately. The temperature of both rose to a boiling point before they broke the kiss.

"Baby, are you hurt? Are you okay? I see you're limping." Lewis looked her up and down to see how she fared. He saw the bruises on her face and neck.

"I'm okay. When Lloyd chased me around the house I bumped into a few chairs and tables, that's all." She replied coolly.

"Chased you around the house? Why was he chasing you around the house?" Lewis frowned as he looked from Francie to Franklin who was downing more Scotch.

Francie nodded to Franklin, "Ask him."

"Franklin, why were you chasing her around the house?" Lewis drew his gun.

"Why do you think I was chasing her around the house?" He threw back another Scotch.

"Is he drunk?" Lewis looked to Francie.

"Ask him." She gestured to Franklin.

"Are you drunk?" Lewis puzzled.

"I hope so." Shaking out more hot sauce on a taco, Franklin then took a bite.

"Tacos? I thought you hated tacos." Lewis made a face.

"I loathe tacos." Franklin replied as he took another bite.

"Then why are you eating them?" Lewis tried to understand, but the bruises on Francie worried him.

"I'm in pain. Eating something I hate takes my mind off it."

Lewis picked up the bottle of hot sauce. "Extra, extra hot sauce?" He shuddered to think how the combination of the condiment and Scotch felt in Franklin's stomach.

"Francie calls it, 'extra flamey'," Franklin tried not to slur his words.

"What happened to your leg? Is this the other pain?" Lewis noticed the split open leg of the jeans as the white gauze peeked through.

"I was chasing her around the house and I cornered her in the kitchen. She had a knife."

"Oh, so she stabbed you in the leg." Lewis squeezed her hand and looked to her. "Good job, baby! Why is he still alive? Why didn't you aim higher?" Lewis pointed the gun at Franklin, but Francie pushed it away.

"He turned back and begged for his life."

"Turned back?"

"He went all Jekyll and Hyde on me. Eyes turned solid black. After I stabbed him, he turned back to himself and I couldn't kill him."

'No, no, that's not why. I told her if she killed me, there would be no one to command the shadows and they would kill everyone, including you. At the mention of your name, she spared my life." Franklin threw back another Scotch.

"So the knife took the romance out of the relationship, huh?" Lewis grinned. Franklin shot him an irritated look as he continued eating and drinking.

Lewis picked up the decanter of amber liquid and sniffed it. "Scotch?" He replaced the container. "Isn't it a bit early for Scotch?"

Franklin didn't reply, but he shot Lewis a dirty look.

"Don't nag him about drinking and don't needle him about the knife," Francie whispered.

"Let me get this straight. He was chasing you around the house to hurt you and you stabbed him in the leg. He begged you not to kill him and you patched him up?"

"What makes you think I patched him up?" Francie wanted to know.

Taking the barrel of the gun, he moved the jean material aside to expose the gauze bandage tie on Franklin's leg. "The way this one is tied off is the same way you tied my bandages."

Franklin slapped the barrel away. "Please sit down. Have a taco. Scotch?" He offered.

"Lewis, please put the gun away. He's not dangerous now." Francie said quietly.

They sat down, but Lewis hung on to his gun.

"If he's alive, he's dangerous. He tried to…to," Lewis just couldn't say it.

"…violate you." Franklin finished the thought.

"Your face and neck are black and blue. How could you not kill him?" Lewis tenderly touched her face and neck, tracing the bruises. Then he held her close and fell silent.

For a moment, he and Francie watched Franklin throw back Scotch and eat tacos with hot sauce. Then, Carver stumbled into the sliding glass door.

"Come in Carver. Sit down, please." Franklin beckoned. Carver moved to an overstuffed chair.

"Why are you sitting around watching him eat tacos and drink…?" Carver glared at Franklin. "You hate tacos and are you drunk?"

"I loathe tacos and yes, I'm drunk."

"He's pretty docile after I stabbed him in the leg." Francie looked remorseful.

"Don't talk about me like I'm not here. Why did you and Lewis come in the back door?"

"We were trying to sneak up on you, but it appears that a lot of debris is pushed up against the door," replied Carver.

"Sneak up on me? You made enough noise to wake up the dead. Anyway, I have something to say since we're all together." He threw back another Scotch. "I want to apologize to Lewis for the slight transgression of trying to kill him."

"Slight transgression? Trying to murder me is not a slight transgression." Lewis turned red and aimed the gun, but Francie pushed it down gently.

"It's an apology. Please accept it." She whispered.

"I will not."

Franklin continued in spite of the contention. "I promised my lady that I wouldn't kill you and I won't even try."

"When did you promise that? Before or after she stabbed you in the leg?" Lewis asked venomously.

Franklin said nothing, but shot him another dirty look.

"I think we should hear him out." Carver said knowingly.

"Has Francie told you who I am?" asked Franklin.

Lewis looked to Francie. "Why are we talking to him? He tried to kill me twice. He tried to hurt you last night. I say let me shoot him."

"Please put the gun away and answer his question." Francie looked into his eyes and Lewis melted. Leaning to the side, he pressed his lips to hers.

Franklin glared at Lewis. He never liked interruptions, especially that kind.

Lewis pursed his lips then replied, "Yes, she said you are a twelfth century knight."

"Did she tell you about her abilities?"

"You told her she was a soul-reading siren." Lewis replied with skepticism.

"Good. Francie asked me how it was possible for me to still be alive."

"Because she didn't stab you a second time?" Lewis added with sarcastic contempt.

"Lewis, don't goad him." Francie hugged his arm.

Franklin glared at him, but ignored the wise cracks and continued. "Carver, please explain."

"It's my fault he's still alive." Carver began. "Please don't say a word." Lewis sat back and pursed his lips again.

"I created an elixir that extends mortality." He pulled a small vial from his inside coat pocket. "When I say extends morality, it will stop the aging and increase the immune system. In other words, the elixir will stop the aging process and make you immune to illness and disease. However, it does not give immortality. As long as it's not natural causes, you can die." Carver paused and looked from Lewis to Francie.

"Franklin would like me to offer this to Francie." He set the vial down on the coffee table on the side closest to her.

Lewis flushed beet red, even behind his ears. "Hold it! You created an elixir that extends mortality. How's that? You and Franklin come from the same time?"

Carver knew Lewis wouldn't take this well. Swallowing hard, he took a deep breath and proceeded to explain. "I was a man of medicine years before I met Franklin."

"Years? How many years?" Lewis narrowed his eyes at his boss.

"Forty BC," came the reply.

"Correction, it's BCE and not BC," Lewis interjected. "Wait! Forty years before Christ? Are you kidding me?"

"Not kidding. I was from a large port city called Corinth. Perhaps you've heard of it."

Francie sat with her mouth agape a moment before she could utter a word. "Corinth? Like in the Bible, Corinth? That's ancient Greece."

"At last, someone older than me," Franklin sighed as he sat back. By now, he'd stopped eating and drinking since his stomach had started burning.

"I was born Telemachus, son of Agapetos. I, like my father, was a man of medicine. Because of my love of science, I created the elixir by accident. My initial goal was to create an elixir of eternal life, but it obviously fell short. First, I used it on myself. No one of my family or friends would entertain the thought of living past their mortal years.

"That is, until I met Franklin, then called Sir Gregory of Cornwall. He never told me the reason he wanted to die. When he found I was a man of medicine, he asked for poison to end his life. I never could understand why anyone would hold such a frail and precious gift of life so carelessly." Carver paused and looked to Lewis and Francie. No one said a word. To hear whispers of such a phenomenon could make one dizzy, but to look a man face to face and hear him admit to being centuries old with a potion that could extend mortal life was jaw dropping.

Carver smiled at Francie. "Care to read my soul?"

"I'll pass. If reading Lloyd/Franklin nearly made my head explode, I can imagine what reading you would be like. Yikes!"

Lewis asked, "He said he wanted to die?"

"Yes. He asked me for poison. Instead, I gave him the elixir."

Lewis couldn't pass up a chance to needle Franklin. "Some friend you are. The man makes a simple request and you deny him."

"Actually, he brought that to mind the other day. He said if I'd been a true friend, I would have honored the request." Carver looked to Franklin. "Why did you beg Francie not to stab you again? I thought you wanted to die?"

Hesitating, Franklin looked to each one in the room. "After seeing the vacant look in her eyes, I changed my mind. I saw no remorse or conscience in them. She would have ripped me open on the kitchen floor. After all the battles I've fought, all the one on one confrontations, I have never been afraid of anyone until now." Franklin shuddered.

Carver and Lewis couldn't help but chuckle at that. Grinning, Lewis pressed him, "Seriously? Francie is the only person that scares you?"

"Yes! You didn't see her. An expressionless face, blank stare, holding a knife over me that dripped my own blood..." his voice trailed as he shuddered again. "In that instant, I really didn't want to die. My God woman, you'll be the death of me yet!"

Even Francie smiled at this.

Now, Franklin picked up the conversation about his offer. "The proposal is that I will let you and Lewis go. Take the vial with you. Drink it if you wish. Should you do so, you would be like me. You could live your life with Lewis until he passes. I will be waiting for you."

"Ah, that's sweet!" Francie felt sad when he said this.

"In the end, he still gets you. What's sweet about it?" Lewis gritted his teeth.

"Lewis, let him finish." Francie hugged his arm and patted his chest.

"Thank you, Francie. The second proposal is if you consent to marry me instead of Lewis, I will stop the experiment immediately. I will put the shadows back where they belong and return the missing people. Monitor me for two months that I may prove whether or not I can control the change. Then, we shall be married."

Lewis hit the ceiling and began shouting. "THIS IS INSANE! We don't have to do anything he says. Why are we listening to him? We can just walk out of here right now."

"Lewis, please stop shouting. Trust me." Francie tried to explain, but he wouldn't listen.

"No! Why do we have to choose any of the proposals? Who died and put him in charge?" Lewis flushed with anger and set the gun down on the coffee table.

"I don't care how bad you feel. I'm calling you out. No shadows, no darkness, no weapons. You and me, Franklin. Outside, now!"

"Are you challenging me?" Franklin seemed genuinely surprised.

"What do you think?" Lewis flushed red as the heat of anger inflamed him.

"Francie, I must accept his challenge. If I don't, I'll be branded a coward." Franklin pushed himself up with Carver's help.

"I don't get it. Francie, he tried to hurt you. He tried to kill me twice. Carver, he had an affair with your wife. How can you just sit here and feel sorry for him? I don't care if he is a Shadow Bender, I want justice." Lewis shook off Francie's hold and stood up.

Francie got up, too. "I don't want any of you to fight. I can make my own choice."

Lewis looked at her incredulously. "Well, it isn't about you anymore. Originally, I came here to rescue you. Now, it's a matter of principle. Come on, Franklin. Outside, now!" With that, he quickly moved to the sliding glass doors and stormed into the gardens.

Franklin looked to Francie.

"I'll try not to kill him, but I must accept his challenge." Franklin stated.

"No!" Francie protested. "I don't want you two fighting."

"Stay here or come outside and watch. However, if you watch, say nothing." After that, Carver helped him out to the gardens, with Francie in tow.

Plenty of sunshine flooded the beautiful land filled with a variety of trees, shrubs and flowers. The fragrance of newly opened blossoms permeated the air.

As they reached a little clearing near a tool shed, they saw Lewis standing on the gravelly part of the area. He kept moving, stretching and flexing his hands.

Carver released Franklin and moved to Francie.

"I know your concerns, but you will have to let the men handle this." Carver tried to explain. Francie didn't reply. She stood in the sun, wringing her hands, while tears trickled down her cheeks.

Lewis bounced around like a boxer warming up for a fight. He threw a few punches into the air then stretched his legs, first the right then the left.

Franklin didn't move. He motioned for Carver. "What's he doing?"

Carver studied Lewis for a moment as he continued moving, stretching and flexing his hands. "I suppose he's warming up." He gave a lopsided smile.

"Warming up for what?" Franklin figured the challenge was a brawl, not a game of sports.

Caver shrugged. "Why don't you ask him?"

Franklin puzzled, but wanted to know, so he said, "Pst...Lewis!"

"What?" Lewis replied, annoyed.

"What are you doing?" Franklin had to know.

"Warming up."

"For what?"

"To fight you."

"To fight me?

"Don't you warm up before going into battle?" Lewis stopped bouncing around.

"Not like that. This appears to be a warm up for an extreme sport instead of a fight."

"Maybe I should've challenged you to a duel of pistols. Twenty paces turn and fire." Lewis said, mockingly.

"No thank you. I've done that twice." Franklin sounded irritated.

Lewis looked at him as if he had grown a second head. "You've dueled with pistols."

"I used to be a riverboat gambler on the Mississippi at the turn of the twentieth century. Dueling with pistols was quite the fashion." Franklin grimaced at the pain in his leg.

Drying her eyes, Francie butted in with surprise, "I didn't know you were a riverboat gambler. I thought you were always a soldier of some kind."

"You never asked a true historical question. All you ever asked was if I'd met Jack the Ripper, had I killed a dragon, did I know the Knights Templar and if they'd found the Holy Grail." Franklin looked at her.

"Francie, seriously, the Holy Grail?" Lewis chuckled.

"Those were my words exactly," replied Franklin.

"Well?"

Franklin had to smile, as did Carver.

"It's in history," Francie weakly defended.

"The Holy Grail is a myth. There is no Holy Grail," Lewis rolled his eyes.

"Okay. Then what name did you go by as a riverboat gambler," Francie asked Franklin.

"Beauregard. Beauregard d'Orsay. As in the station, Gare d'Orsay."

"Not Maverick?"

"Maverick? Huh?" Franklin seemed to have no idea what she meant.

"The old TV show, Maverick. The two brothers were gamblers, Bret and Bart, they had a cousin who was also a gambler, named Beauregard Maverick," said Francie innocently.

"My God! Another film reference of sorts! Lewis, come on. Let's fight. Hit me, please. I can't stand another film reference," Franklin shook his head and gave a wry smile. Carver struggled not to laugh.

Without warning, Lewis charged Franklin. As soon as he entered his opponent's space he threw a punch, Franklin sidestepped and grabbed his extended arm, pulling him through with no effort. Lewis couldn't stop and headed out into open space. Infuriated, he whipped around and came at Franklin again. The same thing repeated, Lewis committed his punch and Franklin sidestepped him and pulled him through effortlessly.

This made Lewis even angrier. "Stop doing that and fight like a man."

Lewis then whipped around and as he got closer, he threw a right jab. Franklin sidestepped again, grabbed the arm with his left hand, shuffled in closer to Lewis, right elbow in the midsection, backhand to the face, and with a sweep, he took Lewis down.

With the wind knocked out of him, Lewis lay in a daze for a moment. Carver held Francie back. The men had to settle their differences without interference.

Knowing the man's ego must be bruised Franklin leaned over and extended a hand to help him up. Seeing his chance to take him down, Lewis took his hand. On the way up, he grabbed a fist full of dirt and threw it in Franklin's face.

"Not fair, Lewis!" Francie cried out.

Instinctively, Franklin threw up both hands before his eyes and turned his head. Lewis threw a punch, but Franklin anticipated it. Catching the fist, he turned quickly, and flipped his opponent over his hip and on to the ground.

"No more dancing. I'm aching all over and my stomach is about to expel the Scotch and tacos. Stay down until I return to the house," Franklin ordered in no uncertain terms.

Then he looked to Carver and Francie. "I kept my promise. I didn't kill him."

He motioned to Carver, "Please help me back to the house."

Francie moved to him, "Are you hurt?" She tenderly touched his arm.

Franklin looked at her hand on his arm and smiled, "No, but I believe I broke open the leg wound. You may attend me in the house. Go to Lewis. I may have rattled his brains." Franklin touched her face lovingly. Then he turned and motioned for Carver to go.

Francie ran to Lewis, still flat on his back on the ground. "Are you hurt?"

"Not physically, just my pride." Lewis rolled over and pushed himself up. Francie tried to help, but he waved her away.

"Why did you go to him first? We both have wounds. I am the one you're supposed to be in love with." Appearing to be upset, Lewis turned and started walking away.

"I'm sorry. He was closest to me and I asked." She tried to keep up.

"I was on the ground. I love you, but I don't think you love me the same way." He stopped and turned to her. "You still love *him*, no matter what. If he had killed me, you wouldn't have to make a choice."

"That's cold! I never wanted you dead. I begged him *not* to kill you," tears welled up in her eyes.

A mix of emotions washed over Lewis. He didn't know what Francie wanted. She saved his life when she found him in the alley. The darkness did give himself and Lon a means to escape and this was due to Francie. On the other hand, she wouldn't let him kill Franklin, after all the evil he'd done. Why?

Back inside the house, Carver sat on the overstuffed chair near the end of the table where the plate of tacos sat. He looked up and saw Lewis and Francie coming toward him.

"Taco?" Carver offered.

"No thanks," refused Lewis. "Where is he?"

"In the kitchen, waiting for Francie to attend his wounds." Carver picked up a taco.

"Why does she have to do that? Why doesn't he get his manservant to do it? Or, go to a hospital," grumbled Lewis.

Francie looked to him, wondering what she should do. He looked at her and waved her on.

Sadly, she went into the kitchen and found Franklin sitting on a chair waiting for her. Chef Jacques and his sous chef Maurice scurried about to prepare lunch for him and his guests.

Francie pulled back the denim to see the blood soaked gauze. In silence, she went to the cupboard and pulled out the first aid kit. She propped his leg on a chair. Then she repeated what she'd done earlier, after removing the soiled bandages. While she cleaned the wound, Franklin looked at her sadly.

"He's upset with you, isn't he? Because I beat him, he's taking it out on you."

No answer.

"I can't apologize enough for what I put you through. I couldn't turn back. Really, I tried, but I had no will of my own. I never meant to hurt you." Franklin tried to make her believe him, but she ignored his efforts. The look on her face told him she didn't want to discuss it.

"Francie, please talk to me." His heart ached seeing her like this. The tension between them pained him almost as much as a knife in the leg, almost.

"I've been talking to you. Sometimes, I don't think you're listening. What was this proposal business all about? You knew that would just agitate Lewis." Now, she started to bandage his leg.

"I was trying to make amends."

"How? By provoking him to fight you? How did that work out? You beat him. Happy now?" She wrapped the bandage a little too tight, he grunted in agony.

"I kept my promise. I didn't kill him." He grimaced a little from the tightness of the bandage.

"Thanks for that. Right now, I think he wishes you had." She tied off the gauze and put the roll back in to the first aid kit.

"I'll take care of that as well." Franklin gave a half smile.

"You can't joke about things like that. You did try to kill him twice."

"I apologized."

"A slight transgression? How is attempted murder a slight transgression?" Francie glared at him then picked up the first aid kit and replaced it into the cupboard.

She slid his leg off the chair and put the chair in place.

"Have you thought about my proposals?" Franklin asked then closed his eyes real tight, bracing himself for the wrath of Francie DeWitt.

The cupboard slammed shut. She whirled around with flame and fire in her eyes. "Have I thought about your proposals? Are you nuts? You went all Jekyll and Hyde on me last night. I'm black and blue from fighting your dark side and you want to know if I've considered your proposals? Ask me again why I don't want to be with you. To coin a phrase from a song you never liked, 'What part of no don't you understand?'" With that, Francie stormed out of the kitchen.

Quickly, Franklin arose, but paused and winced in pain from the leg. However, the ache in his head prevailed over that in his leg, as did the flip-flop of his stomach from the Scotch and tacos with the extra hot sauce.

It took a moment for him to stop reeling. Then he limped out to the living room to find Francie sitting in an overstuffed chair opposite Carver and Lewis who were on the sofa, eating tacos.

No one said anything for a while. Franklin found a seat at the far end of the sofa, nearest

Francie, who cradled the towel concealing the knife, her eyes closed. Carver read a newspaper, while Franklin watched Lewis eat tacos.

"All right, no one has to agree to anything I've proposed. Beginning immediately, I shall put all the shadows back where they belong. When I return to the Underworld, I shall release all the people that disappeared from the movie theatre and coffee shop. Then, if I haven't turned, or as Francie puts it, gone all Jekyll and Hyde, I shall take whatever consequence she and Lewis deem I deserve." Franklin announced in the voice of defeat.

Lewis sputtered and coughed in the middle of chewing his taco. Carver looked over his newspaper as if someone had announced an invasion from Mars. Francie said nothing and didn't even open her eyes.

"Are you serious?" Lewis asked as he threw back the Scotch. Then, he made a face and gasped. "Too early. This would be much better with tequila, anyway." Francie's eyes popped open in accusation of Lewis' statement.

Lewis saw the look on her face. "Just kidding. Franklin, are you serious?"

"Dead serious. When you've finished eating, I'd like to talk to you alone."

Francie interjected, "He can't control when he turns. I say shoot him."

"Francie!" Franklin exclaimed in astonishment. A maniacal smile crept across Lewis' face.

"You can't control that. You will turn again in a week and by the way, I told you there is no Underworld." Francie replied.

"Underworld? Lon mentioned that." Lewis got up, but Carver stopped him.

"What do you need?" Carver asked.

"Milk. The Scotch doesn't stop my stomach from burning."

"I'll ring for Cedric, the butler. He'll bring you some milk." Carver offered.

"Water is better. Milk will just agitate the symptom," said Francie, eyes still closed.

Lewis looked from Carver to Franklin. Both shrugged.

"I'll take water." Lewis gave in. Carver rang for Cedric and ordered water for Lewis and tea for the rest. Cedric, an aged man of sixty or so with short, graying hair bowed and left.

"Does she always tell you what to eat and drink, like that?" Lewis asked playfully.

"Always," replied Franklin. "And there is, without a doubt, a movie reference, or a song for everything in life."

Francie's eyes popped open. This time she looked daggers at both Franklin and Lewis.

At that moment, Cedric carried in a tray filled with sweets, assorted fruit, a teapot filled with hot tea, china teacups and matching saucers, with

169

sugar, cream and lemon on the side. Gently, he set the tray down on the coffee table and removed the plate of tacos and hot sauce.

Lewis gulped down the water. Carver poured the tea and offered some to Franklin and Francie.

Accepting the tea, Francie said, "Go on, Franklin. Tell Lewis about the Underworld."

"He knows. It's in my journal."

"I haven't read anything, except about the gun. What about the Underworld? You know that's mythology." Lewis sat back.

"It's not mythology. The darkness has a path to the Underworld. I've been there."

Lewis looked to Carver, who shrugged. Then he looked to Francie.

"I told him the same thing, but he says he's been there. What can I say?" Francie sipped the tea.

"If I have not changed in a week, we will go to the Underworld and release the people I transferred there." Franklin stirred a little cream in his tea.

Lewis looked at him as if he had two heads. "*We* will go to the Underworld? Who do you mean, *we*?"

"You, Francie and me. Carver will stay here and monitor our progress."

Lewis looked to Francie. She shrugged.

"There is no Underworld. Sudicorp deals with science, not mythology." Lewis reminded.

"Technically, it's more theology. The worship of the Olympians is a religion," corrected Franklin.

"Okay, Sudicorp doesn't deal with *religion*, either. There is no Underworld. I'm not going to a place that does not exist."

"Where do you think I put the people that disappeared?" Franklin sipped his tea.

Lewis and Francie exchanged looks.

"According to Franklin's journal, he has discovered a path to the Underworld through the darkness. If you can disprove it, then we can use that as scientific fact. Otherwise, the Hades experiment has proved that the

Underworld is actually a place and Hades is the ruler. This now becomes fact and not mythology or fiction." Carver stated matter-of-factly.

"Francie, I'd like to speak with Lewis, alone, if you and Carver don't mind." Franklin waited for Francie's reply.

Not sure why he wanted to talk to Lewis, Francie couldn't refuse. Looking to Carver, she arose and set the cup and saucer down. Carver also rose and he and Francie went outside through the sliding glass door.

Franklin set his cup and saucer down, pulled himself up from the end of the sofa, and hobbled to the overstuffed chair where Carver had sat near Lewis.

"You have every reason to hate me. Nevertheless, I know I can trust you to promise to do something for me. You still have the gun, the prototype, don't you?" Franklin began.

"Yes." Lewis replied, appearing to puzzle at where the conversation would lead.

"I want you, Francie and Carver to stay here with me for one week and see if I turn. If I change and cannot control it, then set the prototype on electrical, then to the highest voltage and shoot me with it full blast. It will either reset my brain waves, or…" his voice trailed.

"…kill you." Lewis finished.

"Yes. I can't bear to think what I would have done had Francie not stabbed me in the leg." His voice choked and tears streamed down his face. "I love her so much. I never wanted to hurt her. This, this experiment, or whatever is inside, drove me to pursue her relentlessly. No matter how she pled and wept, I could do nothing but watch myself hurt her and try to force her to do something she didn't want to do. Don't let this happen again, Lewis. Promise that you will make every effort to kill me before this occurs." Franklin shook as he sobbed for the wickedness he'd done and would have done.

Lewis fell silent. He'd never seen Franklin like this.

Franklin continued. "I'm aware of when I change, I could very possibly absorb the blast of electricity. Whether that makes me stronger for better or worse, I don't know. Just make sure you kill me. I don't know what I will become, but I don't want to hurt Francie.

"I know you love her as I do. Take care of her. Make her happy. Make her forget me. I cannot restore the lives of your ancestors, which I have murdered, but I can make sure I don't hurt her or you again.

"Francie is the last stage to my demise. Remember, she is a siren. The Song of the Lorelei was not meant to stir a man's desire or stimulate his libido. It was designed to drive him to self-destruction. Promise you will make sure I don't hurt her?" Franklin wept so bitterly that Lewis felt sorry for him.

"I don't know what to say. I've hated you for some time, but now, I feel for you. Of course, I'll protect Francie. You make it very difficult for me to want you dead." Lewis didn't know how to console him, except to say he would terminate his existence.

"Then you promise to make every effort…" Franklin started.

"…to kill you. Yes, Franklin, I'll do my best to kill you if I have to." Lewis promised. "Now, stop crying. It's not manly. Francie and Carver will think I beat you up. Is your leg hurting?"

Franklin took a hand and wiped his tears away. "Francie hasn't forgiven me." He sniffled.

"How so?" Lewis asked half mockingly.

"She tied the bandage too tight. It's cutting off the circulation." Franklin winced.

"Tell her."

"I don't think so. I've apologized profusely, but it doesn't help."

Just then, Francie and Carver returned. "Did you two kiss and make up? Are you BFF's now?" Carver puzzled at the men talking civilly with each other.

"Not BFF's. We just understand each other," Lewis looked at Franklin sadly. "Why don't we go to the karaoke bar tonight and unwind?"

"Unwind?" Carver couldn't understand this. "You still have wounds to heal, Franklin can't walk and Francie's black and blue. How can you suggest karaoke?"

"I don't know. We've been so serious with all the fighting and trying to kill each other, I just thought singing would help. Besides, if we loosen the bandage on Franklin's leg, I bet it would heal faster," Lewis hinted.

"Are you saying I tied it too tight?" Francie sounded indignant.

Lewis got up and hugged her. "No, not at all. I just meant he may want to dance."

Franklin's eyes widened and he shook his head. Francie saw the logic in the request, so she went into the kitchen and returned with the first aid kit. Opening the kit, she took out the roll of gauze and pulled out a piece she measured around Franklin's leg. Then she cut that piece off from the roll. Inspecting the tied gauze around his leg, she snipped it off then wrapped the new gauze around his leg and tied it looser. Then she put the scissors and gauze back in the kit and closed the lid.

Chapter Twenty-eight
Karaoke bar—Evening

That evening after the four had rested, Francie and Lewis went with Carver and Franklin to the karaoke bar, the one Franklin favored. Lewis didn't want to tell anyone about his talk with the doctor. It seemed best to keep something so emotional as true love and his pact to kill the man, should he turn into the ultimate Shadow Bender, confidential.

Whether the Underworld existed or not, Lewis knew Franklin had found a man who called himself Hades that verified the realm he ruled was called just that. Franklin had rested most of the day, the violent events of the night before having sapped his strength as well as the physical change into a nearly unstoppable monster.

From the corner of his eye, Franklin saw something move, something not human, dark and shapeless. Jerking his head around, he saw a black mass shrink in size and slither away into a crack in the floor. His breathing grew erratic as he tried to muster enough strength to command the shadows. After taking some Ibuprofen, his aches and pains decreased, but he didn't feel he had enough energy to perform the role of a true Shadow Bender if he didn't change. He couldn't control what he did the last time, so what deemed more hazardous, allowing the shadows to run amuck, or changing into an unstoppable creature of immeasurable power with uncontrollable abilities beyond human comprehension?

Carver looked past Francie and Lewis to Franklin. His face looked drawn and pale, a sure sign that he was going to change. Carver reached around Francie and tapped Lewis on the shoulder.

Carver motioned to talk to him. Lewis leaned in behind Francie.

"How's Franklin? He looks pale and distraught. He gets that way before he changes. Where's the gun?" Carver said as he nodded toward Franklin.

When Lewis turned, he saw what Carver meant. Without a verbal reply, he held up his hand to signal he'd find out.

In the background, the DJ, Anatole, warmed up the crowd with an Alan Jackson song, 'Livin' on Love'.

"Hey, you okay? You look a little peaked." Lewis said to Franklin.

For a moment, he labored to catch a breath. Placing a hand to his chest, he tried hard to suck in oxygen. Then he replied, "I saw shadows. Don't have the strength to command them. Trying not to change."

Lewis patted him on the back and offered the man some water. "Calm down and take a deep breath. Then drink some water. You are not going to change."

Franklin took the glass of water and sipped it. Lewis motioned for him to drink more. He obeyed, and his breathing returned to normal.

"Thank you, Lewis. It's generally worse after I change back. Only this morning it wasn't as bad. I don't know why I'm having a spell *before* changing." Franklin finished the glass of water. The color came back to his face.

"What causes these symptoms?"

"My energy is low. I am still mortal, and it is difficult to maintain this much power all the time. When I do have the energy, then it drains me of everything. I used to get a boost from the prototype, but soon that didn't do any good.

"Listen to me. If I can't command the shadows as I am, I may have to turn. I don't want to, but which is better, to allow the shadows free will, or change into what I was last night?" Franklin said.

Lewis' face went blank. "Are you kidding me? That's like asking if I want the firing squad or the gallows. What kind of choice is that?"

"The only one I have to offer. At least I'm telling you in advance. You have to help me. After all, you are Safety and Security." Franklin pushed him.

"Don't remind me. Well, just now, you stopped yourself from changing. That's a start. Now, we know that you can stop it. If you turn, maybe you can make yourself change back." Lewis sounded hopeful.

"If you say so."

"Can you put the shadows back with their objects or humans without going back to the lab?"

"Yes, but, again, I haven't the energy, unless I change."

"You really didn't think this through, did you?" Lewis pursed his lips.

"The experiment is ongoing, you know that. Since I have the extended mortality due to the elixir, I was the best candidate for the experiment."

"Yes, Dr. Jekyll, I got that. We just don't want to deal with the shadows and Mr. Hyde at the same time. If you feel like changing, let me know. I have the prototype in the trunk of the car."

Franklin gave a long sigh. Lewis pushed the list of songs to him. "Pick something. Try and get your mind off of changing."

Franklin said nothing. Knowing the shadows feared him made him feel more secure, but since they communicated with each other, they seemed to be revolting, like any living being vying for its freedom.

Nudging Lewis, Francie asked, "Is he okay?""He sees shadows and doesn't have the energy to command them. He's afraid he'll have to change to make them obey. Maybe you can talk to him. Cheer him up." Lewis motioned for her to walk around him and talk to Franklin.

"Cheer him up? No!"

"Come on. He's trying to be good."

"Leopard changing spots? What did you and he talk about?"

"Francie, please." Lewis pleaded and Francie gave in. She jumped up and scooted between Lewis and the table behind them to reach Franklin. Franklin automatically wrapped his arms around Francie and pulled her down on his lap. She squirmed a little, but seeing the sadness and hurt in his eyes, she placed both hands on each side of his face. She and Lewis exchanged looks. As much as he hated to agree, Lewis shook his head in agreement for her to kiss the man.

Caressing his hair lovingly, she pressed her lips to Franklin's. When the kiss broke, both she and Franklin had to gasp for air.

Lewis bit his tongue, but still he had to say his piece, "I know I agreed to the kiss, but did you have to sit on his lap and take his breath away?"

Franklin clung to her as they both caught their breath. "You told me to cheer him up. Next time, be more specific." Francie sputtered.

For a while, no one saw any shadows independent of their objects or humans. The DJ made a special announcement of their presence and welcomed them back. It seemed that business always increased when they performed.

"We are so happy to welcome back Francie and Lloyd. We know we're assured of a great show when you're here. We see you've brought some friends with you. Welcome as well. I will start the night off with, 'All Night Long.' Feel free to join in," said the DJ. He shook the long curls from his face as he slid in the CD. The lively music blasted the room with happiness and merriment. The DJ started clapping in rhythm to the music. The audience followed suit.

Francie whispered something in Franklin's ear. Smiling, he agreed. "Being with you, having you in his arms makes all his fears and worries vanish. It feels like you've forgiven me. If magic truly exists, it came from your touch," Franklin smiled weakly.

Francie slid off his lap and returned to Lewis at the table behind them. She whispered to Lewis and kissed him, then went backstage with her little black bag of props. The music stopped as the DJ finished the song.

Lewis gave a long sigh. "I think she kisses you with more heated passion than me."

"Of course she does. Please help me backstage. I must have a chair and table for our number." Franklin pushed his chair back and waited for Lewis to help.

"Of course she does? Explain." Lewis felt a surge of anger build up in him.

"She loves me more than you. I need her, you don't." Franklin said matter-of-factly.

"What? You need her. Franklin, don't make me hate you all over again." Lewis arose and helped Franklin to his feet. He looked to Carver, who nodded. Then the two men shuffled backstage. After releasing Franklin, Lewis slid a small square table and chair out to center stage.

Franklin stood at the curtains, stage left, awaiting the musical cue. Lewis grabbed Francie, who was now dressed in a low cut, long black chiffon dress with a slit up to the right thigh. She wore black silk stockings with pumps and a feather boa.

"If he starts to change, get off the stage, my dear. He claims he sees shadows lurking about. And what are you dressed up for? Are you trying to give him and me a heart attack?" Lewis felt his libido stimulate and his heart raced seeing her look so feminine and desirable.

"Keep your eyeballs in your head. I'm still covered up." Francie smiled and kissed Lewis hard on the lips. He wrapped his arms around her, holding tight, kissing her back with all the heat he could exert in a rush. When the kiss broke, they both gasped for breath. The fireworks had been traded for fever.

The DJ announced: "Francie and Lloyd will honor us with a little number they haven't done for a while. I know you're going to love it. Give it up for Francie and Lloyd performing, 'Big Spender!'"

The crowd cheered and clapped vigorously. Most of the patrons knew them from the many evenings previously spent at the bar. Hoots and whistles rang out over the cheers and applause. With her back to the audience, Francie stood center stage, beside the table and chair. Hands on her hips, she moved them rhythmically as the music began. The musical cue hailed Franklin to walk in with his cane in rhythm to the music and sit down at the table. His eyes lit up to see Francie looking so alluring. A big smile spread across his face.

Francie began singing. She moved to Franklin seductively in time to the lyrics and music.

Then she playfully nudged him with her hip and fell into his arms at the first "good time." Franklin couldn't resist, he held her close and kissed her face tenderly.

Gently, she pushed him back to finish the song. She pranced around Franklin, teasing him with the feathered boa before she wrapped it around his neck and gave a big finish with the final "spend a little time with me." When the final note faded, the audience went wild with applause and cheers. Franklin pulled her onto his lap again and pressed his lips hard against hers. Again, she melted into his arms as she pushed her tongue into his mouth.

Forgetting all his pains, Franklin nearly exploded with desire for the woman in his arms. Lewis turned beet red and attempted to get up, but Carver pushed him back. Leaning toward Lewis, Carver raised his voice to be heard above the applause, "Let him go. He will lead us to where the missing people are. I think he'll change tonight and he may never see Francie after this anyway."

Francie tried to push him back, but he wouldn't let go. Finally, she rubbed a hand across his chest and broke the kiss. Whispering in his ear, she reminded him they were still on stage. He smiled and nodded to all the nice people. Then, he released her.

When the applause died down, Francie and Franklin returned to their table in the audience with the help of Lewis, where the question of "what were you doing up there?" begged an answer.

"Let me rephrase that. *Why* were you doing that up there?" Lewis glared at both Francie and Franklin. "It's understood she was trying to cheer you up, but I didn't tell her to sit on your lap and French you. What's up with that? Does that stop you from changing?"

Franklin looked a little sheepish, like a child caught with its hand in the candy jar. Francie turned red with embarrassment. "You said cheer him up. He got carried away with me. It's your fault."

"My fault? Seriously? I didn't tell you to seduce him. Cheer him up means clever conversation. Talk about the weather. Talk about movies. Why do you have to sit on his lap and kiss him?" This time, out of the corner of his eye, Lewis saw a black mass. His head jerked about and there at the end of the stage, caressing the curtains, was an ebony-colored thing that was taking the silhouetted shape of a human. Lewis nudged Franklin and pointed when he got his attention.

In an instant, it had melted into the fabric and vanished. Lewis and Franklin exchanged looks. This time, Francie saw it too.

"Can you command them? Do you know what they're up to?" Lewis bit his lower lip and cracked his knuckles.

"I can hear the murmuring, but can't make it out. We need an EVP recorder to hear them clearly. They only act this way when they want independence." Franklin replied and took a swallow of water. "I still can't command them without changing."

The DJ announced another performer. The crowd applauded and the music began. Carver and Lewis looked around the room. The shadows seemed to come in and out intermittently.

Carver reached around Francie and touched Lewis on the shoulder. "Perhaps we should have Franklin go outside and change, so he can command the shadows. I'm afraid they are going to attack."

At this, Francie turned pale. Lewis didn't want to worry her, but he too feared the worse, a chill ran up his spine.

An hour passed without incident. Carver showed Francie his list of songs, "Help Me Rhonda," "Donna," and "Mandy."

"Don't you know any songs that don't have a woman's name in the title?" Francie tried to smile.

"Not as well as these. Besides, I told you I didn't want to sing."

Lewis heard him and interrupted, "Let's do 'Livin' on Love' with Franklin. Francie can sit in the audience and be our judge." He wanted to be cheerful, but he felt sure cheerful wouldn't be the way the night would end.

After a while, Carver and Franklin joined Lewis on stage for the Alan Jackson song, "Livin' on Love." Everything appeared lively and happy as the audience clapped in time with the music and sang along with them. Nevertheless, Francie noticed shadows on the walls and on the stage floor where no object or person stood to cast it. She shuddered. The night might end badly.

Amid cheering and applause, the men returned to their seats. Other performances came and went. All in all, the evening went well. Franklin physically felt better.

Carver looked to Francie. "If Franklin turns when you do your last number, I'll motion for you to get off the stage. Don't try to save him. Just run. Understood?" Francie nodded in agreement. This didn't sound good.

A few minutes to midnight, the DJ announced the last number of the evening. "Traditionally, when Lloyd and Francie are with us, we invite them to do the last number. Ladies and gentlemen, once again Lloyd and Francie are to do the Bonnie Tyler hit, 'Holding out for a Hero.'"

Francie and Franklin moved center stage as the intro began. On cue, Francie began to sing, "Where have all the good men gone and where are all the gods? Where's the street-wise Hercules to fight the rising odds? Isn't there a white knight upon a fiery steed? Late at night I toss and I turn and I dream of what I need."

As Francie sang, shadows popped up all around the room, unbeknown to anyone but Carver and Franklin.

Seeing the increase of shadow population, Franklin stopped moving with Francie. His eyes flashed into solid black. Red-black charges of something akin to electricity crackled and coursed through his body. He held Francie's arms out stretched, supporting them, but not in dance.

In a loud voice, Franklin bellowed, "Revertimini ad antiquitatem vestram. Sermónem meum servábit. 'Return to what you were. I command it'. Revertimini ad antiquitatem vestram. Sermónem meum servábit. Revertimini ad antiquitatem vestram. Sermónem meum servábit.

After the third command in Latin, the shadows began to quake.

Carver panicked and punched Lewis in the arm. "Hurry, get the prototype. He changed."

Lewis sprang from the chair and pushed his way through the crowd.

In the parking lot, Lewis raced to the car and popped open the trunk. Finding the golf club carrier, he whipped out the gun, slammed the trunk closed and ran back into the bar.

When he got inside, he fumbled with the settings as he pushed past people, chairs and tables. By now, the shadows had disappeared but the roiling mist of darkness answered their master's call. Creeping across the stage, the mist swirled up and around Franklin and Francie. Carver jumped up and down trying to get her attention. He waved his hands and mouthed the words, "Get off. Get off."

Francie continued singing, but narrowed her eyes to see why Carver was waving his arms and jumping up and down. Lewis aimed the gun and pulled the trigger. The prototype jammed. Nothing happened. Again, he fumbled with the settings and the trigger.

When Francie stopped singing, all hell broke loose. Not only did she notice the black mist swirling around her, but when she looked into Franklin's face, she saw his eyes had turned solid black. People started screaming and fleeing from the room as darkness engulfed the stage. Francie screamed and tried to pull away, but Franklin held fast and continued chanting in Latin.

Carver pushed his way to Lewis who still fiddled with the prototype. "Never mind that. Take it with you. Go! The darkness is taking them away. Go now!" Carver pushed Lewis toward the stage.

Amid the screams and scraping sounds of chairs and tables scooting about, Lewis scrambled up on stage with the prototype. The black mist swallowed him, as it did Franklin and Francie. When the mist dispersed, an empty stage remained.

A sinking feeling hit Carver in the pit of his stomach. The bar was empty of people, including the DJ, and reeked with the smell of sulfur and smoke.

Chapter Twenty-nine
Through the Darkness to the Underworld

It was almost pitch black and the air felt heavy as though something had tried to shut off the oxygen. Sounds of skittering and shuffling came from behind her as Francie clung to a fast moving man of darkness. A dim, eerie glow, like diffused phosphorous illuminated the path. The stench of burning wood and what smelled as if someone had struck a match permeated the atmosphere. Brimstone - another name for sulfur. The odor nearly overwhelmed her and she started coughing and struggling for air.

The vice-like grip on her wrist was a reminder that Franklin led them along the path of darkness. From the dimness, she could see red-black electrical charges coursing through his body and arms. Every now and again, a jolt would surge through her, making her jump and scream from the stabbing pain it produced.

Once again, they reached the light, which projected a visual of Franklin's and her trip to Hawaii. He didn't pause long enough for the replay as Lewis and Lon had.

Instead, he pushed on along the path, to where another light projection waited for viewing. At this one, Franklin paused.

The light faded to an overcast sky in a dreary London night filled with fog, a year ago, when he had taken Francie for a visit. Bundled up in coats with scarves around their necks, Francie and Franklin walked arm in arm along the street as others wrapped in winter apparel milled about. Though they were clearly speaking to each other, the audio was mute.

Franklin pulled Francie to him and pointed up to the overcast skies. Fog swirled around them, giving the world the surreal look of a dream.

183

Without notice, Franklin crushed his lips against hers extremely hard and pulled open her coat, his hands roamed her body, and tugged at her clothes. Suddenly, she pushed him back hard and slapped his face.

His facial expressions contorted with surprise and anger. He raised a hand to slap her, but stopped when she slapped him again. Scene faded.

"I remember this," cried Francie wincing at the grip around her wrist. "We were in London. I'm sorry I slapped you."

"I deserved it," was the cold reply in a distorted voice that barely resembled Franklin's. The crackling of the energy outlined his body as he dragged her onwards.

The malodor of fire and brimstone grew stronger when they reached a cavern of immense height and width with large rock formations scattered about. Gaseous vapors rose up from various pockets in assorted boulders. As they entered the cavern, the wall straight ahead of them had a hazy resplendence that served as a backlight to the rocks in front of it.

"This is the entrance to the Underworld," explained Franklin in his distorted voice. From the shadows stepped a man with a shaggy mane of dark hair, dressed in black as if going to battle in ancient Greece. He held a shield with his left hand and a deep amber colored broad sword in the sheath around his waist.

"Sir Gregory, so good to see you again. I trust all went as planned?" asked the man that was dressed in black battle gear.

"It is done. Please release the people I shifted here. They may now return to their homes above." The distorted voice replied.

"Very well." The man waved his hand and the grind of a huge boulder scraped into the ground, opening a passageway. People, dressed in clothes of the present day, poured out of the passageway and halted abruptly. They trembled and no one said a word.

"You may all leave. Follow the dark path back to the world above. Do not stop and do not turn off. Go quickly before the passageway closes," said the man dressed for battle.

Without hesitation, the people pushed and shoved to get through the exit and on to the path. The pounding of many footsteps echoed throughout the cavern. Soon, they all faded into the dark passageway and once again, the cavern hung in crypt-like silence.

The man turned to Francie and bowed saying, "In all the rush, Sir Gregory has forgotten his manners. Permit me to introduce myself. I am Hades, god of the Underworld. Some refer to me as Pluto, others as Osiris. Depends on where you reside."

Francie looked to Franklin, whose eyes were still solid black and his face twisted. He nodded for her to speak.

"I am Frances DeWitt. Please call me Francie, nice to meet you, Mr. Hades." She said as she trembled and her teeth chattered.

"Ah, yes, of course, Francie. You are the siren of whom Sir Gregory spoke. You will reign as his queen."

"Queen?"

"He didn't tell you? Gregory, this is shameful. I must tell her of our pact. Francie, you know that Persephone is my queen and spends six months of the year here with me, so that autumn and winter may arrive. However, the other six months of the year my dear Persephone leaves me to go above so that spring and summer may visit the world, as agreed with her mother, Demeter. Yes, yes, there was a family argument, but that's all behind us. Your brilliant man bargained with me to a joint reign of the Underworld."

As Hades explained the pact, Lewis crept into the cavern unbeknown to anyone and slipped in behind a rock formation as close to Francie, Franklin and Hades as he could.

Hades continued, "This would allow me to go above with my beloved wife for six months. We wouldn't have to be separated. Isn't that generous of Sir Gregory? Yes, yes, indeed, very generous." Hades turned and called out. "Persephone, please join us."

Francie tried to pull away from Franklin, but he tightened his grip on her wrist.

From the dark of the cavern an incredibly beautiful woman emerged, dressed in a dark, flowing dress with ebony, velvet robe. Her coal black tresses were twisted upon her head, with gentle curls that hung around her face.

"This is my wife and queen Persephone." Hades introduced. In the strange state he was in, Franklin said nothing and made no gestures. "My darling, this is Sir Gregory and his queen Francie."

Francie did a little curtsey, but nothing came out of her mouth.

"My pleasure. I have added a feminine touch in the back. I hope you enjoy it. Let us go, Hades. My mother is waiting. I assure you she was in shock when I said you were coming with me." Persephone said as she started to leave without her husband.

"Sorry to rush off. Can't be late for dinner with mummy dearest," he said, referring to Demeter, his mother-in-law. Then he hurried off after his wife and disappeared through the passageway.

Instantly, Francie watched as Franklin turned back to himself. His eyes returned to normal and his facial features relaxed. The crackling of energy ceased and no longer surged through him. Releasing her hand, he turned to Francie.

"I apologize for not telling you about the pact. None of this has been easy for you or me. I know Lewis tried to keep his promise, but the prototype jammed." Before Franklin could say another word, a beautiful woman, dressed in a linen pendent sleeved dress with a silk over-veil covering her raven hair, stood before him. She was followed by a little boy of six years old and a little girl of eight years old.

"Arianna! Rowena! Little Gregory!" Franklin knelt down and hugged each of his children. They in turn embraced him and he sobbed as if his heart would break. Then he arose, hugged Arianna and kissed her.

"Come with us, Gregory. We have waited a long time for you. We've missed you so." Arianna said, on the verge of tears.

"Come with you? You don't want to go with me?" Franklin appeared confused.

"There is nothing in mortality for us. We do not belong. We are dead. Nothing keeps you in that world, except for Francie DeWitt." Arianna looked to Francie.

"He is holding on to you. It is he that cannot choose. I have saved you from him twice. Release him to me and you will never see him again. He will never hurt you." Arianna finished.

Francie broke out in tears. "But he will be dead, won't he?"

"Yes, he will be dead. As well he should have been many centuries ago. Another man loves you dearly. Go with him and leave me with my husband."

"I can't let him die. I won't leave him here," Francie sputtered through tears.

"Francie, do you love my husband Gregory?"

Franklin listened tentatively, hoping and praying that he'd hear what he longed to hear.

"I know him as Lloyd. Others know him as Franklin. Whatever he calls himself, I do love him, just as I love Lewis Avery. I don't want either one to die and I will not release any one to death." Francie dried her tears as she spoke with determination.

Arianna looked to Franklin. "Then you have the final say. Come with the children and me and we will be together at last. If you choose Francie, I will understand. May peace be with you, my husband."

The hurt and sadness appeared in Arianna's eyes. They never had the chance to say good-bye in mortality. Franklin bit his bottom lip and tears rolled down his face.

"For several hundred years, I've looked for a way to free you and the children from death, only to learn you want to stay dead and for me to come with you," said Franklin.

Turning to Francie, he asked, "Do you really love me? Do you truly want me to live?"

"I do love you. I don't want you to die. I won't leave you here." She threw her arms around his neck and pulled him to her.

Lewis watched the scene.

Franklin explained as he pulled back from her gently. "I must honor my pact with Hades. For six months, I must remain in the Underworld and rule as a god. I am now the Ultimate Shadow Bender. As of this moment, I am immortal and I choose to stay with you, only under the conditions mentioned. When Hades returns with Persephone, after six months, then I will return to you in the world above. However, if you need, call out to me. As a god, I will respond to your prayer."

"Prayer? Lloyd, I don't get it," Francie questioned.

Franklin turned to Arianna and the children. For the last time, he embraced each child and kissed them, saying the good-bye he never had the chance to do centuries ago. He and the children stood weeping.

After witnessing all of this, Francie had to ask, "Arianna, I know that you love Lloyd, I mean Gregory, but don't you love him enough to come back into mortality, regardless of the changes?"

"It is defying the laws of nature. The dead have other things to do after mortality. Unless the god who has the authority to resurrect calls us back, we must remain dead. Gregory is now lord of the Underworld." She replied to Francie.

Looking to Franklin, she continued, "It appears it is not my Gregory's time. Go with the one you truly love, my husband. Mourn no more for me and the children." Arianna dried her eyes with a kerchief.

Her last words were to Francie, "Take care of Gregory. He is stubborn, emotional and filled with darkness. Nevertheless, there is goodness in him."

Sadly, Franklin collected Arianna in his arms and kissed her good-bye. "Forgive me for not saving you. Forgive me for holding you back in my grief. Forgive me," he sobbed.

Arianna said nothing but embraced him. Then, she pushed him back and waved him on to Francie. In unison, the children said, "We love you father. We shall be waiting."

As the last words fell from their lips, Arianna turned around to leave with her children. Franklin reached out for them, but they faded into the darkness.

Francie touched his arm. He turned and pulled her to him. Again he asked, "Do you really love me? I've given up something very precious to me, because of you. Can you understand how much Arianna and my children mean to me, but in the end, it's you, Francie. You hold me to mortality, and now, I must reign in the Underworld until Hades returns."

"You know that Hades never stayed down here all the time. Many stories tell how the gods of Olympus visited mortals. I do love you Lloyd. No matter what you are, I cannot release you to death." After saying this, Francie threw her arms around his neck. Looking into each other's eyes, they caressed each-others face and hair.

Teary-eyed, Franklin held her to him. "You don't know how long I've waited to hear you say that. In all the centuries, I've never loved anyone as I love you." Then he pulled back a little and leaned into to her.

Their lips had almost met, when the cavern began to quake and once again Franklin changed. His eyes turned solid black and his face contorted into the fierceness of one possessed. Francie screamed, but he crushed his lips to hers with such a fever, making the red-black electricity crackle violently. She fought and struggled against him, but his hold was like a vice.

In vain, she kicked him. No longer did he react to the pangs of mortality. Pulling back from her, he roared in a distorted voice with the command of a deity, "I am immortal and no longer feel pain. I am a god, the Ultimate Shadow Bender."

With this, he tossed her against a boulder as if she were a rag doll. Francie's head met the hard surface and she fell unconscious to the ground.

Seeing this, Lewis moved out from where he'd been hiding, took aim with the prototype, and pulled the trigger. The blast of electricity came like the lightning bolts of Zeus. Repeated solid beams of high voltage hit Franklin, jarring him violently each time. However, the energy seemed to melt into his body like a sponge sucking up water.

In a few minutes, the prototype drained. It would take time to recharge, and time they didn't have. Lewis ran to Francie and tried to awaken her. A few meters away, Franklin stood unharmed. As feared, he had absorbed the energy, making him stronger and more powerful than before.

With wooden steps, Franklin marched to Lewis who threw up his hands with the gun before him. Franklin slapped them aside as he would a falling leaf. Like a streak of lightning, he caught Lewis by the throat and lifted him off the ground.

"Now you will bother me no more. I shall crush you like an insect," bellowed Franklin as he watched Lewis suffer.

Groggy, Francie rallied and her eyes fluttered to stay open. It took a moment for her to focus on the horrible site of Lewis clawing desperately at the hands around his throat, dangling from Franklin's grip, as he was slowly being strangled to death. The hands around Lewis' throat held him so tightly; he couldn't gasp or cry out. His mouth opened and his tongue protruded in grotesque agony.

A moment of panic seized Francie and she had no voice. Pushing herself up, she strained to make a sound with her mouth. The ghastly smell of fire and brimstone filled the atmosphere, causing her to gag and choke.

She had to sing. No water to drink. No fresh air to clear her lungs. Nevertheless, with all her breath, she started to sing Peggy Lee's - 'Fever'.

At the sound of her voice, Franklin loosened his grip, but not enough to release Lewis. Jerking his head around mechanically, he snarled at her and waved his hand to push a mass of energy her way, but failed as the song of the siren continued.

"What a lovely way to burn. And what a lovely way to burn." The last refrain of the song literally set Franklin on fire.

He dropped Lewis like a hot potato. In a white, burning flame, he turned to Francie, bellowed like a crazed bull, and then charged her. As if a spell had broken, his eyes turned back to normal, Francie sidestepped and Franklin crashed into the rocks. He bounced off the ragged surface and slid to the ground like warm Jello on the side of a bowl. The flame extinguished.

Francie ran to Lewis who floundered about, trying to get up, still holding his throat. He pushed himself to sit up.

He scrambled to follow her to where Franklin lay on the ground, flat on his back. This time, he choked and strained for oxygen. Francie gathered him up into her arms and leaned down, placing her mouth over his, blowing air into his lungs. When his breathing stabilized, the CPR turned into a kiss. Francie gently pulled back, and looked into his weak, sad eyes.

"I am no match for a siren, even as a god. No strength. It's better this way. I shall go with Arianna and you with Lewis." Franklin said weakly. Tears streamed down Francie's face.

"Don't weep for me. I hurt you all the time. Forgive me." Then he looked to Lewis. "Forgive me Lewis." Franklin reached out to the man, who nodded his forgiveness.

"Please take care of her." Franklin requested again. "I love you so much, Francie." Weakly, he caressed her face.

"I love you Lloyd," Francie said between sobs. Taking his hand in hers, she leaned in and kissed him one last time.

When the kiss broke, he took a deep, strained breath, then closed his eyes and fell quiet. Gently, she laid him on the ground and sobbed as Lewis held her to his chest.

A great rumbling echoed throughout the cavern, shaking with a tremendous force. Rocks and shale rained down from the ceiling. Lewis grabbed his darling by the waist and pulled her up. Whatever shook the place would certainly close the portal if they didn't leave now.

Amid all the dizziness and discomfort of being strangled and slammed against a rock, Lewis and Francie ran from the cavern into the dark passageway.

Through the blackness, a hail of pebbles peppered them, blurring their vision even more than the dimness that illuminated the path. At one point, Lewis stumbled and dropped the prototype. Francie helped him up. He tried to grab the gun, but another shower of small rocks rained down on them, and they had to leave it.

From behind, they heard a loud rumble of feet moving quickly upon them. Lewis moved Francie to the wall, and shielded her with his body. Whatever ran passed them, flew by like a bullet, howling like a banshee.

When the thing cleared them, Lewis put his arm around Francie and they started again, hoping to find the light of day or at least a light at the end of the darkness. In the eerie dimness, vague outlines of objects on the ground came into view. A few times, both of them stumbled and tripped on the loose rocks and shale.

Finally, a pinhole glimmered up ahead. The closer they ran, the brighter the hole became. In a matter of minutes, they found themselves back in the karaoke bar. Carver grabbed both of them as they skidded to a stop. Looking back, the path of darkness faded into nothing.

Panting, Lewis asked, "How long, how long we been gone?"

Carver looked from Lewis to Francie. "I don't know. Maybe twenty minutes. Are you all right?"

"Twenty minutes? It seemed like hours," Lewis sputtered, rubbing his throat.

"Franklin, where is he?" Carver looked around them.

"Dead. Francie sang him to death. He sucked up all the juice from the gun, which I lost on the way back. He became what he called the Ultimate Shadow Bender, an immortal. Yet, when he heard the song of the siren, he burst into a white flame and changed back to himself. This time, he said he was too weak and died."

"I am sorry." Carver pretended to lament.

"No, you're not. You've wanted him dead for a long time. In the end, he asked me and Francie to forgive him." Lewis gave him a look of disdain.

"Are you sure he's dead?"

"Why do you ask?"

"If he attained immortality, nothing could kill him."

"Trust me. He's dead. An earthquake hit the place and everything started to fall apart." Lewis narrowed his eyes at Carver and wondered to himself. *Could Franklin still be alive? How so? No one checked his pulse. No one had time.*

Chapter Thirty
A Week Later—Karaoke Bar

For some reason, Drake Carver wouldn't accept the resignation of Lewis Avery. So here they sat again; Carver, Lewis and Francie sitting up front near the stage. This used to be Thomas Franklin's favorite table.

A few minutes before nine o'clock, several customers came into the bar. Lewis looked around and gave a long sigh. He whispered to Francie, "When you want to go, let me know. I don't want to be here anyway." She half smiled and nodded sadly.

Carver looked at his friends. After all they'd been through together, they *were* friends.

"Come on. Franklin wouldn't want you to be sad. Let there be laughter and dancing," Carver tried to sound merry and made hand gestures as if dancing, but nobody smiled.

Shaking his head, he pushed the song list to them. "I'm willing to sing a song. I'm volunteering and I won't choose a song that has a woman's name in the title."

Lewis gave a lopsided smile. "What do you plan to sing; 'Funeral March of a Marionette', 'Nearer my God to thee' or 'Amazing Grace?'"

Caver pursed his lips. "Those are songs for a funeral. We need dance music."

Francie arose and motioned for Lewis. Together they climbed up on the stage and she told the DJ the song selection. Then they walked out to center stage, mikes in hand.

"I am Francie DeWitt and this is my fiancé, Lewis. Some of you remember me with my friend Lloyd Maxwell. He cannot be with us tonight, because an accident took him away." Tears streamed down her face. Groans from the audience echoed her sadness.

She went on, "Tonight, we want to honor his legacy of love by singing, Amazing Grace."

The musical interlude played. Francie and Lewis began singing.

When they finished, the audience applauded and Francie and Lewis took their bow, but just as they handed their mikes to the DJ, they heard a male voice, like a whisper, saying, "Francie, help me! Francie, help me!"

Their eyes widened in surprise as Francie and Lewis exchanged looks. *What just happened?*

Looking around, they found that the audience, including Carver, had heard it too. Everyone looked around, then up to the ceiling, murmuring their concern from where the voice came.

The DJ asked, "Francie was that Lloyd? Is this a joke?"

"N…no. He died. I was with him," she stammered.

"But that was his voice, wasn't it?" The DJ puzzled.

From the depth of darkness, a silhouette strained to sit up. A small porthole of light revealed the inside of the karaoke bar, with Francie and Lewis on stage with the DJ.

A weak whisper escaped the silhouette, "Francie, help me! Help me!"

About the Author

Born and raised in Salt Lake City, Fay E. Simon nurtured and developed a love for writing from an early age. She started out writing short stories for an English class, and took first place in several local short story and poetry contests. In high school, she served as a member of the editorial staff of the creative writing magazine and wrote a number of short skits for her acting class. Fay tried her hand at writing several different screenplays (still in progress), only to return to her first love, writing novels. Today she lives near Los Angeles where she continues to write and coach new writers online.

Also by the Author
at
Rogue Phoenix Press

Behind the Mirror

What would you do if your favorite novel suddenly became a reality? What would you do if the handsome main character of that novel fell in love with you? During a trip to Paris with her friends, nineteen-year-old Emma King walks through an antique mirror and into the embrace of Ehrich de Natois, the mysterious main character of her favorite novel. Unfortunately, whether in books or real life, living happily ever after just doesn't happen. Emma realizes this when she is pulled into the *"in between;"* a place between dimensions, a place much darker and more surreal than she could ever imagine.

An Excerpt

PROLOGUE

The Wilds of Scotland, 1849

The shadows of twilight danced across the lush meadows, stretching dark fingers out to the Mystic Pool of Aire in the garden of Shylah, the Celtic Seer. A tall, hooded figure shrouded in a black robe glided into view. It wore the hood pulled up around its face, leaving only the yellow glint of its eyes visible. Kneeling by the pool, Shylah disturbed the water when the dark shape overshadowed her.

Shylah cast her dark eyes upward to meet the eerily glowing orbs. Still kneeling, she gathered her robe around her, shivered, and offered the dark figure a seat by the pool.

"I know why you've come. You want to know your future," she said in a delicate English accent. Looking back at the pool, she continued to stir the water. When she stopped, the water swirled into a ghostly white mist reaching out its tendrils.

The image of a young woman in her late teens appeared in the center of the mist. She was dressed in clothes different from their time, a white top with writing and dark blue denim trousers. Her soft, brown hair gently framed her face, bringing out the sparkle in her dark, flashing eyes. She laughed and talked with two other young people about her age, a male and a female.

"How very strange," Shylah said. "For you, I see two separate, yet intertwining destinies running parallel to each other. This woman becomes a major part in both sides of your future." Shylah reached out to disturb the vision, but a skeletal hand stopped her. Its shockingly cold touch sent chills through her body, nearly frightening her to death.

"You want to see more of this woman?"

The dark figure nodded, so Shylah stirred until another image formed. "She comes from another time and space. At the moment, she abides in our future, yet she knows you and everything about you."

The vision in the pool showed the woman and her friends watching flickering shadows on a wall where two lovers kissed. The tender moment was interrupted by a dark-robed figure enveloping them.

"I'm not sure how, but this picture moves, telling your story."

A bony finger tapped the side of the pool. Shylah paused, trying to understand what the figure wanted. Again, it tapped then pointed to the vision.

"You want to know how to meet her?" The tapping continued. "I cannot tell. But without her, your second destiny will be final: one of intense hatred, unrequited love, and certain death." Shylah flinched at the icy, death-like touch of the skeletal hand.

"Do you want to see the second woman in your future?" The hooded head nodded. Shylah passed her hand over the pool. White vapors covered the image and dispersed, revealing a new one. A beautiful young woman in her late teens with dark, cascading curls stood on the stage of a grand theater. With a curtsey and a smile, she accepted the applause.

"They call her Cerise. She is the death you cannot escape. She will never love you." Shylah shivered again and reminded, "You cannot change history."

The shrouded figure stood abruptly.

Standing in the presence of a foreboding creature made Shylah turn cold, and knots of anxiety formed in her stomach. She wanted to jump up and flee into the night, screaming, but the creature's eyes gave her second thoughts.

The skeletal hand grabbed her arm. Its angry, vice-like grip brought excruciating pain, sending her to the ground screaming and pleading, reminding the creature that she only prophesied what came from God.

It released her arm. She fell to the ground gasping, clutching her discolored limb. Again, a skeletal finger tapped the edge of the pool.

Shylah rolled over, holding her damaged arm, gasping and biting her lip. The tapping continued until she passed a shaky hand over the pool.

Visions of both young women appeared. The one entwined in a lover's embrace with a black-clad figure. The other wept softly within the walls of a building.

The golden orbs blazing within the hood resembled an artist's concept of the Grim Reaper. Shylah turned her face to the ground, sobbing and pleading, as she cradled her throbbing arm. No longer could she bear to look into its eyes. Her entire body trembled until her heart nearly failed. Suddenly, the hooded figure turned and swiftly melted into the night.

Chapter One

Present Day Paris, France

"*Studio Duchenois, named for its founder Ranier Duchenois, brings to life the very essence of old France in both stage and film.*"

Emma paused in her reading and looked up from the brochure. Something flickered in and around the shadows of the statues on the Studio's roof. She rubbed her eyes for a moment and looked again, but it had disappeared.

"Go on," Doone urged as he playfully yanked on the brochure.

"Hey, stop that." Emma began again. "*Little known to most of the world in comparison to other popular Paris landmarks, the Studio, originally known as le Théâtre Ranier and built in 1870, always housed a rousing play, a passionate reading, or a little-known opera.*"

She paused again. It seemed surreal; she had been waiting to see this building for a long time, or rather, what this building contained.

Twanda, Doone, and Emma all stared up at the exquisite statues that adorned the roof of the majestic building. Emma imagined how it would feel to walk among all the splendor of its Baroque architecture in bygone days.

Emma couldn't believe she was finally here. She had been dreaming of this moment for a long time. Twanda's parents had agreed, as had Emma's, to allow them this little trip before college. Doone...well, Doone was a different story.

She looked back down at the brochure and finished its description. "*Today, Studio Duchenois presents plays both past and present, as well as allowing filmmakers the privilege of using its sets and newly added soundstages.*"

Eighteen-year-old Twanda Evans donned shades as she stepped a little farther back with her camera, trying to capture a shot of the roof.

For an instant, a shadow appeared and flickered through the statues. It remained on the dark side of the roof, as if watching the three friends. Twanda looked up from the camera. Her light brown complexion glistened with tiny pearls of perspiration from the sun's heat.

"Did anybody see that shadow moving on the roof?" Twanda asked, looking up from behind her dark glasses.

"I saw it. Could be a tour up there," answered Emma, visually searching for the flickering shadow.

"Mmm, maybe." Twanda tried to focus her lens.

Emma King wore her short brown hair in layers that met her shoulders and shone almost red in the light of day. With excitement, she turned to Doone, falling into a sword fighting position. "*En garde!*"

"Show off. Just because you took fencing lessons and Shotokan doesn't mean I can't beat you," Doone said as he wielded an imaginary sword.

Emma laughed. "I can beat you no matter what."

Even though twenty-five year old Doone had dropped out of high school, Twanda and Emma treated him like family. He wore his dark hair long and stringy. His thin, lanky frame made for stooped shoulders because of his height. The sun illuminated off his tie-dyed shirt and faded jeans.

Doone watched Emma furtively. He had always let on that he had wanted to come to Paris to walk the path of Ehrich de Natois from their favorite novel, *Dark Tales of le Théâtre Ranier*, and that was part of the truth, but he'd also wanted to be with Emma.

Since Doone could write his music and plays from anywhere, especially since no money came from them, his father had sent him on this trip to get him out of his way. He was tired of dealing with his son picking locks and being arrested.

Unfortunately, the young man habitually picked locks just to see if he could do it. He never stole anything or destroyed what wasn't his, but locks challenged him. However, the people owning the locks did not see lock picking as an exercise, and neither did the police.

"Are we going up to the roof?" asked Emma as she stepped next to Twanda, who was struggling to take a clear picture.

"We'd better. This haunted Duchenois-thing is making us all crazy. I wanna know what it was like for Cerise and Ralph up on the roof when Ehrich came after them. I know he must have been broken-hearted after seeing her with Ralph," Twanda finally snapped the picture.

"I would love to meet Ehrich. He must be so handsome and brave. Especially after he fought all those soldiers for killing his family," Emma said. She smiled and gave a long sigh.

"If you really met him, you'd faint."

"I would not. I would talk to him."

Twanda giggled and started making kissing noises.

"I didn't say kiss him. I said talk to him," Emma smiled shyly, as she playfully defended herself. "Well, maybe a little kiss." Thoughts of scenes from her favorite Ehrich movie filled her mind.

From the shadows of le Théâtre Ranier, Ehrich de Natois watched the lovely Cerise take her bows on stage.

A smiled crossed his lips as his eyes lit up at her beauty. But that smile soon faded as he watched her fly into the arms of Ralph Duchenois, a wealthy patron of the arts. He followed them to the rooftop.

"You were magnificent!" Ralph exclaimed as he kissed her tenderly. "My brougham awaits. We must leave tonight."

"I do love you, my darling. I can hardly wait to be your wife!" Cerise clung to him. Suddenly, a figure sprang from the darkness and overshadowed them and they were gone.

"I wanna be Ehrich. Such a great actor! Knowing all that Magick. All that lurking in shadows and secret passageways and coming in and out of trapdoors. Way cool!" Doone barked in his Valley-boy accent, as he tried to imitate twirling a cloak.

"You are so lame. Do you want to hide away in an old theater?" Twanda snapped.

"Why not? No rent, no neighbors, way cool! Then my dad wouldn't be complaining that I'm good-for-nothing." He half laughed.

Twanda rolled her eyes. Emma motioned for them to follow her inside. "Slow down, Emma," Twanda said.

The lobby and grand foyer exhibited exquisite sculptures of semi-nude females, and intricate carvings decorated the handrail of the grand staircase ascending to upper levels. Sconces reminiscent of the late 1800s illuminated the ascension.

The three friends couldn't possibly have imagined the huge columns and high ornate ceiling. A magnificent chandelier hung high, overlooking the grand foyer with various scenes painted on the ceiling above. Such scenes included angels flying, circling as if keeping watch over their charges.

Emma shuddered with delight. She was here; finally here. She had to see more.

Unfortunately, the Studio only conducted tours of the lobby, and even then only during performances, since filming went on in the soundstages most of the time. With no plays and the soundstages in use, the three milled around the lobby then the gift shop. There just had to be a way to see more of the building.

"Excuse me," began Twanda to the cashier. "We hear you only conduct tours of the lobby during stage performances. But what about the roof? We saw someone on the roof."

The cashier, a mature woman with her silver hair drawn up into a bun at the back of head, frowned a bit. Hesitantly, she replied in a French accent, "You are mistaken. No tours of the roof today."

The girls exchanged puzzled looks. "But we saw someone moving up there," Emma added.

"You are mistaken. No tours of the roof today," came the sharp reply. Puzzled, the girls turned to rejoin Doone.

"I don't get it," mumbled Twanda, checking her digital camera. "Bet I got a picture of whoever was up there." She flipped out the viewer but somehow, her photo was gone. "Shoot! Nothing!" she cried in disgust as she slapped the viewer shut. They left the gift shop and pretended to be interested in the lobby again. They looked down halls and wondered what doors led where.

All of the dressing rooms and seats seemed to be closed to tourists, especially Ehrich's balcony seat at the east end. But they had come all this way. The three had to get inside.

The staircase leading to the balcony seats lay before them in the center of the room a little ways from the guest relations and gift shops. A thick, golden-colored rope blocked anyone from ascending.

A sign in several languages read: *Do not enter. This area currently off limits.*

As their eyes followed the winding staircase, they could see the entrances to some of the balcony seats.

After all, what did "off limits" mean to a guy like Doone?

Emma and Twanda watched him pick the lock. They had to be quick and quiet. No one wanted to get caught. From time to time, one or both of the girls would peek around the corner to make sure no one was approaching.

Carefully, Doone jiggled the pick inside the lock. A shuffling noise caught their ears. For a brief moment, they all held their breath, afraid to look. It seemed Twanda couldn't stand the suspense and tiptoed to peek around the corner, again. A cleaning lady stood on the stairs dusting the banisters and one of the statues.

Taking a deep breath, Twanda quietly went back to the others and whispered, "It's only a cleaning lady. She's not coming up here yet. Hurry!"

Finally, after Doone fumbled for a few minutes, the lock clicked and the door opened. Rich crimson velvet walls caught their eyes first, and clothes hooks lined the wall to their right as they entered the room. A small lamp mounted on the ceiling lit the way. Four seats lay before them, just past the red velvet curtain.

They only spoke in whispers, but mainly gestured to keep from being discovered. Doone immediately went to a column behind the seat to his left. "I feel strange, like I've been there before. When I touched the pillar, its surface seemed so familiar, like I had walked right through it at some point. But no, that could not be."

Emma and Twanda tried out the seats. Emma was giddy with excitement. "Oh, Ralph, come to me, my darling. Take me away from here and from Ehrich," teased Emma in a high-pitched voice.

Twanda looked to her with exaggerated gestures, reaching out and making kissing noises.

"My carriage awaits, my sweet Cerise. Come away with me now." The two playfully faked an embrace.

Doone took the opportunity and raised both hands, comically pretending to hypnotize them. "I am Ehrich, the Master of Arts. Look into my eyes. Look, look!" Then he mimed twirling a cloak he didn't have.

However, a solemn moment occurred during their pretense. As if in a trance, Emma arose from the seat and locked eyes with Doone. Twanda sat motionless, her eyes focused between them, not sure what was happening.

Doone seemed to become very serious, drawing himself up to his full height. He extended his hand, and she walked to him.

When their hands touched, it was electric; he drew her close and leaned down to taste her lips. She leaned upward to meet his. The sweet scent of sandalwood swirled around the lovers. Twanda, exasperated, jumped up and separated them. "No, no, no. None of that!" The scent of sandalwood vanished.

Trying to dismiss what nearly happened, they headed for the exit.

As the door closed behind them, a flickering shape with blazing orbs hovered in the shadows. In a moment, a quiet rustle stirred near the column.

"Now, that was lame!" exclaimed Twanda nervously as they wandered around the lobby. "Just a bunch of seats."

"It was Ehrich's balcony. I liked it." Both girls turned to Doone and frowned. "Way cool!" he finished.

"We saw an empty balcony. What's cool about that?" Twanda retorted.

Once again, curiosity got the better of the girls, so they began searching for the dressing room of Cerise St. Clair where Ehrich had allegedly recited words of love from the mirror.

Doone sat this one out, distracting an employee by arguing about what the tour covered while Emma and Twanda sneaked up the gorgeous, winding staircase.

Both girls had wanted to see Cerise's dressing room. *Dark Tales of le Théâtre Ranier* described a full-length antique gold mirror that Ehrich used to enter and exit. This was a must see.

On the first level, they found all the dressing rooms and storage areas locked.

They wandered aimlessly through the corridor for a few minutes. Emma stopped short when she heard the faint voice of someone reciting the soliloquy from Hamlet.

"You hear that?" asked Emma. Twanda froze in her tracks to listen. The voice stopped.

"Don't hear anything. Let's go." Twanda started for the lobby; Emma froze. She heard it again. Wrapping itself around her, the mesmerizing sound of a male voice pulled her on.

Entranced, Emma moved toward the door a little ways down.

"Where are you going? Come back," whispered Twanda.

No answer.

Emma proceeded to turn the door's handle.

Surprisingly enough, the door swung open at Emma's touch. A dim wall lamp in the back of the room provided the only light. A few scattered stuffed chairs filled the room, as well as a table near the door. Deep inside the chamber stood a beautiful full-length mirror, with a gilded frame and gold leafing, beckoning to her.

Twanda timidly moved inside with Emma.

"Is this Cerise's room?" Twanda wondered aloud.

No answer.

The mirror seemed to summon Emma. Carefully, she examined it, running her fingertips along the sides and bottom.

"We'd better go. We've been gone too long." Twanda moved into the corridor.

Emma ignored her. The voice began again. It filled her soul and engulfed her mortal body. When she closed her eyes, the world as she knew it vanished while her mind and soul soared to the ethereal realm of the gods.

As the voice continued, Emma opened her eyes, and for an instant, she stared at her reflection. But as she did so, the mirror grew dense with roiling clouds, creating a vortex.

The soft, sweet voice floated up through the vents and again filled the air with strains of a recitation that thrilled her to the very bone. The scent of sandalwood waltzed all around her. A spark of light crackled and flashed as she walked into the mirror and the watery entrance to another dimension.

Gone.

The mirror now stood clear and alone.

**VISIT OUR WEBSITE
FOR THE FULL INVENTORY
OF QUALITY BOOKS**:

http://www.roguephoenixpress.com

Rogue Phoenix Press

Representing Excellence in Publishing

*Quality trade paperbacks and downloads
in multiple formats,
in genres ranging from historical to contemporary romance,
mystery and science fiction.
Visit the website then bookmark it.
We add new titles each month!*